Mark Morris's fi~~rst~~ published in 198~~9~~ sixteen novels, in~~cluding~~ and four books in the popular *Doctor Who* series. He also edited *Cinema Macabre*, a collection of fifty horror-movie essays, for which he won the 2007 British Fantasy Award. Mark is currently working on a novel-ization of the 1971 Hammer movie *Vampire Circus*. He lives in North Yorkshire. To find out more, visit www.markmorriswriter.com

DEAD ISLAND

Mark Morris

BANTAM BOOKS

LONDON • TORONTO • SYDNEY • AUCKLAND • JOHANNESBURG

TRANSWORLD PUBLISHERS
61–63 Uxbridge Road, London W5 5SA
A Random House Group Company
www.transworldbooks.co.uk

DEAD ISLAND
A BANTAM BOOK: 9780857501035

First publication in Great Britain
Bantam edition published 2011

Addresses for Random House Group Ltd companies outside the UK
can be found at: www.randomhouse.co.uk
The Random House Group Ltd Reg. No. 954009

The Random House Group Ltd supports The Forest Stewardship
Council (FSC®), the leading international forest-certification organization.
Our books carrying the FSC label are printed on FSC® certified paper.
FSC is the only forest-certification scheme endorsed by the leading
environmental organizations, including Greenpeace. Our paper
procurement policy can be found at
www.randomhouse.co.uk/environment

Typeset in 11/14pt Palatino by Falcon Oast Graphic Art Ltd
Printed in the UK by CPI Cox & Wyman, Reading RG1 8EX

2 4 6 8 10 9 7 5 3 1

DEAD ISLAND

PROLOGUE

'Bring her.'

In his full ceremonial regalia, the witch doctor was a terrifying sight. His leathery body, bedecked with rattling beads, was painted in symbolic swirls of white and red. Over his shoulders was a cape of cured crocodile skin and his long, matted hair was entwined with twists of coloured cloth. He wore bracelets and anklets made of human bones, and on the belt around his waist, resting on his stomach, was a grinning human skull.

He led the procession uphill, on a winding path through the bamboo and the lansan trees, through riotously coloured clusters of plumbago and allamanda and the red, saw-toothed lobster claw. Here in the jungle the vegetation grew quickly, and often the young men had to dart in front of the witch doctor to slash a path through the undergrowth with their machetes.

The girl the witch doctor had referred to had ropes tied round her wrists and was being dragged along by two powerful men who wore nothing but loin cloths, and whose muscular bodies were painted in the same swirling ritualistic symbols as those displayed by the witch doctor. The girl, by contrast, though her skin was dark like that of the natives around her, wore western clothes – jeans and a thin white cotton shirt. The clothes were torn and dirtied, however, and her face was bruised and bloodied. Her fingernails were ragged from clawing and scrabbling in vain at the bodies of her attackers. She was weeping and begging for mercy, arms stretched out in front of her, stumbling along in bare feet.

In a straggling line behind the girl came the villagers, chanting and muttering the sacrificial incantations that had been passed down through generations. They swayed and jerked, their eyes glazed, as though they had been entranced or enchanted.

Finally, bringing up the rear, tied together at the necks and wrists and ankles, their mouths gagged with thick vines to stop them biting, came the *zombi*. There were sixteen of them and they shuffled and stumbled along, their eyes bleached of colour, their skin discoloured by death and blotched with green and white patches of rot. Four men, two at each side, lashed them with horse-hair whips to keep them in line and moving. The crack of the whips resounded through the air, mingling with the squawk of parrots overhead and the frogs calling somewhere off in the denser jungle in their clear, bell-like voices.

It took almost four hours to reach the burial site. It was situated halfway up a bare, jagged-peaked mountain, which rose from the thick green mass of the jungle, and was connected to a further range of mountains stretching into the distance. Up here the sun beat down mercilessly, and the girl, parched and exhausted, was almost out on her feet. For the last thirty minutes she had stumbled and fallen again and again, and her wrists were raw and slick with blood from being yanked continuously back to her feet by her captors.

The burial site itself was fronted by a vast stone mausoleum, constructed around the entrance to a cave which stretched deep into the mountain. The mausoleum had been built hundreds of years before, with stones that had been hacked from the living rock and then lovingly chiselled and hewn until the slabs fit snugly together like pieces of a three-dimensional jigsaw. Ancient symbols similar to those daubed on the witch doctor's body had been carved into the walls of the mausoleum – symbols that were intended to protect the departed from evil spirits and ensure their souls a swift and safe journey to the afterlife.

Walking up to the mausoleum, the witch doctor placed his hands on the huge rock that had been rolled across its entrance. He muttered a few words, requesting ingress from the spirits of the dead, then he turned and raised his arms.

Instantly the chanting of the crowd subsided and the cracking of whips ceased. The only sound was the agitated shuffling and grunting of the shackled *zombi* captives and the soft trilling of insects in the dry and patchy undergrowth.

'My friends,' the witch doctor proclaimed in the centuries-old language of the Kuruni people, 'we have come here today in order to lift the curse on our village.' He pointed at the girl, who had dropped to her knees and whose head was slumped forward like a supplicant bowing before her god.

'This one,' he said contemptuously, 'has brought shame and misery upon us. By her selfish and foolhardy actions, she has angered the spirits that watch over us all and has brought their wrath down upon us in the form of pestilence and plague and banishment from their divine realm. There is only one way we can appease the spirits and lift this curse.' He paused dramatically. 'We must offer her to them, body and soul, so they may enact their punishment upon her.'

The people cheered and clapped and chanted.

'No,' the girl muttered. 'This is wrong. This is murder.' Unheard, drowned out by the uproar, she shook her head slowly, her face hidden beneath the swaying curtains of her dark hair.

A couple of younger men stepped from the throng to take the ends of the ropes binding the girl's wrists, while the two men who had dragged her through the jungle and up the mountain stepped forward to flank the witch doctor. At a nod from him, they reached out and began to push at the rock covering the entrance to the mausoleum. Sweat gleamed on their muscular bodies and thick veins stood out on their foreheads and biceps as they heaved with all their weight and strength. Finally, with a gritty grinding sound, the rock began to shift. At first it tilted and then, powered by its own momentum, rolled to one side.

The people fell silent again, as if half-expecting to

see the spirits of the dead come swooping and curling from the depths of the mountain. Revealed behind the stone was the mausoleum's arched entrance, beyond which only shadowy darkness could be seen.

'Bring her forward,' the witch doctor said, pointing at the girl. The two men who had pushed aside the rock lumbered forward, took the ends of the ropes from the young men who had momentarily been watching over her, and then wrenched savagely on the ropes, causing the girl to scream in pain and sprawl face-first on to the dusty ground.

'Get to your feet,' the witch doctor commanded, his voice rising above the girl's sobs. 'If you do not walk to your fate, we will simply drag you there.'

Still sobbing, the girl clambered awkwardly to her feet. Blood was running down her hands now, dripping from her fingers on to the ground. The two men gave another tug, and she stumbled forward a few steps. Beaten and bloody, but still clearly defiant, she raised her head, hair falling away from her face, and suddenly screamed, 'This is barbaric! Can't you see that? There are no spirits! There is no curse! All you are doing here today is committing *murder*!'

The people gasped, but the witch doctor merely grinned in savage triumph and raised his arms once again.

'You see!' he cried. 'You see how the darkness within her tries to trick us even now?'

The people nodded and muttered. Her anger momentarily spent, the girl's shoulders slumped, but she fixed the witch doctor with an accusatory glare. 'How can you do this?' she muttered. 'You of all people?'

The witch doctor sneered at her, exposing teeth that had been filed into sharp points. 'Do not talk to me, demon,' he said. He looked at the two men and nodded towards the cave entrance. 'Take her inside.'

Pleading for mercy, for her captors to see reason, the girl was dragged into the cave. The witch doctor followed, while the people waited outside, silent and expectant. After a minute the girl's cries for mercy changed to screams of panic. As the sounds tore out of the cave entrance and echoed around the mountainside, the people looked at each other, nodding and murmuring in satisfaction. Eventually the girl's screams became muffled, and a moment later the witch doctor and his companions emerged from the cave entrance.

'It is done,' the witch doctor said. As the men rolled the rock back into place, he raised his hands and spoke the ritualistic words of allegiance and devotion. He offered his hope that the spirits would accept their sacrifice as penance and release them from their terrible burden of suffering. When he had finished the incantation, the people muttered the words of response, before lapsing into silence. The witch doctor looked out over the throng for a moment, his face grim. Then suddenly he grinned and cried, 'Let the feasting begin!'

The people cheered and turned as one, jostling for position in an effort to gain a good view of the ritual slaughter. The four men who had been herding the group of *zombi* tucked their whips into thick animal-hide belts around their waists and produced gleaming machetes, which they brandished in the air in acknowledgement of the crowd's cheers. Then, with the practised skill of butchers or executioners, they stepped forward and began hacking at the *zombi*, severing their heads quickly and neatly from their shoulders. The people laughed as the *zombi* fell and the slaughterers' faces and arms and chests were spattered with stinking black-red blood. The heads were collected up and passed through the crowd, to be placed in a row at the witch doctor's feet. He nodded in approval as each head was propped on its dribbling stump of a neck before him. Finally sixteen heads were lined up, their eyes glazed and white, their slack mouths hanging open.

Now a child was pushed forward from the throng, a small boy of four or five years old. The people muttered encouragement as he walked shyly up to the witch doctor, carrying a cloth-wrapped bundle in his outstretched arms. The witch doctor thanked him solemnly and carefully unfolded the layers of cloth. Nestling within was a curved knife with symbols etched into the handle. The witch doctor took the knife and held it up. The people cheered.

Sitting cross-legged on the ground, the witch doctor picked up the first of the *zombi* heads and propped it between his knees. He then rammed the knife into the *zombi*'s temple, just above its eyes, and began to hack and saw at the dead meat and the bone beneath, cutting around the top of the skull. It took several minutes of vigorous work before he was finally able to lift the skull-cap aside. When he did, exposing the grey-black putrefying brain within, the villagers went into raptures.

Grinning, the witch doctor dug his long fingers into the *zombi*'s head and scooped out a porridge-like gobbet of brain matter. He held it out towards a little boy, who was still standing in front of him, wide-eyed with wonder. The boy looked at him uncertainly, but the witch doctor smiled and nodded. Encouraged by whispers from his mother, the child stepped forward, opened his mouth and sucked the glistening lump of brain from the witch doctor's fingers.

A sigh of contentment ran through the crowd. 'Eat!' the witch doctor cried and dug his fingers into the *zombi*'s head once more. As the villagers queued up for their share of the feast, he offered another portion of this most sacred of delicacies to the second recipient.

'Eat!' he cried. 'Eat! Eat!' When the first head was empty he reached for the second.

Behind him, in the tomb, drowned by the excited clamour of the feast, the muffled screams of the girl went ignored.

Chapter 1

IN-FLIGHT ENTERTAINMENT

'Hey, you! Get me another of these, will ya?'

The guy with the short dark mohawk, both of his arms sleeved in tribal tattoos, leaned so far out of his seat that he almost tumbled into the aisle as he tried to grab the attention of the passing flight attendant. He reached out, and instead of grabbing her attention he accidentally grabbed her blue-skirted bottom as she bent over to talk to an elderly passenger who couldn't get his headphones to work.

'Whoa, sorry,' sniggered mohawk guy, hauling himself back into his seat and holding up his hands innocently as the stewardess glared at him. 'Didn't mean to do that. Truly. Nice ass, though.'

Having dealt with the elderly passenger, the stewardess turned back to mohawk guy. 'Is there something you need, sir?' she asked flintily.

Immediately the guy's smirk faded and his expression grew stony. 'There are many things I need, sweetheart,' he said, 'and one of them is for you to remember who the paying fucking customers are here.'

Smiling sweetly, the stewardess said, 'Oh, I do, sir. I remember that at all times.'

'Yeah? Well maybe you should remember to leave your shitty attitude at home too.'

Still smiling, the stewardess said, 'And maybe you should remember to keep your hands to yourself, sir. In this job molestation is still a crime, regardless of who's paying.'

'Hey, it was an accident, right?' mohawk guy said, loud enough to turn heads. 'I lost my balance.'

'In that case I accept your apology,' said the stewardess.

Mohawk guy scowled. 'I ain't apologizing to you. I got nothing to apologize *for*.'

The passenger sitting next to him was a young, muscle-bound black man with a sculpted, neatly trimmed beard. He was dressed in baggy jeans, a skinny black T-shirt and a red bandanna. Although he had given all the indications of being asleep, he now opened his eyes and removed the headphones from his ears.

'Why don't you stop giving the nice lady a hard time?' he rumbled.

Mohawk guy turned to look at him, sticking his jaw out pugnaciously. 'Who the hell asked you?'

'Nobody asked me,' said the black man. 'I'm jus' sayin'.'

'Yeah, well, butt out, brother. This has got nothing to do with you.'

The black man grinned, displaying a gold-plated upper canine among a mouthful of clearly expensive dental work. ' "Brother"? Is that some kinda racial slur?' he enquired.

Mohawk guy rolled his eyes. 'What is this? Character assassination week? First she accuses me of being a sexual deviant, now you accuse me of being a damn racist.'

'I didn't accuse you of sexual deviancy, sir,' the stewardess said.

'Molestation, you said. Pretty much amounts to the same thing.'

'Well, you *did* grab the lady's butt,' said the black man.

'I was trying to attract her attention is all,' mohawk guy protested. 'All I wanted was a damn drink.'

'How about I get you a drink and we say no more about it?' suggested the stewardess. She eyed the array of miniature scotch bottles on the passenger's fold-down table, all of them empty. 'Same again, sir?'

Mohawk guy hesitated. For a moment he looked as though he wanted to prolong the argument. Then finally he nodded. 'Yeah, sure. And take these empties away, will ya?'

'Certainly, sir,' said the stewardess politely.

When she had gone, mohawk guy turned to the black man, who was eyeing him as if he was a weird and particularly repellent form of pondlife. 'What?' he said.

The black man shook his head slowly and deliberately. 'Nothin'. Nothin' at all.'

He reached for his headphones again, but before he could put them on mohawk guy said, 'Hey, don't I know you?'

The black man winced slightly. 'Probably not.'

'Yeah, sure I do. You're that rapper. Sam something.'

'Sam B,' the black man conceded with a sigh.

'Sam B! That's right! You had that song, didn't you? Back in the nineties. What was it now? "Voodoo Hoodoo"?'

' "Who Do You Voodoo, Bitch," ' Sam corrected him.

Mohawk guy gave a gurgle of laughter. 'That's the one! Jeez, I loved that song when I was at school.' He paused, his eyes – the whites pink from the alcohol – narrowed shrewdly. 'So what happened to you, man?'

'Nothin' happened to me,' replied Sam. 'I'm right here.'

Mohawk guy laughed, as if he had made a joke. 'Sure you are. But how come you didn't do no more music after that one song?'

Sam closed his eyes briefly. He had answered this question so many times that he had grown to dread being asked it.

'I was young,' he said. 'Young and stupid. At nineteen I thought I knew it all. Took me a long time to realize I didn't know shit. That song was a blessing and a curse, y'know? It was a hit all over the world, made me an instant star, but it was too much fame too quickly.' He tapped the side of his skull with his forefinger. 'I was just a dumb kid from New Orleans and success went straight to my head. I lost track of my roots, deserted the friends I'd grown up with to party with the rich and famous.'

'And you stopped writing music?' asked mohawk guy.

Sam shrugged. 'I couldn't take the pressure. The more people told me I needed to come up with another hit, the more it paralysed me. I started off playing big hotels in Vegas, then seedy lounges in Reno, then third-rate cruise ships.' He shook his head. 'But why the hell am I telling you this?'

'Because you recognize a kindred spirit?'

Sam snorted a laugh. 'Yeah, right.'

The stewardess returned with mohawk guy's drink. 'Anything for you, sir?' she asked Sam.

Sam shook his head. 'I'm good, thanks.'

The stewardess smiled and walked away. Mohawk guy opened the miniature bottle and took a swig. Smacking his lips, he turned back to Sam. 'You don't recognize me, do you?'

'Should I?'

Mohawk guy paused and said, 'I'm Logan Carter.'

Sam looked at him blankly.

The other man, Logan, looked a little put out. 'The football star, Logan Carter? First round NFL draft pick?'

Sam shrugged. 'Sorry, man. I don't follow sports.'

Logan gaped at him. 'You don't follow sports? That's like saying you don't follow life.'

Sam shrugged again. 'Sorry.' He was silent for a moment, and then, almost reluctantly, asked, 'So . . . you still play?'

Logan's face darkened. He drained the rest of the bottle in one gulp. 'No, I . . . er . . . had to retire.'

'Why don't you tell him why?' said a voice from the seat in front.

Logan blinked and jerked upright as though someone had slapped him. 'Excuse me?'

The passenger turned and knelt on her seat, her

head rising above the seat back. She was startlingly beautiful, her skin the colour of teak, her hair a silky black waterfall. She had a snub nose, plump, almost purple lips that Sam guessed could be wide and smiling but were currently pursed in something like disapproval, and wide, dark, penetrating eyes.

'I said why don't you tell him why you had to retire?' the girl repeated, her voice husky and warm.

'What the hell has it gotta do with you?' Logan asked.

The girl pointed at him. 'He didn't recognize you, but I do. I know what you did.'

'What I did? I didn't do anything.'

'You killed a girl.'

The accusation was so blunt that for a moment nobody moved or spoke. Then Logan, his face reddening with anger, spluttered, 'I didn't kill nobody.'

'No?' said the girl, tilting her head to one side. 'So what would *you* call it?'

'I'd call it an accident. And that's what the judge called it too. So get out of my face, lady!'

For the first time the girl turned her attention to Sam. He felt a stirring in his gut as her dark-eyed gaze swept over him, a sensation somewhere between desire and unease. The girl was incredibly beautiful, but in the way a panther was beautiful. Sam had a feeling she could be predatory, dangerous.

'*You* ever killed anyone, Sam?' she challenged.

Sam's first instinct was to ask her how she knew his name, but then he realized she must have been listening in on their conversation. He shook his head. 'Nope.'

20

'Glad to hear it. The guilt of it twists you up inside. Isn't that right, Mr Carter?'

Logan glared at her. 'What part of "get out of my face" didn't you understand?'

Sam raised his hands. Peacemaker wasn't a role he was accustomed to, but then again he wasn't often in the presence of people who seemed even more fucked up than he was. 'Let's just cool it down a bit here, OK?' he said, turning to Logan. 'Listen ... Logan. Why don't you tell me what happened?'

Logan gave a bad-tempered sigh, glancing balefully at the girl. She smiled.

'Yeah, *Logan*, why don't you do that?'

'I don't have to justify myself to you,' Logan said to the girl.

She shrugged as if she couldn't care one way or the other, a faintly amused expression on her face. Sam touched Logan's arm briefly.

'Hey. *I'd* like to know, man. I'm interested. And I got an open mind here. Hell, I'd never even heard of you till ten minutes ago. No offence.'

Logan almost smiled at that. Then he pushed himself upright in his seat and said, 'I need another drink.'

'Why don't we *all* have one?' proposed the girl. 'On me. Sam?'

Sam shrugged. 'I'll have a soda, I guess.'

'Nothing stronger?'

He nodded at the empty miniature scotch bottle on Logan's table. 'I had enough problems of my own with that stuff. I ain't going there again.'

The girl attracted the attention of a stewardess and

ordered their drinks – same again for Logan, a soda for Sam, a white wine spritzer for herself.

When the drinks arrived, she said, 'So, Mr Carter?'

Logan squinted at her. 'What are you, a cop?'

'Used to be,' she admitted.

'That figures.' He took a small sip of his drink – having poured the scotch into a plastic cup this time – and said to Sam, 'I guess, like you, I was young and stupid. Unlike you, though, I had it all. I was a football star in high school and college, so I was . . . protected.'

'Spoiled, you mean?' said the girl.

Logan scowled. 'Look, who's telling this story? Me or you?'

The girl held up her hands, as if allowing him the floor.

Still scowling, Logan said, 'We don't even know who you are.'

Shrugging as if it was no big deal, the girl said, 'My name's Purna.'

'Purna?' repeated Logan. 'What kind of a name's that?'

'It's Australian,' said the girl. 'Aborigine actually.'

'You're an Aborigine?' said Sam, interested.

'Half – on my mother's side.' She turned her attention back to Logan – and suddenly smiled. Sam almost gasped. Her smile was every bit as radiant as he'd imagined, like the sun coming out from behind a cloud. 'You were saying, Mr Carter?'

For a moment Logan looked bemused, as if he'd been bewitched by her smile too. Then he nodded briefly and said, 'So . . . er, yeah. Like I say, I was pro-tected. I had pretty much whatever I wanted – fame, money, women, fast cars.' He grimaced. 'That last one was my downfall. Well . . . those last two, I guess. I shoulda looked after myself more, but well . . . there were a lot of parties back then. A *lot* of parties. Anyway, this one night, I'd had too much to drink, snorted some coke . . . you know how it is. And this one guy, he started ragging me about my car, calling it a piece of shit, all that.'

'What kind of car was it?' Sam asked.

'Porsche Spyder. Like James Dean used to drive. Classy car, man . . .' For a moment Logan's face softened and he looked almost as if he was going to cry.

Sam nodded brusquely. 'Sure thing. So what happened?'

Logan took a deep breath. 'I challenged him to a race. His fucked-up old Buick against my Spyder. I mean, he had no chance, but the dumb fuck took me on.' He shrugged. 'I wanted to teach him a lesson. Not just beat him, but *really* beat him, you know.'

'But you ended up beating yourself, didn't you?' said Purna softly.

Logan snorted a laugh, but it was hard, without humour. 'You could say that. Took a bend too quickly. Lost control. Hit a wall at . . . I dunno. . . eighty, ninety miles an hour?' He shuddered, took a drink. 'Shattered my knee. End of my career. But that wasn't the worst part.'

Sam glanced at Purna, and then back at Logan. 'The girl?' he asked.

Logan nodded. 'Her name was Drew Peters. She came along for the ride. She took the full impact . . .'

'But you got off,' said Purna, her voice unreadable.

Logan nodded and glanced at her, his face almost defiant. 'Yeah, I got off. What can I say? I had a good lawyer.'

'Money talks,' she said, and this time there was a definite bitterness to her tone.

'It's what makes the world go round, baby,' Logan murmured. 'Always has, always will.'

Before Purna could respond, there was a crackle from the intercom and the voice of their pilot, who had introduced himself earlier as Captain Avery, announced, 'Ladies and gentlemen, we will shortly be beginning our descent to Banoi Island airport. Could you please now return to your seats, put on your seat-belts and return your tables to the upright position. It's a beautiful day on the island today, with temperatures in the region of 27 degrees Celsius, that's 80 degrees Fahrenheit, and the local time there is currently 11.52 a.m. In a few moments we will be descending through cloud cover, whereupon those of you on the right-hand side of the plane will be able to see the island as we begin our approach. I hope that you have all had a pleasant flight, and on behalf of New Guinea International Airlines, I thank you for flying with us today.'

The pilot's voice clicked off, and a few seconds later the engines began to rise in pitch. Purna, Logan and Sam strapped themselves in, Sam gripping the arms of his seat and looking out of the window as wispy white clouds billowed past the aircraft. He was not a nervous flyer, but he was anxious about what awaited him on the island. The gig at Banoi's top resort hotel, the

Royal Palm, had fallen into his lap like manna from heaven and he was determined not to blow it. This could be his last chance to prove he was not a joke, maybe his *only* chance to showcase his new material in front of a sizeable audience. And who knew, if even one or two of the record executives his manager had informed about the gig made the effort to turn up, it could even lead to a new record deal, his first in over six years. He was desperate to show the world he was not a one-hit wonder, that there was far more to him than 'Who Do You Voodoo, Bitch'. He swallowed to clear the pressure in his ears as the plane swooped towards the ground, but his mouth was dry.

'Hey, would you look at that!' said Logan beside him, craning forward as far as his seatbelt would allow. Sam followed his gaze and saw a lush tropical paradise below, surrounded by an ocean so placid and clear it seemed to sparkle like a plain of blue-white diamonds. On the nearside of the island was the resort area – hotels, restaurants, bars and stores clustered around a vast beach of pristine white sand. Beyond that, covering a good seventy per cent of Banoi, was dense tropical jungle, which eventually gave way, on the far side of the island, to a bare and jagged mountain range, rising up from the greenery like the gnarled back of some prehistoric beast.

'Looks like paradise, all right,' Sam said, though he still couldn't quell the nerves in his belly.

Logan pointed to the right of the island. 'What's that?'

Maybe a couple of miles offshore was a much smaller island, little more than a rock maybe half a mile in circumference, with a grey rectangular build-ing situated on a plateau in the centre. The building resembled a huge but grim-looking office block, and was dominated by a flat-roofed tower at one end that jabbed up into the glorious blue sky like an accusatory finger.

'Looks like a prison,' Sam mused, noting the high electrified fence that encircled the building.

Purna's face appeared in the gap between the seats. 'It's Banoi high-security prison,' she confirmed. 'Full of psychos and terrorists. The locals call it ... well, I can't remember the actual word, but it translates as "hell in heaven".'

'How come you know so much?' Logan said.

'I read a lot,' replied Purna. 'You should try it.'

The prison wheeled away from them as the plane banked slightly on its final approach to the island. Logan looked at Sam with eyes a little bleary from drink.

'Welcome to paradise,' he said.

Chapter 2

FAMILY HONOUR

'Royal Palm Hotel. How can I help you?'

As she dealt with the customer request, Xian Mei wondered, not for the first time, what she was doing here. She hated living a lie, hated being out on a limb, and most of all she hated the fact that her life currently seemed to have no direction. She had been told that she was doing 'important work for her country', but what was so important about observing the habits of a bunch of wealthy western tourists? Banoi wasn't exactly the front line, and being a receptionist on the desk of a luxury hotel in the middle of nowhere, far from her family and friends, was a long way from how she had envisaged honouring the memory of her father.

Xian Mei still remembered that terrible night in October 1999 as if it were yesterday. She had been twelve at the time, at home with her mother, Jiao, her homework spread out on the kitchen table of their sixth-floor apartment in Beijing. She had been trying to finish early because her grandmother, Li, was coming to visit. When the front-door buzzer sounded, Xian

Mei had at first assumed her grandmother had arrived early. Jiao, who had been preparing mutton dumplings for supper, raised her eyebrows good-humouredly at Xian Mei and strolled out into the hallway, drying her hands on a cloth. When she answered the buzzer, Xian Mei had been surprised, and initially a little relieved, to hear a man's voice crackling from the intercom. Her first thought had been that she might have time to finish her homework before her grandmother arrived after all. She had no way of knowing at that moment that her homework would never get finished, that the mutton dumplings her mother had been preparing so lovingly would never get eaten, and that her life, and that of her mother's, would never be the same again.

The visitor was her father's friend and partner, Detective Sergeant Paul Ho. Many a time Paul and his pretty wife Huan had been guests at her parents' house, and their evenings together were full of laughter and good fun, and often – for the adults – a little too much wine. Xian Mei liked Paul, not only because he was full of jokes and compliments, but also because he often brought her a little present – a bow for her hair, a pocket-doll for her collection, a money box in the shape of a fat smiling cat.

Paul did not bring her a present on this evening, however. Nor was he full of jokes and laughter. It had been raining and when he turned up on their doorstep he had water running down his face and dripping off his jacket. He mumbled an apology, but Jiao told him not to worry. She fetched a towel, and as he dried his hair and face she asked him in a hushed voice – almost as if she was afraid of the answer – what was wrong.

Looking back, what Xian Mei now particularly remembered about that evening was the strange and uncomfortable tension that accompanied Paul's arrival. It was almost as if it clung to him, a kind of darkness that caused her stomach to tighten, her mouth to dry up, the ends of her fingers to tingle unpleasantly. She felt it as soon as he stepped through the door. It was so strong that it drew her, almost unwillingly, from the kitchen. She felt as though Paul was a magnet and she was a shred of metal being dragged helplessly towards him. She sidled into the hallway but held on to the edge of the door, the only way of anchoring herself. Paul glanced up and saw her standing there, peering almost fearfully at him, and his eyes filled with such sadness and pity that it terrified her.

'Can we talk privately?' he asked Jiao.

Jiao flinched and clenched her fists, as if his words had punctured her like a flurry of arrows, but she nodded. She glanced briefly at Xian Mei, who was shocked to see that her mother looked as frightened as she herself felt. As Jiao ushered Paul towards the lounge, Xian Mei stepped forward. Though her mouth was dry she forced herself to speak.

'What's happened to my father?'

Once again, Paul turned those desperately sad eyes on her. Usually so confident, at that moment he looked lost, uncertain what to say. Jiao saved him from having to say anything by stepping in front of him.

'Go back into the kitchen and finish your home-work,' she muttered almost angrily.

'But—' Xian Mei began.

'No arguments! Just do as I say. Your grandmother will be here soon.'

Jiao all but pushed Paul into the lounge and closed the door. Xian Mei retreated into the kitchen but she didn't finish her homework. Instead she sat cross-legged in the open kitchen doorway, listening. She heard Paul speaking, but his voice was too low and muffled for her to make out the words. Then he fell silent, and there was a pause that seemed to Xian Mei to stretch out for ever.

And then – suddenly, shockingly – her mother cried out. It was a harsh sound, the kind you might expect to hear from someone who had been stabbed through the heart. It made Xian Mei jump, then wrap her arms around herself protectively. But although the cry was bad, the sound that followed was much, much worse. Xian Mei had never heard her mother weep before, but now she began not just to weep, but to *wail*, almost to scream. It was an awful, heart-rending sound; to Xian Mei it seemed to encapsulate all the despair and misery that existed in the world. Frightened by the intensity of her mother's grief, she clapped her hands to her ears and squeezed her eyes tight shut. If she had any doubts before, the noises her mother was making now had confirmed without question that whatever had happened tonight was the very worst thing ever.

The rest of the evening seemed to pass in a terrible, murky fog. When the door to the lounge finally opened, it wasn't Jiao who emerged, but Paul Ho. He let out a huge sigh and rubbed a trembling hand over his face. Then he realized Xian Mei was sitting in the kitchen doorway, staring at him. For a moment he looked almost guilty, as if he had been caught doing something he shouldn't, then he walked across and knelt beside her. His damp jacket smelled of the city – of rain and petrol and dark places.

'You're going to have to be very brave and look after your mother, OK?' he said quietly.

Xian Mei looked up at him. His skin was saggy and his eyes were red, and for the first time she thought he looked old.

'Where's my father?' she asked.

Paul hesitated. 'You need to ask your mother that question.'

'Is he dead?' Xian Mei persisted.

Paul made a face as if he'd tasted something sour. Then he leaned forward and kissed Xian Mei gently on her forehead. 'I'll see you soon,' he said.

Xian Mei couldn't get her mother to speak to her. She tried, but Jiao had locked herself in the bathroom. She didn't emerge until grandmother Li arrived almost half an hour later. Even then the two women went into the bedroom and Xian Mei was forced to wait outside. When they finally came out, both were pale and grim-faced. Jiao told Xian Mei that Li would look after her, then she went out without answering her daughter's questions.

'Why is Mother being so mean to me?' Xian Mei said.

Her grandmother shook her head wearily. 'She's not being mean. She's just upset. She's protecting you.'

'I don't need protecting,' Xian Mei said. 'I'm strong.'

Li smiled. 'Maybe you are.'

'I *am*,' Xian Mei insisted. She looked at her grand-mother. 'Won't you tell me what's happened?'

Li averted her gaze. 'Maybe in the morning.'

'*Now*,' Xian Mei said. When her grandmother didn't reply, Xian Mei said almost defiantly, 'Father's dead, isn't he? Something happened to him tonight, and now he's dead.'

Li's eyes brimmed with tears, and she nodded. She wiped her face with a trembling hand. Eventually she said, 'He was very brave. He died a hero.'

It wasn't until the next day, or the day after that, that Xian Mei found out the full story. Her father had been killed in the line of duty, shot dead while trying to apprehend a gang of drug smugglers. It wasn't until he was gone that Xian Mei really discovered how loved and revered her father had been. In the days following his death, many people came to the house to pay their respects, and each of them had a story to tell about her father's courage, or humour, or kindness, or loyalty. As Xian Mei helped her mother prepare the house for his funeral – covering the statues of deities with red paper, removing the mirrors so the reflection of the coffin would not be glimpsed in the glass and bring bad luck, hanging the white cloth over the door-way and placing a gong to the left of the entrance – she vowed she would honour her father's name by follow-ing in his footsteps.

It was a vow she neither forgot nor relinquished. For the next few years, driven by a steely determination and a single-mindedness she liked to think she had inherited directly from her father, she strove for excellence in all areas of her life. Always a good student, she now became an exceptional one, achieving the highest grades possible in every subject. But she knew that academia alone would not secure her a place in one of the toughest and most ruthlessly efficient police forces in the world, so she took up Changquan and trained tirelessly, day after day, pushing herself through physical barrier after physical barrier, until she became one of the foremost martial artists for her age and gender, not only in China but in the world.

The day she was inducted into China's first all-female Special Forces squad was the greatest day of her life. Throughout the ceremony, as she stood there in her beautiful black and grey uniform, she thought only of her father and how proud he would be. Indeed, she strongly believed his spirit was there with her, standing at her shoulder, revelling in her success.

It took almost no time at all for the dream to turn into a nightmare.

What became apparent to Xian Mei and her fellow inductees very quickly was that China's first all-female Special Forces squad was, in effect, little more than a glorified PR stunt. Xian Mei had had high hopes of becoming a pioneer, of helping to usher in a new age of equality in China, but almost as soon as the induction ceremony was over, the squad was broken up and its members distributed around the globe on 'special assignments'. Xian Mei's assignment was to come here, to the Royal Palm Hotel in Banoi, and to spy on the decadent rich, using her receptionist's job as cover. What Xian Mei found particularly insulting was that her superiors didn't even bother to *pretend* she was doing vital work. It was abundantly clear to her that she had been shunted aside simply for the sake of convenience – a case of out of sight, out of mind.

Although it was another gloriously sunny day in Banoi, Xian Mei felt her spirits plummeting as a bus pulled up outside the main doors, transporting the latest batch of holidaymakers from the airport. Although she planted a smile on her face, she wondered what her father would think if he could see her now. Would he be ashamed of his daughter or angry on her behalf? If the latter, she wished his spirit would give her some guidance on how to escape from this trap. Not only was she under strict orders to maintain a constant vigil and supply her superiors with weekly reports (reports in which she was finding it increasingly hard to say anything of value), but her government had paid for everything – her flights, her expenses – and she could not leave without their say-so. Even resigning from the Special Forces squad and flying home by scraping together her own meagre savings was out of the question. She would be ostracized and labelled a trouble-maker, and it would bring great shame on her family. Despite the idyllic surroundings, therefore, in many ways she felt just as much a prisoner as the rapists, murderers and terrorists incarcerated in the high-security jail a couple of miles offshore.

The bus was disgorging its passengers now. As always, they looked bleary-eyed, sweaty and flustered from all the travelling, but many of them were peering around with wonder and satisfaction. Xian Mei was not surprised. There was no denying Banoi was beautiful. It was a place of sunny skies, white sand, sparkling blue seas, palm trees and flowers in abundance. For a tourist resort, the pace of life was laid-back, relaxed, and the atmosphere – even at night – was relatively peaceful. The soundtrack was one of insects, birds and the sighing of the tide, rather than of loud music, drunken shouting and people throwing up.

The first of the holidaymakers were trudging into the hotel now, carrying their suitcases or dragging them on wheels behind them. They were pretty much the same as any other group of holidaymakers, as far as she could see, the majority of their number composed of families and couples. Banoi was a location that appealed to all age groups, which meant that in any sample selection of customers you would find young honeymooning couples, middle-aged couples on a romantic break and elderly couples hoping for a week or two of rest and gentle recreation. Xian Mei had been led to believe that westerners were conniving and deceitful, and so shamelessly decadent that they posed a serious threat to the world's very stability, but in the three months she had been here she had seen little evidence of that. On the contrary, once you looked beyond their loud, revealing clothes and their open, sometimes abrasive manner, they were not that dissimilar to her own people. Unless Xian Mei was missing something, all they really seemed to want were healthy, happy, fulfilled lives for themselves and their families.

Occasionally people would arrive here alone, and it

was this group that Xian Mei observed most keenly. For the most part, though, they too seemed harmless, and in fact she often ended up feeling sorry for them as they took their meals alone, or went for solitary walks along the beach, or spent their days sitting silently by the pool, their heads buried in a book. Sometimes she would strike up a conversation with one of them, find out they were a widow or a widower, or treating themselves to a quiet break after a painful divorce. Or sometimes they were single simply because they chose to be, content with their own company.

As ever with a batch of new arrivals, the first hour was a flurry of activity. Xian Mei and her three colleagues, who were often interchangeable depending on their shift patterns, tried to get through the check-in procedure as quickly and efficiently as possible. They all knew there was nothing more annoying for customers who had spent the whole day travelling, and who were desperate to freshen up and relax, than having to wait in yet another queue. But however efficiently she worked, she knew it was inevitable that one or two people out of a group of fifty or sixty would give her a hard time. In this case, it was a young, muscular, tattooed man with a flushed face and a slight limp. He thumped his elbows on the desk and leaned in towards her with a leer. Xian Mei tried not to recoil at the smell of alcohol on his breath.

'So where can a guy get a little action around here?' he said by way of introduction.

Xian Mei gave him a professional smile. 'That depends what you mean, sir. There is an abundance of restaurants and bars on the island.'

'That so?' said the man thoughtfully. 'And I guess you'd know all the best ones?'

Xian Mei hesitated. 'I don't go out too often. I work long hours here, and I'm usually very tired at the end of the day.'

'Sounds to me like you could use a little R'n'R,' said the man, leaning in even closer.

'As I say, I work long hours,' said Xian Mei. She focused on the monitor in front of her. 'Do you have a reservation, sir?'

'I do indeedy,' said the man. He grinned and leaned back, like a hunter who had failed to bag his target on this occasion but knew it was only a matter of time.

'Could I take your name, please, sir?'

The man pushed out his bottom lip, feigning offence. 'You mean you don't recognize me?'

Xian Mei glanced at him. 'I'm afraid not, sir.'

Next to her, her colleague, Lan, was dealing with the reservation of a young black man wearing a red bandanna. The black man glanced over at Xian Mei's customer and shook his head. 'You givin' *this* nice lady a hard time now?' he drawled in a voice as deep and warm as melted chocolate.

The tattooed man spread his hands. 'I'm just being friendly is all.'

The black man raised one eyebrow. 'There's different types of friendly. I don't think the nice lady likes *your* particular flavour.'

Xian Mei smiled, genuinely amused. 'It's really not a problem, sir.'

'You see!' said the tattooed man triumphantly. 'Not

a problem.' He turned back to Xian Mei. 'I think you and me are going to hit it off just fine.'

Xian Mei smiled, but didn't comment. Instead she said, 'So if I *could* take your name, sir?'

The tattooed man sighed theatrically. 'It's Carter. Logan Carter. *Football star*, Logan Carter.'

'*Ex*-football star,' muttered the black man.

Logan scowled. 'Just like you're an *ex*-rapper, you mean?'

The black man turned and gave Logan a cool, appraising look. 'We'll see about that, won't we?'

'Yeah,' Logan said. 'I guess we will.'

Xian Mei typed Logan's name into her keyboard and pressed Enter, and immediately his details scrolled up on her monitor, together with a flashing red symbol in the top left-hand corner. Because of her briefing from her manager that morning, she recognized the symbol as the logo for the US National Blood Drive Campaign. Looking up, she said, 'I see you're one of our blood drive people, Mr Carter?'

Logan nodded. 'Sure am. Helped promote the blood donation campaign, what with being a nationally-known face and all. Had my picture taken giving an itty bit of blood and got an all-expenses-paid holiday in return. Sounded like a damn good deal to me.'

Beside him the black man said, 'Snap.'

Logan turned. 'Pardon me?'

'I'm in on that blood drive deal too. Gave some blood at a celebrity event in New Orleans. Next thing, I get a call offering me a two-week gig here in Banoi. Pretty cool, huh?'

Before Logan could respond, a voice behind the black man said, 'Double snap.'

Both men turned to reveal an elegant and strikingly beautiful dark-skinned woman in a short, sleeveless, green summer dress. The woman waved her plastic room key, on which was stamped the red National Blood Drive Campaign logo.

'After I gave blood I didn't even know I'd been entered in a sweepstake till I got a call to say I'd won an all-expenses-paid holiday. Thought it was a scam at first.'

The black man turned to Xian Mei. Nodding at their fellow guests who were still waiting in line to check in, he said, 'Hey, are *all* these dudes here because of this blood drive thing?'

Xian Mei tapped a couple of keys on her keyboard. 'No, just the three of you,' she said.

'Hey,' said Logan, 'we're like a club. Well, ain't *that* nice?'

The black man looked at Purna and raised an eyebrow. 'Yeah,' he said drily. 'Maybe we should all get ourselves some T-shirts.'

Chapter 3

WHO DO YOU VOODOO, BITCH

'Well, now, ain't this somethin'!'

Logan stood out on the balcony of his hotel room, looking at the view. He had showered and changed, and was now ready to have himself a little fun. He swirled his scotch and soda round in his glass, liking the way the ice cubes tinkled and chimed. He had popped some Prozac a while ago and was currently feeling mellow, relaxed. His knee had been throbbing some after the flight, but a couple of Tramadol had taken care of that. He thought about the cute Chinese girl on reception and wondered what time she finished work. Despite her resistance earlier, he still had high hopes of reeling in *that* particular fish. In his experience, it was often the initially shy and reluctant girls who ended up being the wildest between the sheets.

Ten minutes later Logan was sitting at the hotel bar, his gaze roaming around the room. The place was full of couples and families, all dressed up for dinner. There were no single women here, not even that Purna chick. Maybe he should have knocked on her door on the way down – he, Purna and that rapper guy, Sam, had been given adjacent rooms, just as they had been given seats together on the plane, almost certainly because of that blood drive bullshit – though something told Logan he wouldn't make much headway in *that* direction. The woman was stunningly beautiful, sure, but she was also tough and angular and had a don't-fucking-mess-with-me look in her big brown eyes. In Logan's view women should be docile and vulnerable and sweet if they wanted to attract men, not opinionated ball-breakers.

He had a couple more drinks at the bar and then decided to move on. He knew if he stayed in the hotel he could have free drinks all night, not to mention a free dinner, but he would rather put down a few of his own hard-earned dollars if it meant getting himself a little action.

'Same again, sir?' the bartender asked.

'Maybe later,' replied Logan. He stood up and began to make his way towards the exit, but then something occurred to him and he turned back. 'Hey, I don't suppose you know what time Sam B is doing his thing, do you?'

'Ten p.m. I believe, sir.'

'Thanks, buddy.'

It wasn't until the fresh air hit him that the world started to spin. He paused a moment, blinking. Must be the jet lag. That and the fact that he hadn't eaten in hours. He began to weave away from the hotel, heading for the bright lights of the main street. It was beginning to get dark now, streaks of lilac cloud appearing in the blue sky.

Every fisherman knows there are days when the fish

41

just don't bite, and such was Logan's luck that night. He trailed the bars of Banoi's main street for over two hours before deciding to head back to the hotel. He had talked to a few likely looking girls, had even persuaded a couple of them to accept his offer of a drink, but somehow they kept slipping the line before he got the chance to reel them in. By the time he arrived back at the Royal Palm, with nothing to show for his evening but a lighter wallet and a smear of seafood sauce on his shirt from the crayfish sandwich he had eaten in a bar called the Sailing Boat, he was foul-tempered and so drunk that the ground was tilting and yawing beneath him like the deck of a ship.

Noting blearily that the little Chinese girl was no longer on reception, he decided to make for the bar for an on-the-house nightcap or two. Then he heard the thump of music coming from somewhere off to his right and remembered all about Sam and his gig. Moving carefully so as not to trip over his own feet, he changed direction and followed the pulse of the beat. He was going not out of any sense of loyalty to his new-found blood drive buddy, but because if there *was* any decent and available pussy here in the hotel, then this is where he would be most likely to find it.

The main ballroom, where the gig was taking place, was hotter than a sauna. Logan breathed in the heady scent of sweat and perfume, his head swimming. All around him, people were gyrating or nodding in time to the music. The heavy bass throbbed in his teeth and chest like a second heartbeat. The darkness of the room, combined with the ever-changing light display up on stage and the alcohol in his system, seemed to scramble Logan's senses, to blur individual bodies into a single pulsing mass of humanity. Feeling a little overwhelmed by it all, Logan felt instinctively he should head for the light, and so began to push through the crowd towards the stage, at first muttering 'Excuse me' as he barged his way through, and then, following his ball player's instincts, simply lowering his head and charging forward.

If anyone protested or tried to stop him, Logan wasn't aware of it. He simply kept pushing until there was nothing left to push against. When he finally raised his head it felt like surfacing from a warm pool. He was drenched in his own and other people's sweat, his shirt sticking to him like another layer of skin. Right in front of him, level with his face, was the edge of the stage. The music was so loud now that his whole body seemed to be convulsing with it. He looked up.

And there was Sam B, prowling from one side of the stage to the other like a caged tiger. He was scowling aggressively, jabbing at the audience as he spat out his lyrics. He looked much angrier up on stage than he did in real life. He was bare-chested, a huge, gold 'B' pendant swinging on a chain round his neck. There was more bling round his wrists, and his stomach was imprinted with a tattoo – a black skull above a pair of crossed Uzis. He looked fit and predatory, totally in his element.

Logan was impressed in spite of himself – and more than a little envious too. He turned and peered drunkenly into the crowd. They were clearly enjoying themselves, grinning and bouncing and punching the air. There *had* been a time when Logan himself had enjoyed this kind of adulation – crowds cheering and whooping; girls wanting to fuck him; guys wanting to *be* him. All at once, standing there alone, he felt a wave of self-loathing sweep over him. Not quite knowing why he was doing it, he turned and waved his arms.

'Sam! Hey, Sam!' he yelled.

It was only when the rapper carried on as if he wasn't even there that Logan realized he *did* know why he was trying to grab his attention. It was because he wanted Sam to acknowledge him, to bathe him in a little reflected glory. The fact that Sam didn't even look at him caused a red mist to descend in front of his eyes.

'*Fuck you!*' he screamed at the stage. Then he turned and barged his way back into the crowd. 'Out of my fucking way!' he snarled.

People took one look at his wild eyes and stepped aside. Logan wondered how many of them recognized him, or half-recognized him, or maybe thought he looked vaguely like someone they might once have known. Fame was the best thing in the world when you were standing on its summit, looking out at the view. But he couldn't believe there was a worse feeling than sliding back down the mountain and realizing there was nothing to stop you from hitting the bottom. To have been famous once and then to have lost it was surely worse than never having been famous at all. It was worse too, in its way, than the end of a relationship, or even the death of a loved one. In Logan's opinion it was easy to find love again – people did it all the time. But how many famous people, once they had hit the slippery slope, managed to reverse the fall and make it back to the top of the mountain?

He was halfway through the crowd when he spotted Purna. She was standing alone, arms folded, eyes fixed intently on the stage. Making a snap decision, he staggered towards her.

'Hi,' he shouted above the music.

She looked momentarily startled, which gave Logan a vicious ripple of satisfaction. She'd seemed so in control before that it felt good to scratch her veneer a little bit.

'Hi,' she said guardedly.

He nodded towards the stage. 'So whaddya think?'

'He's good.' She shrugged. 'It's not my kind of music, but . . . yeah, I appreciate the artistry.'

Logan sneered. 'Artistry?'

She looked at him a moment before replying, as if weighing him up. 'You don't think it's an art?'

'Fuck, no!' He spat the words with such venom that he stumbled forward and Purna had to reach out with both hands to steady him.

'Hey, you OK?' she said. 'You don't look too good.'

'I'm fine,' he said. 'Just . . . hot. I've been up at the front. Thought I'd get a drink. You want one?'

'No, I'm good, thanks.'

She turned away, as if dismissing him. Logan felt that red mist prickling at the edges of his vision again.

'Why do you do that?' he snapped.

She glanced at him, puzzled. 'Do what?'

'Turn away like . . . like I'm a piece of shit on your shoe?' He knew that analogy didn't quite make sense, but he felt as though he'd made his point.

She looked exasperated rather than defensive. 'I don't. It's your imagination.'

'Fuck that,' he said. 'You think you're so fucking superior to everyone.'

'I really don't.'

'Yeah you do. You're doing it now. Treating me like I'm some . . . some bum pestering you for a dollar.'

'You're drunk,' she said. 'I think you should go and lie down.'

'Yeah? Well, why don't you come and lie down with me?' He reached out to grab her wrist.

Before his hand could make contact, Purna somehow managed to step both to one side and closer to him. Her right knee came up swiftly, crushing his balls. Despite the dulling effects of alcohol, the pain was so unbelievable that for a moment Logan felt sure he'd been ripped in two. As he doubled over, she grabbed his arm and twisted it up behind his back. He howled in agony.

She leaned in close to him and murmured in his ear. 'I really think you should take my advice, Logan. Go back to your room, drink lots of water, then sleep it off. You'll thank me in the morning.'

He tried to twist out of her grip, but that only caused fresh pain to shoot up his arm. Pain so acute that he felt on the verge of passing out. 'Let go of me,' he wailed.

'Only if you promise to do as I say.'

Black sparks were dancing in front of his eyes now and the sweat on his body was turning clammy.

'Promise me,' she repeated.

Thoroughly humiliated, his balls and arm hurting almost beyond endurance, Logan gasped, 'I promise.'

Immediately he felt his arm released. He staggered forward and fell on his knees.

All the shit he had been through over the past few years suddenly seemed to rush in on him, to coalesce in that moment. He felt utterly wretched, more wretched even than he had felt alone in his hospital bed with his busted-up knee, the painkillers wearing off, and the knowledge that an innocent girl was dead because of him.

Without looking back, he began to crawl away. He felt like a maggot, something to be reviled and crushed. It was only when a wave of nausea rushed through him that he felt compelled to rise to his feet. He spotted a sign for the restrooms and staggered towards it, the hand that Purna had twisted behind his back hanging limply, the other cupping his throbbing balls.

He passed beneath an arch into a short corridor, where a pair of doors faced each other on opposite walls. Choosing the left one at random, he all but fell against it. It opened and he stumbled into the rest room, vomit already boiling up through his oesophagus. The pain and the alcohol and the need to puke had diminished his senses, the music now no more than a mushy throb in his ears, his eyesight narrowing to tunnel vision. Ahead of him he spotted a sink, the silvery gleam of a mirror above it. Somehow he forced his feet into a rickety, lopsided run. He had barely gripped the edge of the sink when his head lurched forward and what felt like gallons of stinking liquid ejected itself from his system.

The liquid burned as it rose up through his stomach

and throat. The fumes from the regurgitated alcohol were like a toxic irritant, making his eyes water, his nose run. He puked so violently that it spattered back off the porcelain walls of the sink, peppering his face and hands and shirt. The shirt was pale blue with little white palm trees on it. He had only bought it that week and was wearing it for the first time.

Slowly he raised his head and looked at himself in the mirror. He looked ghastly, his skin like old dough, his eyes peering from deep hollows. He looked just like his grandpa Buck had done in the last stages of his battle with liver cancer. Leaning forward to prop himself against the sink, he tentatively released his grip so he could turn on the cold tap.

After scooping several handfuls of water over his face and into his mouth, Logan felt a little better. A little, but not much. He had now reached the point where all he craved was a soft bed and sweet oblivion. Hoping enough strength had returned to his legs to support his body, he pushed himself upright and stepped back. As he did so, the reflection in the mirror showed him more of the room, and he was surprised to discover he was not alone.

There were two women on the floor by the toilet cubicles. One was lying on her back, and the other was on her knees, leaning over her. Logan guessed they must have been here the whole time, but he had been so preoccupied he hadn't even noticed them. He turned now and looked at the women properly; he couldn't see either of their faces. The one who was kneeling had her back to him, and was leaning forward at such an angle that she was obscuring the face of the other.

It took him a moment to realize the kneeling woman looked familiar. She was petite and slender, with glossy, black, shoulder-length hair. She was wearing the white blouse and knee-length red skirt of a Palm Hotel receptionist. Unless he was mistaken, this was the cute Chinese girl who had checked him in.

'You OK?' he asked.

The girl turned her head, her raven-black hair swishing like a curtain. It *was* the cute Chinese girl, and she looked worried.

Not questioning the fact that Logan was in the ladies', she said, 'I think this woman's having some kind of seizure.'

Logan stepped forward and saw the other woman's face. 'Whoa,' he said.

The other woman looked . . . weird. Her eyes were glazed and white, the pupils having shrunk to little more than pinpricks. Her teeth were clenched and she was frothing at the mouth like a rabies victim. Moreover she had begun to snort and growl like an animal, her head thrashing from side to side. Even as Logan watched, her body was seized by a series of shuddering convulsions, her hands becoming rigid, fingers curling into claws.

He was about to say something when, without warning, the woman snarled and sat up. The cute Chinese girl was still looking over her shoulder at Logan and so was slow to respond. Before Logan could shout a warning, the woman lunged at the Chinese girl, grabbed her arm and bit her hand. The Chinese girl screamed and pulled away, but not before the woman had done some damage. Logan was shocked to see blood mixed with froth dribbling from the woman's mouth, and a crescent of teeth-marks on the fleshy pad of the Chinese girl's hand. He thought again of rabies, of infection. As the woman sprang to her feet, suddenly lithe as a monkey, he made for the door.

The Chinese girl was right behind him. Logan wrenched open the door and they scrambled out together. He had barely got the door shut when the crazy woman hurled herself against the other side of it. Logan clung to the handle as she screeched and battered at the door, trying to yank it open. He wondered whether he ought to let go and make a run for it. There were so many people in the room that she would probably attack someone else.

'We ought to try and help her,' the Chinese girl shouted above the thud of the music.

'Are you kidding?' Logan yelled back. 'Unless you've got a tranquillizer gun she'd rip our fucking faces off.' He noticed blood dripping from the Chinese girl's hand and shrank back from it. 'You should get that looked at. It might be infectious.'

The girl looked around. 'I'll do it in a minute. Wait here.'

'Where are you going?' Logan shouted as she moved away.

'To get help,' she said and slipped into the crowd. On the other side of the door, the barrage of blows from the screeching woman continued. Logan clung desperately to the door handle and wondered if this was finally it, his divine punishment not only for killing Drew Peters but also for getting away with it. If

you could call the loss of both his career and his repu-
tation 'getting away with it', and, personally, Logan
didn't think you could; he felt he had already suffered
more than enough. He'd heard all that Old Testament
stuff about God being vengeful and full of wrath, but
sending some crazed, psychotic bitch after him to
make his life even more crap than it already was was
just fucking overkill.

He decided that if the Chinese girl wasn't back
within a minute he'd let go of the handle and take his
chances. If the psychotic bitch jumped him and ripped
his head off, at least she'd be putting him out of his
misery. He started to count, but had barely reached
twenty when the Chinese girl came running back
with two hefty security guys in tow. The security
guys looked dubious and a little amused – they
wore expressions which clearly conveyed that whatever the girl had told them, they believed she was
exaggerating.

'She's in here,' Logan said. 'Be careful, she's crazy.'

The security guys lumbered forward. Both Chinese,
like the rest of the staff here, they were built like Sumo
wrestlers and sported identical buzz cuts.

'Move away from the door please, sir,' one of them
said confidently.

'I don't think that's a good idea.'

'Just do it, sir,' said the other security guy. 'We'll take
it from here.'

'Well, if that's what you want . . .' Logan said, and
let go of the handle.

He didn't hang around to see what happened next.
The instant he let go, he turned and ran for the exit. It

might have been his imagination, but over the pounding beat of Sam's signature tune, 'Who Do You Voodoo, Bitch', Logan thought he heard screams. But he didn't look back until he was safely in his room with the door closed and locked behind him.

Chapter 4

UNKNOWN NUMBER

'Help meeee!'

It was almost 4 a.m. when Purna awoke to screams.

Alert in an instant, she jumped out of bed and ran lightly across to the double doors leading on to the balcony. The screams had come from outside, she was sure of it. In her job it paid to be attuned to her surroundings even when asleep. She turned the key in the lock and stepped on to the balcony in her bare feet.

From here she could see the swimming pool below, its inset lighting creating strange ripples and reflections. Beyond the environs of the resort, away to her right, was the lower end of the main street. Purna was just in time to see a woman, running, being chased by . . . what? In the quick glimpse she caught of it before both the woman and her pursuer disappeared around the edge of a building, Purna thought the figure looked and moved like an ape – an ape wearing dishevelled and possibly blood-stained clothes.

The woman screamed again, her voice echoing back along the otherwise deserted main street. Purna knew she couldn't just stand by and do nothing. Stepping back inside the room, she ran across to the phone beside her bed and lifted the receiver. She had already pressed '1' for Reception when she realized the line was dead. What the hell? Exasperated, she replaced the receiver in its cradle.

Training and experience had taught her to remain clear-headed, unflustered. She dressed quickly, pulling jeans and a light zip-up jacket on over the shorts and vest top she wore as pyjamas. She put trainers on over white sports socks, her fingers deft as they tied the laces. Grabbing her room key from the dressing table, she crossed the room, opened the door and stepped into the corridor.

Despite the time, the corridor was not deserted. At its far end was the bellhop who had brought her luggage up earlier. He was a young, polite Chinese guy in a grey uniform, but there was clearly something wrong with him. In fact, he looked as though he had been in a fight or had an accident. There was a lot of blood down the front of his uniform and on his face.

He was moving strangely too, tottering like a drunk, his body hunched over and his hands twisted into arthritic claws. Purna noticed that it was not only his face and clothes, but also his fingers that were smeared with blood and clots of matter, as if he had been tearing up raw meat.

Purna licked her lips, torn between offering help and treating him with caution. Though her instincts were generally good, she was finding it hard to decide whether the bellhop was acting like a victim or an aggressor. If the latter, then he was clearly confused –

perhaps he was drunk or high on drugs? As a cop, Purna had dealt with domestic incidents involving horrific violence, only for the attacker to be utterly bewildered by his or her actions afterwards.

In the end, thinking of the distressed woman in the street, and knowing she would have to approach the bellhop to get to both the lift and the stairs, she stepped forward and said, 'Are you OK?'

The bellhop's head snapped up, and for the first time Purna got a look at his eyes. They were almost white, the pupils the size of pinpricks. The bellhop opened his mouth and snarled, something red and lumpy sliding from between his lips and spattering to the floor, then he started towards her in a shambling run.

He was parallel with the lift and Purna was adopting a defensive stance to meet him when the door beside her opened. A rumpled-looking Logan stepped out, having clearly crashed out on his bed fully dressed, and looked at her sleepily.

'What's all the fucking—'

'*Look out!*' yelled Purna.

Before Logan could respond, the bellhop was on him like a wild animal. The Chinese boy leaped on his back and frenziedly began to bite at his shoulder and neck, tearing at his flesh with his teeth. Taken by surprise, Logan staggered and almost fell, then began to scream and thrash about, his arms flailing in an effort to dislodge his attacker. Within seconds the shoulder of his pale blue shirt was soaked in blood.

Moving forward, Purna grabbed Logan's flailing arms and, displaying both strength and composure, clamped them to his sides. Then she slammed Logan backwards as hard as she could, so that the bellhop's body was crushed between the ex-football star and the wall. She heard a satisfying *clonk* as the bellhop's head impacted with the wall and a crunch that she hoped was a couple of his ribs giving way. Before the bellhop could recover, she yanked Logan forward again and shoved him aside, out of harm's way. The bellhop slid down the wall and landed in a heap on the blood-spattered carpet, like an insect whacked with a newspaper.

He should have been dazed enough to have had the fight knocked out of him, but almost immediately he scrambled to his feet. Springing across the corridor, Purna grabbed a fire extinguisher from the wall, brandishing it in such a way that showed she clearly meant business.

'Stay down or I'll bash your fucking brains out,' she warned.

The bellhop ignored her. Whatever he had taken, it had clearly made him think he was invincible. He seemed not even to notice the extinguisher as he sprang upright and leaped at her, clawed hands extended.

With an almost balletic fluidity, Purna stepped back and then thrust forward with the fire extinguisher. The base of it smacked into the centre of the bellhop's face, smashing his nose and knocking him backwards. The blow would have been enough to incapacitate a normal man, but after tottering back a few steps he lurched upright once more. Seemingly impervious to pain, he snarled at Purna through a thick, red mask of blood and hurled himself towards her in a fresh attack.

Purna stepped to her right and swung the fire extinguisher into the side of his head. As he staggered into the wall, she followed this up with two more blows – another directly into the centre of his face, pulverizing his nose still further, and the other a side-swipe across his forehead, the sound of impact like a coconut hitting a brick wall.

No matter *how* many uppers the guy had been taking, this latest trio of blows should have been more than enough to render him unconscious, if not put him into a coma. However, like a puppet jerking back into life, he rose to his feet again almost immediately, blood drooling from his shattered face like molasses from a cracked pot.

'Fuck,' Purna breathed and whacked him again. She didn't want to kill the guy if she could help it, but the way things were going he was giving her no alternative.

On a sudden impulse, she pulled the pin from the fire extinguisher, aimed the hose at the bellhop and squeezed the trigger. A highly concentrated jet of fire-retardant foam shot from the nozzle, directly into his face. He flailed and thrashed, but Purna grimly kept up her attack, concentrating on his eyes and mouth so that he could neither breathe nor see. The foam dripped down the front of his grey uniform, running red with blood, making it look as if he had met with a particularly nasty shaving accident. When she had forced the bellhop to retreat about ten metres, she upended the extinguisher, smashed it into his face once more, and then threw the extinguisher aside and ran back down the corridor.

Logan had slumped against the wall and was now semi-conscious, breathing stertorously and clutching his bleeding shoulder. Purna wrapped her arms around him and dragged him into her room. As soon as his feet had cleared the doorway she lowered him carefully to the carpet, then ran across and closed the door. Now, unless the bellhop had the strength to break down a sturdy hotel room door, they were safe – at least for the time being.

Crossing back to Logan, Purna heaved him up on to the bed. She lifted his head gently and slid a pillow underneath it. He was sweating, his eyes were fluttering, and blood was still pumping out of his shoulder.

'Logan,' she said. 'Can you hear me?'

His eyes drifted open, flickered around. 'Where am I?'

'In my room.'

He considered this, then his lips twitched into a smile. 'Knew I'd make it into your bed eventually,' he murmured.

She laughed suddenly, a release of tension after what had just occurred. 'Dream on, lover boy,' she said.

In the en-suite bathroom she grabbed all the towels hanging over the rail. The hand towel she ran under the tap, wringing it out so that it was wet but not dripping. She went back into the bedroom, dragged a chair up to the edge of the bed and sat down. Logan had closed his eyes again but was breathing a little more steadily than before.

'You still with us?' she asked gently.

He licked his lips. 'Just about. Feel a bit woozy.'

She clicked on the bedside lamp to examine his shoulder better. 'Are you in much pain?'

'Not as much as I was when you kicked me in the balls,' he replied.

She snorted another laugh. 'Yeah, sorry about that ... Actually, no I'm not sorry. You deserved it.'

'Guess I was being kind of a doofus,' he conceded.

'At least you can admit it.' She was silent for a few moments as she ran her eyes over his wounds. There were several deep bite marks as far as she could tell, each of which was still oozing blood. 'Listen, Logan, I'm going to patch you up as best I can,' she told him, 'but I'll have to clean the area up first. It's probably going to hurt a bit.'

'Thanks for breaking it to me gently,' he muttered.

'My pleasure. Now I want you to be a brave little soldier.'

She pressed the wet towel to his shoulder, soaking up as much of the surface blood as she could. He winced a little, but otherwise didn't react.

'How do the wounds feel?' she asked as she folded the wet towel over and began, gently but firmly, to wipe the excess blood away.

'Weird,' he replied. 'Numb, but they also kind of sting a little. Like a jellyfish sting.'

'Hmm,' she said.

'What do you mean "hmm"?'

'Nothing. Just hmm.'

Logan was silent for a moment, then he asked, 'What was wrong with that guy?'

Purna finished cleaning away the blood and dropped the wet towel on to the floor. Picking up a fresh dry towel, she folded it in half once, then twice more. Pressing it to his shoulder, so that the towel covered his still-seeping wounds, she said, 'Can you hold this for me? Press as hard as you can.'

'Sure,' he said, and did as she asked. 'You didn't answer my question,' he grimaced, as she took another towel and tore it into strips.

Purna looked him in the eye. 'I don't know. I have no idea what was wrong with that guy. Maybe he was sick. Maybe he was high on something.'

'You know what I think?' said Logan.

'What?'

'I think it's finally here. I think this is the fucking zombie apocalypse.'

There was a beat of silence – and then Purna barked a laugh. 'Yeah, right.'

'I'm serious. Did you see that guy's eyes? And he tried to eat me, man.'

'He tried to *bite* you,' Purna corrected him. 'There's a difference.'

Logan shook his head, then gasped when pain shot through the side of his neck.

'Keep your head still,' Purna ordered.

'Sorry, nurse,' Logan said. He clenched his teeth as he adjusted position slightly. 'But like I was saying, that guy wasn't on drugs.'

'How do you know?'

'Because he wasn't the first person I've seen like that tonight. There was a woman at Sam's gig. Same weird eyes, and just as crazy.'

'But I was at the gig, remember?' said Purna. 'I didn't see anything.' Then her eyes widened.

'Hang on – this wasn't near the lavvies, was it?'

'If you mean the restrooms, then yeah, it was. Why? What did you see?'

'Nothing much. They were closed off, that's all. Rumour was a couple of security guys got attacked. Someone said something about a nutjob with a knife.'

'It wasn't a knife,' said Logan. 'They were attacked by a zombie. Like that one out there.'

Purna made a dismissive *t'cho* sound through her teeth. 'There's no such thing as zombies,' she said irritably.

'I know a zombie when I see one,' said Logan stubbornly. 'I've seen the movies.'

'Exactly!' replied Purna. '*Movies*. As in *fiction*. Now hold still while I do this.'

Using a number of the torn strips she secured his makeshift dressing in place, then with another towel made Logan a sling, which she tied at the back, next to his armpit, to stop the knot digging into his wounded shoulder.

'My arm isn't broken,' he told her.

'No, but it's heavy,' she said. 'The sling will take the weight and keep the wounds from reopening, give them chance to heal.'

He sighed, and said glumly, 'They aren't going to heal.'

'What? Course they are,' she replied.

Instinctively he shook his head, and immediately winced again. 'No they're not. I'm infected now. Soon as it reaches my brain I'll become one of *them*.'

'Don't talk shit,' she said. 'You'll be fine.'

'You don't sound too sure.'

She scowled. 'I *am* sure. Even if that guy has got . . . well, something infectious, he's not going to pass it on to you. We'll get you to a doctor, get you the right treatment, the right medication . . .'

'There *is* no treatment,' Logan muttered.

'Bullshit!' Purna snapped, angry now. 'Stop talking like you *want* to get sick!'

'Sorry,' Logan said. 'Of course I don't want to get sick. It's just . . . oh, this is seriously fucked up.'

Purna leaned over him, and to his surprise took his face in her hands. For a moment he thought she was going to kiss him, but she simply fixed her dark eyes on his, staring at him until she had his full attention. Then, quietly but with such conviction that he couldn't help but believe her, she said, 'You're going to be fine, Logan. I promise. I'll make *sure* you're fine. OK?'

When he didn't respond immediately, she said it again, more forcefully. 'OK?'

'OK,' he agreed.

'Good.' She released his face and stood up, stretching herself to her full height. She turned her head towards the door, graceful as a gazelle. 'Wonder if our friend's still out there.'

'You're not going to look, are you?'

She shrugged. 'How else are we going to find out?'

'But—' Logan began, and at that moment his cell phone rang.

It wasn't only *his* phone that rang, though, but Purna's too. They came alive at precisely the same instant, Logan's blasting out the old Survivor hit, 'Eye Of The Tiger', Purna's simply giving a no-nonsense double-buzz every couple of seconds. Purna raised her eyebrows curiously at Logan and slid her sleek black phone from her jeans pocket. 'Unknown number,' she muttered, and raised the phone to her ear just as Logan was doing the same. 'Hello?'

The line crackled, full of static, then a clipped, precise voice said briskly, 'Don't talk, just listen. I have a certain amount of information to relay, and at this juncture I simply don't have time to answer questions. This call is going out to four separate numbers, and I see from the information I have here that all four of you have answered. This is good, very good. However, due to circumstances beyond my control, our lines of communication are limited. In fact, this signal could die at any moment – so please, all of you, listen very carefully . . .'

As if to illustrate the caller's point, his voice was suddenly overwhelmed by a burst of white noise. Purna and Logan both flinched and held their phones away from their ears. After a few seconds the white noise settled back into a more bearable fuzz of static, out of which rose the caller's voice, like the auditory equivalent of a ship looming from thick fog.

'First of all, Mr Carter, could you tell me how you are?'

Logan looked shocked. Purna stared at him in wide-eyed puzzlement.

'Er . . . fine,' Logan muttered, 'but how did you—'

'Please be more precise, Mr Carter,' the voice cut in. 'What are your symptoms?'

Logan scowled. 'I was attacked, OK? I have bites. They hurt.'

'But you have had no seizures? No wild impulses? You are not suffering from lockjaw?'

'Would I be able to talk if I was?' Logan snapped. Then he sighed. 'No . . . none of those things.'

'Excellent!' said the voice. 'And you, Miss Mei? How are your symptoms?'

A voice came over the line – young, female, hesitant. 'I'm fine too. My hand aches and I felt a little dizzy earlier, but I'm better now.'

'Splendid!' said the voice. 'Oh, that is truly splendid!'

'Can't say how glad I am that you're stoked—' Logan began drily, but the voice cut him off.

'Please, no talking unless I ask you a direct question. Now listen very carefully. There isn't much time.'

There was a pause, as if the caller was taking a deep breath, and then he said, 'There has been . . . an outbreak on the island—'

Instantly, despite his instructions, a voice cut in that both Logan and Purna recognized. 'What kind of outbreak?' asked Sam B.

'Please,' said the voice, sounding pained. 'I understand your desire to ask questions but try to resist, all of you. I'll endeavour to explain the situation as best I can, but before I do, I must warn you that what I'm about to say will almost certainly sound unbelievable. But you *must* believe me when I tell you your lives will depend on how you respond to my instructions. You must trust me completely and do everything I tell you. I really cannot stress that point strongly enough.'

Once again the voice paused briefly, as if allowing his words to sink in. Then he continued, 'Now, as I was saying, there has been an outbreak on the island. A constantly mutating form of a particularly aggressive virus is cutting a swathe through Banoi's population. The first victim was identified in the downtown area of Moresby city just under six hours ago. It was initially hoped that the virus could be isolated and restricted to a small area, but unfortunately this has not been possible. Since the victim first exhibited symptoms of the virus, it has spread at an alarming rate throughout the city and beyond. The current estimate is that the virus has affected around eighty thousand people – over sixty per cent of the population – though numbers are rising so fast that frankly we're finding it difficult to keep up.'

His words were met with a collective gasp and a babble of questions. 'Please,' the caller shouted, and then had to shout twice more before a modicum of order was restored.

'I realize how shocking this information is,' he said, 'and how anxious you all must be. However the reason I am speaking to you now is not to alarm you, but to equip you with the facts you will need in order to negotiate the hazards ahead. Our ultimate aim is to get you off the island, but to do that I'm afraid you must come to us. Already the exceedingly virulent nature of the pandemic has resulted in the instigation of extreme emergency procedures, as a result of which Banoi has been declared a no-go zone for outside agencies.'

There was a renewed crackle of static and both Purna and Logan held their breaths, fearful they were about to lose contact with what might prove to be not merely their only source of information, but a possible means of escape from the island. Then the static died and the voice came through again.

'. . . furnish you with full and frank information as to the nature of the virus itself,' it said. 'I know that three of you have already had isolated encounters with infected individuals, and so are aware that symptoms of the virus include extreme psychosis, manifesting in a constant and intense desire to devour the flesh of the uninfected. What you possibly don't realize, however – and I'm aware that this information may prove particularly . . . ah, indigestible – is that the virus acts by first killing the host body and then by reanimating the dead flesh. In effect, therefore, it is a parasitical—'

'Zombies!' cried Logan, his manner almost triumphant. 'You see! I *was* right!'

'Zombies my ass,' rumbled Sam B. 'This is bullshit.'

'Please, ladies and gentlemen,' appealed the voice once more. 'Zombies is such an . . . an emotive word. Not to say . . .'

'Cheesy?' suggested Purna.

'I was about to say "inaccurate",' said the voice.

'So what would *you* call them?' Sam asked.

'We prefer to think of them as the "reanimated dead".'

'Same difference,' said Logan.

'He's right,' said Purna. 'It's just a question of semantics.'

'Yeah, what she said,' muttered Sam.

'Please be quiet, everyone,' Xian Mei piped up suddenly. 'I want to hear what the man says.'

66

'Thank you, Miss Mei,' said the caller. 'Now, in order to make it safely off the island you will need to head inland. To prevent the spread of infection, the airport has been locked down and the main harbour is being patrolled by offshore gunboats. Those trying to escape by sea are being ordered to turn back. Any vessels that don't comply are simply blown out of the water. All conventional exit routes have therefore been closed off while the authorities try to come up with a solution to the problem.'

'That's barbaric,' said Purna.

'It's necessary,' replied the caller. 'Would you rather this became a worldwide pandemic?'

'Of course not. But what about the forty per cent of people on the island who *aren't* affected?'

'That number is dropping all the time – and rapidly.'

'It's still a lot of people. So what are they? Collateral damage?'

'We're doing our best in a difficult situation,' said the voice tightly. 'We're trying to help you now, aren't we?'

'Yeah, and why you doin' that?' said Sam. 'Why just the four of us? How come we're so special? And who the hell are you anyway?'

'Someone will be waiting for you downstairs,' said the voice, ignoring Sam's questions. 'He will help you. But you need to go now. The situation is worsening all the time. And you need to arm yourselves.'

'With what?' asked Sam.

'With whatever you can find.'

Chapter 5

SINAMOI

'He's gone.'

Having stuck her head warily out the door, Purna stepped into the corridor, brandishing a splintered chair leg. The walls and carpet were still covered in drying blood and foam from earlier, but the bellhop who had attacked them was nowhere to be seen.

'How many times did you hit him?' asked Logan, emerging from the room with a leg from the same chair.

'Enough to put any regular guy in the emergency ward,' she said.

Logan pulled a face. 'You think these freaks abide by the normal zombie rules?'

'Well, I dunno,' she said, frowning. 'I guess that all depends on what the "normal zombie rules" are?'

'You know – destroy the brain, chop the head off . . . all that shit.'

Purna looked at him in disbelief. 'I really hope we don't get into a situation where we have to find out.'

She tapped lightly on the neighbouring door. 'Sam, it's us.'

Immediately it opened and Sam appeared.

'Hey, I'm loving your weapon,' Logan said drily.

Sam was holding what appeared to be a giant modified egg-whisk. He looked both proud of it and faintly embarrassed at the same time. 'Made it by twisting together all the coat hangers in my wardrobe,' he explained, 'then straightening out the ends. Figure if those fuckers come for me I'll stab their fucking eyes out.'

'Plus it can double as a back scratcher,' Logan said.

Sam scowled at him, then glanced at his makeshift sling. 'So you got bitten, huh?'

'Yes, and I know what you're thinking,' said Logan. 'If I get even the teeniest desire to chow down on your brains I'll let you know.'

Purna was already moving stealthily down the corridor, warily eyeing each door. 'What do you reckon?' she asked. 'Stairs or lift?'

'If the lift's empty we should be able to get all the way down to the ground floor in it,' said Logan.

'Fuck that,' said Sam. 'If the door opens and reception is full of those fuckers we'll be like sardines in a can.'

'More like meatballs,' said Logan, and looked at Purna. 'Talking of which, I think you've given me a hernia.'

Sam raised his eyebrows. Purna pursed her lips and shook her head. 'It's not what you think.'

By mutual consent they bypassed the lift and halted outside the heavy fire door, above which a perspex sign read: IN CASE OF EMERGENCY USE STAIRS.

'Ready?' whispered Purna, wrapping her hand round the door handle.

With his stained shirt, makeshift sling and pasty, hollow-eyed appearance, Logan looked anything *but* ready. However, he raised his chair leg gamely. 'Bring it on.'

Purna yanked the door open with one hand and thrust her chair leg forward with the other. The first flight of stairs was empty, and there were no obvious sounds of activity from below.

'So far so good,' she said.

They crept down the stairs and Purna peered around the curve of the banister at the bottom. 'Clear,' she whispered.

The third flight was similarly clear, and so was the fourth. Their rooms had been on the ninth floor, which meant that with two flights to each floor, they had eighteen flights to descend in all.

'Quiet,' Sam said when they were halfway down the fifth flight.

Purna halted. 'What have you heard?'

'No, I mean *it's* quiet. I thought there'd be more . . . shit goin' down, y'know?'

'It's 4:30 a.m.,' Purna said. 'Most people are probably still asleep.'

Sam considered. 'You think we should warn them?'

She shrugged. 'We can't warn everyone. Besides, what would we say?'

'We could . . . I dunno. Tell them to stay in their rooms.'

'For how long? They've got no food in there, and I'm pretty sure room service is no longer an option.

70

Besides, people would start asking us questions, wanting to know what's going on – and if we told them, how many would believe us?'

'Fuck,' muttered Sam, as the full implications of what they were faced with occurred to him.

'It's a dog-eat-dog world,' said Logan. 'Every man for himself.'

'That so?' said Sam heavily.

'You better believe it,' Logan replied. 'Anyway, what are you – the caring, sharing gangsta? I thought you rapper dudes didn't give a shit?'

Sam gave him a disgusted look. 'Don't listen to a whole lotta rap, do you?'

'I'm more of a Springsteen man myself.'

Sam rolled his eyes. 'Rap is all *about* giving a shit. That's why we're full of such righteous anger all the time.'

Logan nodded seriously. 'So – "Who Do You Voodoo, Bitch". That some kind of social comment, is it?'

Sam sighed. 'That song's gonna haunt me the rest of my life.'

'Don't take it to heart,' said Logan. 'If the zombie apocalypse is really going down, then the rest of your life will likely be over before you know it.'

'Can't quite put my finger on why,' said Sam, 'but that thought don't give me a whole lotta comfort.'

They crept down the next two flights in silence. They had almost reached the fire door that would have led them out on to floor six when Logan halted. 'Shit.'

'What is it?' said Purna, her body tensing.

'Aw, man,' said Logan.

71

'*What is it?*'

'I left my pills in my room.'

'Your what?'

'My pills. My drugs. I forgot all about them, what with being attacked and all.' He considered a moment. 'Maybe I should go back.'

'What? You crazy?' said Sam.

Logan looked stubborn. 'I *need* my pills.'

'What you need them for? You got some kind of condition?'

'Yes, I've got a condition,' snapped Logan. 'It's called needing my fucking pills!'

Purna stepped forward and put a hand on his arm. 'We'll get you some more pills,' she said reasonably.

'Oh, you really think it'll be that fucking easy?'

'To get painkillers and antidepressants? Maybe.'

He looked astonished. 'How did you—'

'I'm good at reading people,' she said crisply. 'Now shall we go?'

The words were barely out of her mouth when the door to floor six flew open and a woman in a white, blood-spattered nightgown appeared. Purna, Sam and Logan reacted instinctively, each of them raising their weapons and dropping into a defensive stance. Seeing them, the woman jerked to a halt, her face etched with terror and shock. Then, with a screech, something flew at the woman from behind, hitting her back with such force that she slipped on the blood pooling beneath her bare feet and went down in a graceless flurry of limbs.

At first Sam thought the thing that had attacked her was some kind of monkey. Weirdly it reminded him of

72

the Tasmanian Devil in the old Bugs Bunny cartoons. That fucker had moved in a blur, like a living tornado. This thing was similarly ferocious, tearing at the woman's back and neck with claws and teeth as she lay half in, half out of the open doorway. The woman was screeching horribly; she sounded more like a tortured animal than a human being. The creature was tearing chunks of flesh off her, just stripping them from her and stuffing them into its mouth. There was blood everywhere, spraying and flying in all directions. It was only when Purna stepped forward that the creature raised its head to look at them and Sam was shocked to see, through its thick mask of blood, that it was a little girl.

She was four, maybe five, and she had a long, stringy lump of chewed skin and meat dangling from between her clenched teeth. She might once have been cute, but now she looked savage, demonic. Her pyjamas and her blonde hair were clotted with chunks of shredded flesh and skin. Sam saw that even now the girl's fingers were buried deep in the bowl of pulped, bloody meat that the woman's back had become. In fact, the girl had ripped so many layers from the woman's back that she had exposed the white, blood-smeared nubs of her vertebrae.

Sam took all of this on board in one, maybe two seconds. Then Purna swung her chair leg with both hands and smashed the girl across the face with it. There was a crunch and the girl's face seemed to cave in. As she fell backwards into the carpeted hotel corridor, limbs flailing like a giant white spider that had lost half its legs, Sam saw with a kind of dreamy horror that beneath the coating of blood and gore she was wearing *My Little Pony* pyjamas.

Without hesitation, Purna followed up her attack, jumping over the woman and battering the girl around the head again and again with the chair leg, not giving her time to recover. Despite the ferocity of the attack, the girl's body twitched and heaved and scrabbled, as if she was not only trying to raise herself but also trying to fight back. Grimly Purna kept whacking the girl's head until her skull was nothing but an unrecognizable pulp and her body was still. By the time she stood back, panting and sweating, she was spattered with blood from head to toe, and the chair leg was coated with a viscous gruel of blood, flesh, bone, hair and slick, porridgey gobbets of brain matter.

Sam glanced at Logan, who was shaking, white-faced. Catching his eye, Logan muttered, 'Man, that was *intense.*'

Stepping over the still-twitching, keening body of the woman, grimacing at the gore squelching beneath his size eleven Reeboks, Sam walked up to Purna and put his arm round her shoulder. She flinched slightly but didn't resist.

'Hey,' he said, 'you OK?'

She looked at him. Her eyes were over-bright, her face a little too composed. 'Fine,' she said.

'You don't have to be,' he told her. 'I'm not sure I am.'

Purna clenched her jaw and looked almost callously down at the sprawled, now-pathetic body of the little girl. 'Then I guess you'd better learn to be. This is something we're all going to have to get used to.'

Shrugging off his arm, she turned and marched back to the woman, who was gasping and juddering now, her eyes wide with trauma, her breath coming in wheezy, panicked gasps.

Squatting beside her, Purna said, 'We can't leave her like this. Either she'll turn or more of those things will get her.'

'You think we should take her with us?' asked Sam, frowning.

Purna shook her head. 'She's beyond help and she'd only slow us down. We need to put her out of her misery.'

Sam blinked. 'You serious?'

'No, I'm joking,' she snapped. 'There's nothing better than a good laugh to lighten a serious situation.'

Sam raised his hands. 'OK, OK. Sorry.' Turning his head and lowering his voice, he said, 'So . . . how we gonna do it?'

'We haven't got time to debate or draw straws,' Purna said. Then, putting her gore-covered chair leg aside, she reached out and took the woman's head almost tenderly in her hands. Leaning over her, she murmured, 'It's OK, don't worry.' Then, with a practised twist, she broke the woman's neck.

'Jesus,' muttered Sam.

Standing out on the landing between staircases, Logan looked as if he was trying not to throw up. 'Where did you learn to do that?' he asked in a faint voice.

'Girl Guides,' replied Purna. She picked up the chair leg and without another word stepped back over the

75

body of the woman and started down the next flight of stairs.

Logan scurried after her, Sam bringing up the rear.

'You think that'll be enough?' Logan said. 'Breaking her neck, I mean?'

Purna halted briefly to glare at him. 'You wanna go back and hack her head off? If so, be my guest.'

Logan tried to smile, but it came out as a grimace. 'That's OK. I'll pass.'

They descended the next few flights in silence, Sam all too aware of the stink of blood and raw meat coming off Purna's clothes. He was aware too that Purna was still at the head of the group, and therefore would be in the front line if any more action went down. Pushing past Logan, he caught up with Purna a couple of steps ahead of him.

'First to the bar buys the drinks,' Logan called.

Sam glanced back at him. 'Just thought I'd take pole position, if that's OK with you? Figured Purna here had done her share of zombie-bashing for now.' He looked askance at Purna. 'That fine with you?'

Purna was looking straight ahead, face set, jaw clenched. When she caught Sam's eye her features softened slightly. 'Sure,' she said. 'My arm *is* pretty tired.'

Sam gave a nod and stepped in front of her. They were descending the stairs below the landing to floor three when he halted, holding up a hand.

'What is it?' Purna asked.

'This time I *do* hear something,' Sam said. 'Listen.'

They all stood still and listened. From a flight or two below them came a shuffling, snorting sound.

Immediately Logan was reminded of a football camp his mom and dad had sent him on when he'd been twelve or thirteen. One night he and a couple of guys had gone camping up in the hills and had been awoken in the early hours by a bear snuffling around their tent, looking for food. Logan had been shit-scared, but like the other guys he'd scrambled out of the tent and run at the bear, yelling and waving his arms. The bear, which it turned out had been only a cub, had taken fright, turned tail and fled. Logan and his friends had stayed awake the rest of the night in a state of nervous excitement. Next day, back down at the camp, they had bragged to the rest of the guys about how they had faced down a full-grown grizzly and survived.

Logan knew that the thing below them now was not a bear, and nor would it run if they yelled at it. For the first time he wondered how much of a survivor he truly was, and how far he would have to push himself, both mentally and physically, in order to get through the coming ordeal. Could he bash the brains out of a little kid or snap the neck of a fatally injured woman like Purna had just done? True, he didn't give much of a shit about anyone but himself, but that didn't auto-matically mean that he'd be prepared to do anything to save his own skin. He usually liked to leave the dirty jobs to other people, to operate under the radar, so to speak. However, he had a feeling that wouldn't be an option from now on. Like he'd told Sam, it was a dog-eat-dog world now; kill or be killed.

All the same, there was nothing to be gained in *inviting* trouble, or rushing headlong into it. Sidling up to Purna, he whispered, 'Maybe if we stay quiet, that thing, whatever it is, will go away.'

Purna, still spattered with the girl's blood, shook her head. 'I don't think so. It's coming towards us.'

Sam turned and glanced briefly at her. 'Maybe it can smell all that shit on you.'

'Let's head back upstairs then,' said Logan. 'We can go through the door and wait in the corridor. Maybe it'll lose the scent.'

'I'm not going backwards,' said Purna. 'If we keep hiding from those things we'll never get anywhere.'

'Amen to that,' said Sam, and hefted his multi-pronged coat-hanger weapon. 'Let's do this.'

Leading the way, he descended towards the sounds of movement, step by careful step. Reaching the curve of the banister, he whispered, 'Y'all ready?'

Purna nodded. Logan tried to think of something scathing and witty to say, but both his mind and his mouth were dry.

Sam braced himself, then swung around the corner on to the next flight, Purna shadowing him. A second or two behind them, the first thing Logan saw was a hulking figure eight or nine steps below. For a split-second he thought it was a bear – a bear dressed in human clothes.

The figure looked up and Logan saw that it was only a man after all. It was even a man he recognized, one he had seen already this evening. It was one of the two security guys who had turned up with the cute Chinese girl after they had been attacked by the woman in the rest room. Beneath his buzz cut, the man's pudgy, round face was smeared with blood and clots of matter. He resembled a giant baby after a particularly grotesque meal.

The mess down the front of his padded black jacket made it look as though he had had a bucket of animal guts thrown at him. He looked too as if he was wearing red gloves, albeit ones that were liquefying. In his fat right fist he was clutching a lump of raw meat that looked as though it might have been torn from a thigh or even a buttock. As soon as he saw Sam, Purna and Logan standing above him, however, he lost interest in the meat, which slithered from his hand and hit the floor with a wet splat, and lurched towards them, snarling.

It was only once he got closer that Logan realized that under its coating of gore the collar of the man's jacket was shredded and a sizeable chunk of meat was missing from the left side of his neck. Indeed, the entire left side of the man's head looked as though it had been savaged; his ear was gone completely and many of the stringy muscles and tendons beneath what would normally have been his cheek could clearly be seen. Additionally the missing flesh had revealed the teeth in the left side of his jaw, which gave the impression he was bestowing them with a wide, lopsided grin.

'Come on then, you big motherfucker,' Sam said, waiting for the dead man to get close enough. When he did, Sam lunged forward, jabbing his home-made weapon into the zombie's face.

With the first thrust, one of the splayed metal spines entered the creature's eye and punctured it. There was a faint pop, and the eyeball tore like a soft-boiled egg, releasing a gluey colourless substance that ran down the zombie's cheek and mingled with the blood around its mouth.

Despite this, Sam's attack didn't even slow the creature down. Seemingly oblivious to pain, it roared not in agony but in rage and hunger and kept on coming, blood-stained fingers reaching out.

Sam thrust again, a knight with a splintered metal lance, and this time most of the spines went into the zombie's mouth. They punctured its tongue and gums, scraped against its teeth, even skewered its top lip and tore a little of it away.

Yet still the zombie advanced, its sheer bulk and momentum driving it forward. Sam's weapon at first bent beneath its weight and then began to snap, metal spines remaining in the zombie's flesh, jutting from its cheeks, lips and gums like strange piercings.

Sam yelled in panic and anger as the zombie's fat fingers closed around the sleeves of his jacket. It bore down on him, growling, its breath reeking sourly of blood, its torn mouth opening and closing as it snapped at him. Pushed backwards, Sam stumbled and fell, the steps of the staircase jarring the breath out of him, digging painfully into his back. He tried to bring his arms up to defend himself, but they were pinned to his sides, his weapon useless in his hand. Frantically, craning his head back to stop the zombie from tearing his face off with its teeth, he brought up his knee, ramming it into the creature's fat belly. It was relentless, however, crushing him like a human steam-roller. In desperation he lowered his head and thrust his upper body forward, head-butting the zombie in the face. He heard a satisfying crunch as its nose broke, but the only result was that his head and face was showered with rank, hot zombie blood.

Suddenly the zombie's head snapped to Sam's left as something smashed into the side of it. Sam felt the creature's weight shift, its left hand tearing loose from his jacket, enabling him to move his right arm. Gripping his weapon tightly, he managed to work it free, then rammed it into the side of the zombie's throat, where much of the flesh had already been torn away. The spines, some of them now either bent or foreshortened from having snapped off under the creature's weight, passed easily through the ravaged meat, sliding forward until they scraped against bone. Unsure whether the bone was the zombie's spine or the underside of its jaw, Sam withdrew the weapon then thrust it forward again, stabbing it back and forth in quick, short jabs. The spines peppered the exposed meat of the creature's neck like wave after wave of buckshot, severing tendons and threads of gristle.

Meanwhile Purna moved into Sam's peripheral vision on his right-hand side, clearly trying to find room and space to once again slam the splintered end of the chair leg into the side of the zombie's head. Sam tried to aid her by withdrawing his weapon, his right hand now as slick with blood as the zombie's own, and ramming it directly upwards into the creature's throat, between its jaw and its Adam's apple. Skewered on the end of the weapon, its torn neck stretched, the creature gave a gurgling snarl and tried to work itself loose. However, instinctively seeking its prey, it pushed downwards instead of pulling up, and so succeeded only in driving the metal spines in deeper. They slid up through the bottom of the creature's mouth, harpooning the underside of its blackening tongue and causing congealed blood to burst from the wounds and spurt out from between its lips.

Seizing her chance, Purna slammed the end of the chair leg into the side of the zombie's head again, and then again. After the fourth blow there was a gristly tearing sound, and like a hinged lid, the zombie's head toppled over to one side, twisting Sam's weapon from his hand with such force that it drew a strip of skin from his palm. The head swung down grotesquely in front of the zombie's chest like a bowling ball in a stocking, held in place by nothing more than a few stubborn ropes of stretched skin and tendon. It swung, in fact, into Sam's face, the prickly buzz cut scraping across his cheek, causing him to cry out in revulsion. Convulsively the zombie's hands began to open and close, enabling Sam to free his left arm, and then, with Purna's help, to scramble out from under the creature's dead weight. Battered and bruised, and drenched stickily in the zombie's foul blood, he watched numbly until the creature's almost decapitated body ceased twitching and became motionless.

'Thanks,' he muttered finally, glancing at Purna.

She gave a brisk, brief nod. 'Don't mention it.'

'Did it bite you?' asked Logan, sitting on the stairs a little above them, like a spectator watching a football game from the bleachers.

'No,' said Sam. 'Just bled on me a little.'

'Zombie blood is probably contagious,' Logan said.

Sam scowled. 'In that case, I'll try to resist the temptation to lick myself clean.'

'Just saying,' Logan said.

With more than a little distaste, Sam placed his foot on the zombie's almost-severed head and yanked his now bloody and mangled weapon from its throat. He held the weapon up ruefully. 'Soon as I get the chance, I'm gonna trade this motherfucker for an Uzi.'

'You want me to take point again?' asked Purna.

Sam glanced up at Logan, narrowing his eyes. 'Ain't it his turn?'

'He's only got one arm. Plus he got bit. Which means he's not exactly in the best of health.'

Logan did his best to look contrite and apologetic. Sam grunted. They continued on down the stairs, trying not to slip in the zombie's blood, which was fanning out from beneath its body, overspilling the edges of the stairs and dripping on to the steps below. They reached the ground floor without further incident, halting at a door marked RECEPTION. Already they looked a pretty battle-weary bunch, wounded and spattered with blood.

'OK,' said Purna. 'We need to be ready for this. We don't know what's out there.'

'What if there's hundreds of them?' said Logan.

'There won't be. Lucky for us, the outbreak only reached this part of the island when most people were already in bed.'

'You reckon that guy who called us up was telling

the truth? That there *will* be someone waiting to help us?' said Sam.

Purna shrugged. 'Who knows? Let's just take it one step at a time.'

'Who was that guy anyway?'

She raised her eyebrows. 'You really want to discuss this now?'

'Guess not,' he said.

'So what's the plan?' asked Logan.

Unhesitatingly Purna said, 'We'll take it nice and slow. No point drawing attention to ourselves. You guys ready?'

'Not in the slightest,' muttered Sam.

'I'm *always* ready,' said Logan laconically, swinging his chair leg.

'Then let's go.'

She pushed open the door just wide enough to ensure there were no zombies in the vicinity, then stepped forward, gesturing to the others that it was safe to emerge. The door to the stairs was situated at the end of a short corridor to the right of the main reception area. From here they could see most of the lobby, including the main doors about fifteen metres away to their left, and the long reception desk just beyond that, occupying the wall directly opposite them. In the centre of the wide expanse of carpet was a fully grown palm tree, encircled by a number of curved, interconnecting leather seats, which gave the impression the tree was at the centre of a giant black wheel.

Although the area was quiet and currently deserted, there were several indications this had been anything but a normal night. There were streaks of blood across the surface of the blond-wood desk and the light-coloured carpet – streaks long enough and dark enough to suggest that this had been heart-blood jetting from a severed major artery. There was more blood on the inside of the hotel's glass frontage, including a smeary handprint. Most distressing of all, there was the body of what they could just about make out had been a young Chinese woman, dressed in the hotel's staff uniform of white shirt, red tie and red skirt, lying on her back close to the central seating area in an ungainly sprawl of limbs.

The young woman had been attacked so savagely that she was almost unrecognizable as human. She had been almost ripped apart, as if by a mob. Her left leg was attached to the rest of her body by nothing more than a shred of skin, her right arm was missing completely from the elbow down, and her intestines had spilled from a jagged rent in her stomach and were now lying on and around her in glistening purple-grey loops.

Seeing her, Logan said, 'Excuse me,' and promptly threw up into one of two small potted palms flanking the doors of the lift a few metres away. Purna patted him on the back and glanced up at the lift indicator. It was frozen at floor 5, and she wondered for a moment what terrible dramas had unfolded up there.

'You OK?' she whispered as Logan straightened up.

He looked more ghastly than ever, his complexion deathly pale, but he nodded.

'Thought the girl might be ... well, the one who checked me in, and was with me when the woman attacked us ... but I'm not sure.'

Sam joined them beside the lift. Although they could see most of the lobby from here, they couldn't see all of it. They couldn't, for example, see the area at the back where the lobby divided into corridors leading to other rooms on the ground floor, such as the restaurant, the main bar and the ballroom where Sam had had his gig.

Thinking of the gig, Sam couldn't believe that five hours ago he had been up on stage, playing to a large and enthusiastic crowd. The event seemed like a lifetime ago now. Strange to think that back then he had been worried about nothing more than how his new songs would go down with an audience, and whether this was his last shot at a new record contract, the only chance to resurrect his career.

'We good to go?' he muttered.

'Logan?' asked Purna.

Logan ran his tongue over his teeth and spat the last of the vomit from his mouth. 'Let's do it.'

Like thieves they crept to the end of the short corridor and peered around the corner. The area at the back of the lobby showed corridors angled in all directions, many of them curving out of sight. Purna nodded and they broke cover, hurrying across the carpet to the main doors. Standing in the well-lit lobby, they were uncomfortably aware of how visible they were from outside. However, the forecourt of the hotel seemed deserted and was fringed with tall palms and thick bushes.

'Guess those fuckers have gone where the food is,' Sam muttered, indicating with a jerk of his head that he meant the infected had probably gone deeper into the hotel in search of the still-living guests holed up in their rooms.

'Luckily for us,' said Purna, glancing outside and swiping her plastic keycard through a reader to the right of the doors.

With an obliging hum the automatic doors parted and the trio stepped outside. Cool, scented air washed over them, taking away, temporarily at least, the stench of raw meat and zombie blood. Logan swayed slightly, as if the air was a little too rich for him.

'Uh-oh,' said Sam, turning, as two dark, silhouetted figures detached themselves from a black screen of bushes on their left.

Purna raised her weapon, but the taller of the two figures slowed its advance, raising a hand.

'Is OK,' it announced. 'We not sick.'

Though she lowered her weapon, Purna still looked wary, watching as the two figures moved out of the shadows and into the light from the hotel. The one that had spoken was a tall, slim, dark-skinned man of about twenty-five, wearing an orange surfing T-shirt, blue knee-length shorts and canvas beach shoes. He was holding a machete in one hand and had a stubby silver pistol with a wide nozzle stuffed into his waistband.

His companion was a slim, pretty Chinese girl with a bandaged hand, who was wearing the now-familiar hotel receptionist's uniform. Seeing her, Logan exclaimed, 'Hey! You're OK!'

The Chinese girl nodded, her face expressionless.

Indicating the bandage, Purna said, 'You're Miss Mei, right? The girl on the phone?'

Again she nodded. 'My name is Xian Mei.'

'And you were bitten? Like him?' Purna jerked her head towards Logan.

'Yes.'

'But you're OK?'

'Yes.'

'Right,' said Purna thoughtfully.

The young man stepped forward. 'Come. I take you to safe place.'

'What's your name, man?' Sam asked.

The young man smiled. 'Sinamoi,' he said.

Chapter 6

THE SAFE PLACE

'We are here.'

Sinamoi, with Xian Mei in tow, had led them through the potentially treacherous resort on a circuitous route, avoiding the main thoroughfares where the tourists hung out and sticking to hidden paths and back alleys. Although Purna, Sam and Logan had followed him without question, Purna in particular had remained wary, constantly alert to the fact that, for whatever reason, their guide might be deceiving them or leading them into a trap. They had seen one or two zombies wandering about, but had managed to remain out of sight and undetected.

'Very quiet now, but tomorrow this will not be good place,' Sinamoi hissed at one point, after they had lain low for a couple of minutes while a clearly infected black man – scrawny, old and white-bearded – had shambled past, snarling and twitching.

They finally emerged from a winding, tree-shrouded path to find themselves on the main route down to the shore, though it was evident from the way the soughing of the waves had been growing steadily louder over the past ten minutes that this was where they had been heading. Purna half expected to see the lights of a boat twinkling out on the black water, ready to whisk them away, but instead Sinamoi led them to a grey one-storey building with barred windows, squatting on the dunes that overlooked the powder-white beach.

'What's this?' she asked.

'Lifeguard station,' Sinamoi replied. 'Very strong building. Very safe.'

'How do we get in?' Sam wanted to know.

Sinamoi grinned, reached into his pocket and produced a key. 'I am lifeguard,' he said.

He unlocked the door and they went inside. The station was well equipped with tables and chairs, a two-way radio and even a small camping stove. There was all-weather gear hanging on hooks on the wall, a metal first-aid box the size of a small suitcase and a camp bed in one corner.

Sam nodded at the camp bed. 'You live here?'

Sinamoi laughed, as if Sam had made a joke. In his broken English he explained that one of the duties of the lifeguards was to stay in constant touch with the fleet of offshore fishing boats, which operated out of Moresby harbour. If a boat got into difficulties, it was the responsibility of whoever was on night-duty to alert the other lifeguards so that a rescue boat could be launched.

'And it's your turn now, huh?' said Logan tiredly, looking drawn and exhausted.

Sinamoi nodded and grinned.

'So who told you to come looking for us?' asked Purna.

Sinamoi pointed at the radio, which was scratched and battered with chunky, old-fashioned knobs and dials, and headphones that looked as though they were held together with heavy-duty parcel tape. Happily crackling and buzzing away to itself, it looked like the sort of lash-up you only ever saw these days in old war movies.

'Man on radio,' he said. 'He try to . . .' He imitated holding a cell phone up to his ear.

'To call us?' said Sam.

'Yes. But signal gone. So he call me. Much stronger signal. Promise me much money if I bring you here.'

'Did he now?' said Purna. 'And did he say *why* he wanted you to bring us here?'

'To keep you safe. Also he have message.'

'What message?'

Sinamoi frowned. 'He say go inland. Past jungle to other side of island. Go to prison island. Top of tower will be helicopter. It fly you away.'

'Is that all he said?' asked Sam.

Sinamoi nodded. 'Yes. Except he try to call if he can.' He mimed holding up a cell phone again.

Sam sighed. 'You ever spoken to this guy before, Sinamoi?'

The lifeguard shook his head. 'No.'

'So you've no idea who he is?'

'No. But he want to save you. So is friend, yes?'

'I hope so,' said Sam. He propped his weapon against the wall, pulled a chair out from under the table and sat down with a grunt. 'Wish we knew who he was, though.'

Following his example, Purna and Logan also laid their weapons aside. Purna sat down too.

'I've got a few ideas,' she said.

'Care to share them with the group?'

'Sure. I could do with cleaning up a bit first, though, and we could all do with a drink. Need to keep our fluids up. Sinamoi, you got any water?'

The lifeguard nodded eagerly. Crossing the room, he pushed aside the all-weather gear to reveal a door, behind which was a tiny cubicle containing a primitive toilet and wash basin.

'Much water. But this no drink.' He put a hand on his stomach and stuck out his tongue, miming sickness. Then he crossed to the workbench on which the radio sat, knelt down, reached underneath it and dragged out a plastic, almost full five-litre water container. 'This drink,' he said.

As he poured water into a variety of chipped and grubby-looking mugs, Purna went into the toilet cubicle to clean up as best she could. Accepting a mug of water, Sam looked at Logan who was slumped against the wall. 'You look wasted, man.'

'I feel it,' said Logan. Turning to Sinamoi, he flipped a thumb towards the camp bed and said, 'Hey, mind if I crash a while?'

Sinamoi nodded vigorously. 'Rest. Sleep.' Then his brows beetled in concern. 'You sick?'

'Just tired,' said Logan. 'Lost some blood.' He glanced at Sam, who was staring at him intently, and raised his right hand. 'On my honour, man. It's not the fucking virus. I've got no designs on your black hide.'

Unexpectedly Sam grinned. 'Think you'd find my

meat a little too refined for your palate anyway, white boy.'

Logan chuckled, trudged across to the camp bed and all but crumpled on to it with a groan.

'You need medicine?' said Sinamoi.

'Sure,' said Logan wearily. 'I'll take anything you got.'

Five minutes later, dosed up on painkillers, he was snoring quietly in the corner, mouth open. Sam, Purna, Xian Mei and Sinamoi were sitting around the table, hands curled not round mugs of water this time, but hot black coffee. Sam blew on his coffee before sipping it, then sat back with a sigh. Although he normally took his coffee with cream and sugar, he murmured, 'Man, that's the best cup of coffee I've ever tasted.'

Purna turned to Xian Mei, who so far had barely said a word. 'So what's your story?' she asked.

Xian Mei looked defensive. 'What makes you think I have one?'

Purna nodded at Sam, then over at Logan asleep in the corner. 'I can see the connection between the three of us, but you're the odd one out; the unknown quantity.'

'You mean the blood drive?' said Sam.

'Yes. We're all here because we gave blood and won ourselves holidays in Banoi. It therefore figures that our mysterious caller is something to do with the NBDC.' She stared at Xian Mei, narrowing her eyes. 'But who are you? His spy?'

Xian Mei tried not to react, even though the Australian girl had come startlingly close to guessing the reason she *was* here. Matching the girl's intense stare with one of her own, she said firmly, 'I'm nobody's spy. Maybe I was included because I gave blood too.'

'You did?' said Sam, surprised.

'In which part of the US?' asked Purna.

Xian Mei shook her head. 'Not in the US. In China.'

'China?' said Sam. 'I thought this blood drive campaign was an American thing?'

Xian Mei shrugged. 'There was one in China too. But it was organized by the Chinese government.'

'Or at least, that's what you were told,' said Purna.

'What do you mean?' asked Sam.

'Think about it. Logan got bit. Xian Mei got bit. We've both been sprayed with zombie blood, which means we've almost certainly ingested some – but none of us are infected.'

Sam frowned, assessing the implications of her words. 'You mean we're immune?'

'Not only that, but the NBDC, or whoever's behind this thing, *knew* we were immune before we came here. That's the reason we *are* here. It's not random chance. Our names weren't drawn out of a hat. It's because of our immunity.'

Sam's eyes widened as the terrible truth dawned on him. 'But that means . . .'

Purna nodded grimly. 'It means that whoever sent us here knew about the virus before we arrived. It means they knew this was going to happen.'

Xian Mei shook her head. 'No.'

Purna looked at her sharply. 'What do you mean, no?'

'I mean that whoever is responsible for us being

here didn't simply *know* that this was going to happen. That's too much of a coincidence.'

'Fuck, you're right,' said Purna.

'You mean they did it deliberately?' muttered Sam. 'They created it?'

Both girls nodded in unison.

'But why?' Sam asked.

Xian Mei shrugged. 'To use as a weapon? Biological warfare?'

'Motherfuckers,' snarled Sam. 'So why throw us into the mix?'

'As guinea pigs?' suggested Purna. 'To see how immune we really are? They've already got our blood, remember, so we're expendable.'

'The question is,' said Xian Mei, 'is our mysterious caller working *for* the people who put us here or working *against* them?'

'So what we talking about here?' asked Sam. 'Rival governments?'

Purna spread her hands. 'Who knows? Our guy could be appalled by the fact that we've been thrown into the lion's den and is genuinely working in our best interests by trying to get us out, or he could be working for an enemy government who want to develop a vaccine from our blood in case the virus is used against them.'

'Or maybe he has a different agenda entirely,' suggested Xian Mei.

'Whatever the reason, we're being manipulated,' said Purna. 'Moved around like pieces on a chess board.'

'So what do we do?' Sam asked. 'Go along with it?'

Purna looked at Xian Mei, who shrugged. 'For the time being,' Purna said. 'I don't see that we've got much choice.'

They fell silent for a moment, each of them wrapped in their own thoughts. Sinamoi, who had been following the exchange with apparently little comprehension, now said, 'More coffee?'

All three nodded and he crossed the room to heat more water on the stove.

Making it sound less like a challenge this time, Purna looked at Xian Mei and said, 'You still haven't told us the full story. You're not a hotel receptionist at all, are you?'

Xian Mei sighed. 'Is it really that obvious?'

'Blindingly,' said Purna.

'OK,' said Xian Mei. 'I'll tell you my story if you tell me yours.'

Purna hesitated a moment, and then said, 'Agreed.'

While Sinamoi made coffee, Xian Mei told Sam and Purna the truth about her father, and the Special Forces squad, and her 'special assignment'. When she had finished she looked at Purna. 'Your turn.'

Purna sighed and sat back, as though wondering how and where to start. Finally she said, 'When I was sixteen, I joined the Sydney Police Department. Nothing to do with my dad. I just . . . I guess when I was growing up I didn't see a whole lot of justice and I wanted to redress the balance. But being young, and female, and half Aborigine, and – I guess – a bit of a looker, I had to put up with a whole lot of shit. Not just sexism and racism – though there was plenty of both, believe me – but people thinking I was dumb or that I couldn't handle myself, that I was a soft touch.'

She paused, as if reflecting briefly on her past, then she said, 'So anyway, all that crap . . . it just made me stronger. I was determined to prove myself, to be just as tough as the guys around me, if not more so. I'd been in the police force . . . five years, I guess, when I was assigned to this child molestation case. It was a bad one –' she barked out a harsh laugh – 'I mean, when are they not, hey? But this one was *really* bad. Nine victims we knew of, ranging from seven to thirteen. High level of brutality . . . I won't go into details. Anyway, we found the perp. The evidence was irrefutable. He was a twenty-two-year-old rich kid called Jeffrey Lucas. Heir to Lucas Industries, a big pharmaceuticals company. On the surface he was a normal kid – privileged background, good school record, no previous, plenty of friends, girlfriend . . . the works. But underneath –' she shook her head – 'a moral vacuum. I mean, seriously. He was worse than any sociopath I've ever come across. He knew he was doing wrong, he understood the concept of human pain and terror, but he just didn't care. He hadn't killed any of the girls he'd harmed, but he'd brutalized them so badly that . . . well, let's just say that if any of them manage to live normal lives after what he did, it will be a major fucking achievement.'

She was breathing hard and made a concerted effort to compose herself before continuing. After ten seconds of silence, punctuated only by the constant buzz and crackle from the radio, she said, 'And the thing is, if he'd been allowed to continue he *would* have killed someone eventually. There's no fucking doubt in my mind about that.' She waved a hand almost casually. 'Anyway, we arrested him, built up a rock-solid case against him, brought him to trial ... and the bastard got off. Basically he was legally untouchable because of his wealth and connections. Top-drawer lawyer, money changing hands, a few words in the right ear ... whatever. Fact is, he got off and he *laughed* at us. He fucking laughed. He thought it was all just one big game. So I hounded him, followed him everywhere. I got told to lay off. And when I didn't I was threatened; someone broke into my house and smashed it up. And then one night ...'

Her voice tailed off. She licked her lips.

'One night?' prompted Sam.

'I killed him. Shot him right through the eye.' She looked at Sam almost fiercely. 'Best fucking thing I've ever done.'

'You caught him in the act?' asked Sam.

'No. I followed him. And when he was alone I killed him. Simple as that.'

'You executed him,' said Xian Mei.

Purna rounded on her. 'You criticizing me for that?'

Xian Mei held up her hands. 'Not at all. I would have done the same thing.'

Purna stared at her intently, as if trying to work out from her expression or the tone of her voice whether she really meant it.

'So what happened then?' Sam asked.

'I lost my job. Everyone knew I'd killed the guy, but I made sure I left no evidence at the scene, so they couldn't pin it on me. I was drummed out of the force quietly, pushed out the back door. Psychologically unfit for service.'

'What about the guy's family?' asked Sam. 'Didn't they come after you?'

'You know, I think in a way they were relieved. Jeffrey was an embarrassment to them, and a sexual scandal was the last thing they wanted. A family tragedy, though . . . that brings people together, doesn't it? Engenders a lot of public sympathy. To them, it was better that Jeffrey was in the ground than in jail.'

'So when did all this happen?' Xian Mei asked.

'Three years ago.'

'And what have you been doing since?'

Purna pulled a face, as if confronted with a bad smell. 'I've been working as a bodyguard for so-called VIPs in various war zones and politically unstable countries throughout the world.'

'You make that sound bad,' said Sam. 'Like you a hooker or something.'

'Maybe because that's how I feel,' Purna said. 'I get a lot of work because, to be honest, fat, ugly, wealthy men like showing up with a pretty girl on their arm. It gives them a feeling of status, of power. And most people tend to assume that as well as protecting my clients I'm also fucking them, that it's a double-whammy deal.' She shook her head in self-disgust. 'I make a lot of money, but I don't mind admitting that what I do makes me feel dirty. I joined the police because I wanted to help those who couldn't help themselves. But instead I've ended up as a servant of the rich and the spoiled . . . and sometimes that feels to me like Jeffrey Lucas has won, after all.'

'You mustn't think that,' Xian Mei said firmly, 'because it's not true.'

'She's right, man,' said Sam.

Purna smiled. 'Thanks. But that doesn't stop me hating myself sometimes.'

'Yeah, well, I guess we all hate ourselves a little bit,' Sam said.

Over in the corner Logan groaned and shifted in his sleep. They all glanced over at him and it was as if a spell had been broken, as if being reminded of their surroundings had snapped them back into the present.

'So what do we do now?' said Sam.

Purna frowned a little. 'Why ask me? I'm not the leader.'

Sam spread his hands. 'Hey, I was just throwing the question out. Far as I'm concerned, this is a democracy. But if you want my opinion . . .'

Both girls nodded.

Sam sighed and said, 'Much as I'd like to stay here till this shit-storm blows over, I think the only way we gonna get rescued is if we rescue ourselves. Far as I can see, the two main things we gonna need are transport and proper weapons – preferably guns.'

Purna nodded. 'And provisions – food and water.'

'Medical supplies too,' added Xian Mei.

Sam glanced up at one of the small barred windows. The glass was grimy but he could see the sky was lightening from black to a hazy, washed-denim blue.

'In which case we should head out now before the world wakes up and we're faced with more infected out there than we can handle.'

100

'What about him?' asked Xian Mei, nodding at Logan.

'We'll leave him here,' said Purna. 'He got bit pretty badly and needs to recover. It won't do him or us any good to take him along.'

The three of them pushed back their chairs and stood up. Sinamoi, who had given the impression he had been following their discussion closely, now looked surprised. 'Where you go?'

'We need a car,' Sam said, and mimed turning a steering wheel, 'to do what the man says. Plus we need weapons.' This time he mimed shooting a gun. 'We gonna go look for some.'

Sinamoi looked concerned. 'You not go. Dangerous.'

'We got no choice,' Sam said, spreading his hands.

Sinamoi held up a hand, finger pointing upwards. 'Weapons. I got. You wait.' Once again he dropped to his knees in front of the workbench supporting the radio and scrabbled underneath. He dragged out a battered cardboard box, the contents clinking together as they shifted. He indicated the box with a flourish, like a magician introducing his glamorous assistant. 'You see?'

Inside the box was an assortment of knives and other tools that a lifeguard might need. There were several large, serrated diver's knives, machetes for hacking aside foliage (and maybe, thought Sam, fighting off man-eating fish), a couple of crowbars with curved ends, and two stubby silver guns like the one Sinamoi had been wearing in his belt when he had first encountered them – and which Sam now realized were flare guns. Kneeling beside the box, he glanced across at his coat-hanger weapon, matted with now-dried gore, which was still propped against the wall, and wished it a silent goodbye.

'Can we take some of this shit with us?' he asked, looking at Sinamoi.

Sinamoi looked uncertain. 'You not go.'

'Your concern is touching,' said Sam heavily, 'but we got to. But we'll be back to pick him up.' He pointed at Logan.

Sinamoi was still shaking his head. Purna said, 'I hate to burst your bubble, Sam, but I think he's more concerned about the money he was promised than he is about us. He probably thinks if we go out there and get ourselves killed he won't get paid.'

Sam considered a moment, then reached into his pocket and pulled out a handful of blue, red and orange bank notes. He held them out to Sinamoi.

'Here you go, man. Plenty kina. You take it and we get to choose what we want from here.' He indicated the weapons.

Sinamoi still looked uncertain. Sam pressed the money into his hand.

'That's all I got on me. OK?'

Sinamoi looked momentarily puzzled, then smiled. 'OK.'

'Cool,' said Sam. He looked round and waved a hand at the box as if it was an open treasure chest. 'Ladies, choose your weapons.'

Chapter 7

BARE NECESSITIES

'You ever see *The Warriors*?'

Purna glanced at Sam. He was just ahead of her, walking along the road, a machete in one hand, a flare pistol in the other. Though his face was now clean, his red bandanna, jacket, jeans and trainers were still heavily stained with dried blood.

'The old seventies film about New York gangs? Sure.'

'How about you, Xian Mei?'

She shook her head. 'Where I grew up, western culture was considered decadent and subversive. Although,' she added almost proudly, 'when I was a little girl my father did once bring home some video tapes of *Sesame Street*.'

Sam laughed. 'Well, that's kinda like *The Warriors*, I guess. Except with slightly less violence.'

'What's your point?' asked Purna.

Sam shrugged. 'When I first saw *The Warriors* I was maybe eleven, twelve years old. I mean, I thought it was cool and all, but . . . guys painting their faces like clowns? Gangs on roller skates? Even back then it seemed kinda dumb.' He hesitated. 'It's weird, but I kinda feel the same now. Like this is unreal. Like it can't really be happening. I mean, look around you. We got palm trees, and peace and quiet, and all that holiday shit, and pretty soon the sun's gonna come out and it's gonna be another beautiful day. I mean, that just don't equate with people killing and eating each other and coming back from the dead. Here we are, walking along like we're going into battle when we should be heading down to the beach. It's crazy, man.'

' "In war, it's best not to think, it's best just to do, because thinking clouds your judgement",' said Purna.

'That right?' said Sam, looking at her strangely.

Purna shrugged. 'Or so someone once said anyway.'

'Oh yeah? Who was that?' asked Sam.

'I can't remember. All I know is I read it somewhere, and it seemed like sound advice at the time. It still does.'

Sam grunted.

Above them the sky was lightening in jags and streaks, as if the night sky was merely a cloth that was splitting apart as it shrank, revealing the paler blue of a new day beneath. Out on the horizon the sea shimmered like gold, and looking at it Sam couldn't help but think how quickly the world could turn, how nothing was ever predictable. This time yesterday he'd been thinking that his first full day on Banoi would maybe involve a swim, a little sunbathing, perhaps a cocktail or two by the pool. Aside from his daily routine of sit-ups and push-ups, he had envisaged nothing more strenuous during his time here than some windsurfing and scuba diving, possibly an occasional light jog along the white sand before settling down to breakfast on his hotel balcony.

On Sinamoi's advice they were currently following the low beach road into town, which was a little longer and more uneven than the main thoroughfare, but considerably quieter. It was, in truth, barely more than a dirt track, maybe wide enough for one car but certainly not two. To the left of the track was a sandy verge populated with low-lying, shrub-like eucalyptus trees, and dotted with occasional clusters of tin-roofed fishermen's huts, all of which had been bleached and weathered by the elements. Beyond this, when the land dipped, they caught brief glittering glimpses of the sea, which appeared to be growing bluer and brighter with each minute that passed.

To the right of the track the foliage was thicker, rough-barked palms crowding together to form a wall whose spade-like leaves would provide welcome shade later in the day. Brightly coloured butterflies zigzagged through the air, and tiny brown and green lizards scurried across the path ahead of them as they walked. Above their heads, intermittently glimpsed birds of paradise screeched and clucked and cawed, and unseen insects crooned in the undergrowth. For the rest of nature it was business as usual, the latest in an endless succession of identical days. But for humankind it was a new and terrible dawn; the beginning of the end.

As if to confirm this, there was a sudden ratcheting scream, which caused a flock of multi-coloured birds to take flight, and a woman appeared from behind one of the fishermen's huts on their left. She was a young, dark-haired, olive-skinned woman, naked but for a pair of peach-coloured bikini briefs. One of her smallish breasts was hanging in bloody tatters, and further bites had been taken from her right arm and her abdomen.

Not that her injuries seemed to worry her, or slow her down in the slightest. She came at them like a rabid fan that had broken through a barrier at a pop concert. Except that in her eyes there was not adulation but a murderous, ravenous rage, and her scream was not an expression of excited hysteria but a primal, anguished howl.

Sam raised the flare pistol he was holding and pulled the trigger. There was a loud *phut* sound and the flare hurtled from the nozzle in a flash of fire and smoke like an avenging angel. It hit the woman full in her screaming mouth and seemed – to Sam at least – to briefly illuminate the inside of her head like a Halloween pumpkin. The woman's head snapped back as if she had run full-tilt into a hidden wire positioned at neck-height, her feet skidding from under her. As she went down on to her back, hands clawing at the air, Sam rushed forward, and before the woman could recover, he raised his cleaver and brought it down with all his strength.

His intention was to sever her head with one blow, but he misjudged slightly and the blade hit her just below the nose, bisecting her face. Blood spurted up with such force that it splashed the underside of his chin and trickled down his neck. He swore as the machete jammed in the front of her skull, almost overbalancing him. As the woman's clutching hand grabbed and tightened around his ankle, Xian Mei glided forward and with ruthless efficiency lopped off the woman's arm at the wrist.

'Godammit!' Sam grunted, yanking and twisting the machete free of the woman's mangled face. Stepping back, he raised it and brought it down again and this time his aim was true. The blade sliced through her neck all the way to her spine. A further blow severed the spine itself and life went out of the woman abruptly and permanently, her body slumping, becoming still.

'And so it begins,' said Purna, her eyes darting everywhere, alert for further attacks.

Sam wiped the blade of his machete on the furry bark of a nearby palm tree and reloaded the flare pistol. 'Least they let us know they're comin',' he said. 'One thing they ain't is sneaky.'

They continued on, Sam muttering about how he'd only just cleaned last night's blood off his skin, and now here he was, all covered in it again. 'And I ain't even had my breakfast yet,' he said.

'What? You hoping to find somewhere we can stop off for a latte and a croissant?' teased Purna.

'Hell no. In light of the situation I'd settle for grits and a soda.'

Purna snorted a laugh.

They knew they were nearing the main street when the ground rose abruptly, curving away from the sea. Suddenly the path became a set of stone steps, caged on both sides by a waist-high chain-link fence.

'We need to be extra vigilant from now on,' Purna said. 'Try not to get hemmed in anywhere.'

107

'Like here you mean?' said Sam, eyeing the surrounding foliage nervously.

'We don't have much choice here,' said Purna. 'Let's just move quickly and stay alert.'

They hurried up the steps, weapons at the ready. Near the top they heard the sound of voices. Sam raised a hand and they paused a moment, listening.

It sounded like two men talking, though what Sam, Purna and Xian Mei found puzzling was that they were making no attempt to keep their voices low. However, although the voices were loud, they had a muffled quality to them, indicating they were indoors rather than out in the open.

'What the hell is—' Sam began, then they all heard a sound that answered the question he was about to ask: canned laughter.

'It's a TV show,' Xian Mei said.

Sam frowned. 'But who'd be watching TV at a time like this?'

'Maybe someone who has no idea what's happening,' Purna suggested.

'Then I guess we ought to tell them,' said Sam, 'before they find out the hard way.'

The blaring of the TV grew louder as they ascended the last dozen steps. Though the infected had probably had hours to check out the noise, it still made all three of them nervous to be so close to something that could potentially attract attention. The top of the steps opened out into a back yard, behind what Sam guessed was one of the buildings lining the long main street. From what he had seen of them, the bars, restaurants and retail outlets were not only crammed together in a jumble of shapes and sizes and styles, but they were also in various states of repair, as if the street had grown up organically, rather than being planned as a tourist-serving *fait accompli* from the outset.

This particular building was a shabby clapboard affair sandwiched between two taller and more austere edifices constructed of steel, glass and polished wood. Ominously there was an overturned dustbin in the yard, spewing rubbish, and the screen door at the back was half open. A narrow alley to the left of the building provided access to and from the main street.

'This doesn't look good,' said Xian Mei.

Sam glanced at her. 'Think we should check it out?'

'It would probably be foolish,' said Purna.

'But?' said Sam.

She sighed. 'But if someone *is* in there, oblivious to what's happening . . .'

Sam nodded. 'They might as well be banging a dinner gong.'

He took the lead, crossing the yard quickly. At the screen door he paused and knocked.

'Hey,' he called softly. 'Anyone in here?'

There was no reply.

'I'm going in,' he said. 'And before you say it, yeah, I'll be careful.'

'I'm coming too,' said Purna.

Sam frowned. 'Someone should stay out here in case of visitors.'

Xian Mei pulled an 'oh well' face and shrugged, as if she had drawn the short straw.

'Yell if you need us,' Purna said, placing a hand

briefly on Xian Mei's arm, then she slipped into the building behind Sam.

If this was a store of some kind, then it didn't seem like it from the back. Clearly the rear of the building was given over to living quarters, indicating that this was a home as much as a place of work. The first room they entered was a kitchen, modest and shabby, but also clean and neat. There was nothing out of place here, nothing to indicate that anything untoward had been happening.

The blaring TV was located somewhere deeper in the house. Sam and Purna crossed the room swiftly to the inner door, Sam placing his ear against it to see if he could make out any other sounds. Unable to do so, he glanced at Purna and she nodded. He opened the door, gritting his teeth against the creak it made, and stepped through quickly, looking every which way to assess the terrain. The TV was now so loud that Sam was able to tell which show was playing – it was a rerun of *Friends*. He even recognized the episode; it was the one where Ross and Rachel get married in Vegas after drinking themselves insensible.

The noise of the TV was coming from a room beyond an open door to their right. In the centre of the opposite wall was another door, closed and with a key in the lock. Sam guessed that this one must lead into the retail/public area at the front of the building. The left-hand wall was dominated by a narrow wooden staircase stretching upwards into shadows. Sam moved forward, but stopped after a couple of seconds when Purna put a hand on his arm.

'What is it?' he hissed.

'I know what you're thinking. You're thinking that if there were any infected in there you'd hear them moving about.'

Sam said nothing. That *had* been what he'd been thinking, but he waited for her to go on.

'But just remember,' she said, 'that although the infected are probably not cunning enough to set traps, people *are*. And in situations like this people get desperate.'

Sam couldn't imagine why anyone would *deliberately* want to draw attention to themselves, but he nodded nevertheless. 'Don't worry,' he whispered. 'I won't get sloppy.'

He slid along the wall to the open door and peered into the room beyond. He couldn't see much. The curtains were closed and it was still a little too early for daylight to seep in and make much of an impact. The constantly flickering gleam from the TV made what he *could* see shimmer and shift queasily. Somewhere among the shadows and the jumpy, ice-white light, he made out a sideboard, a small side table and the back of what appeared to be some kind of recliner – a tank of a chair at any rate, upholstered in some kind of rough, hessian-like material. From the slithering fall of light on the planes and angles of the walls and furniture it seemed reasonable to assume that the recliner was facing the TV. Constantly alert for movement, Sam crept further into the room, raising the flare pistol as he approached the back of the chair.

He was maybe a metre from it when something crunched beneath his foot. Looking down he saw broken glass, and a further glance revealed a table

111

lamp on the floor, its bulb shattered and its wire-and-fabric shade, which was lying several feet away, mangled and crushed as though it had been trampled by uncaring feet.

'If there's anyone here, let me tell you that I'm armed and I ain't taking no shit,' Sam said loudly. As an afterthought he added, 'I come in peace.'

From behind him, Purna said, 'Brace yourself. I'm turning the light on.'

There was a click and the room was suddenly filled with harsh electric light. The first thing the two of them saw, which had previously been concealed by the gloom, was the blood.

It formed a thick, red sticky pool – almost an island – on the green carpet around the chair. Looking down, Sam realized that the toe of one of his Reeboks was mere centimetres away from the edge of the pool. He stepped back quickly, as if afraid it might reach out and grab him.

Also revealed by the light was a hand, a withered old lady's claw, sporting a diamond-encrusted wedding ring. It was hanging limply over the arm of the chair, the blood that was dripping from its fingers making a very faint *plip* sound as it added to the pool below.

Sam and Purna looked at each other, already resigned to the sight of another atrocity, and slowly rounded the chair on opposite sides, forming a wide arc to avoid having to step in the blood. Sitting in the chair, the TV remote control still resting on the side cushion within reach of her right hand, was a scrawny woman in her eighties or maybe older. She had wispy, nicotine-yellow hair and inordinately showy diamond studs in the fleshy lobes of her ears. The skin of her face, which had remained untouched by her killer, was like crumpled brown paper, and there was startlingly pink lipstick edging the yawning O of her open mouth.

Although her face was untouched, the same could not be said of her torso. From her throat to her groin she had been torn apart, the damage so extensive it was as though a grenade had detonated in her belly. There was barely anything left of her bodily contents but a few shreds of bloody pulp clinging to the inside of a torn sack of human skin. She was so insubstantial she looked as if she could be folded up and packed in a suitcase.

'Well, I guess there's nothing—' Sam began, and then the old woman opened pale, cataracted eyes and made a horrible hissing gurgle, as if she was sifting wet gravel through her throat.

Sam jumped, his eyebrows shooting so far up his forehead that they became lost beneath the rim of his red bandanna. 'You have got to be *kidding* me!' he shouted, watching in disgust as the woman's quivering hand rose from the chair and clawed feebly at the air in an effort to reach him.

Stony-faced, Purna raised the heavy crowbar she was holding and brought it down mercilessly on the woman's skull. There was a crack and the skull split open, releasing a gush of thin, brownish blood which ran down the woman's face and into her milky eyes. Two more swift blows were all it took to shatter the skull completely, and a further two caused sufficient damage to the brain for the woman to slump and become still.

Sam stared down at the wreck of the old woman's body, appalled.

'It was a mercy killing,' said Purna, as if she felt a need to justify her actions. 'I couldn't stand the thought of her just sitting here, day after day, full of that . . . that *hunger*.'

'I know,' said Sam, his voice clogged with revulsion. He cleared his throat. 'You did the right thing.'

'Come on,' Purna said, 'let's get out of here.'

Sam nodded. 'Gladly.'

Although they had only been in the house for a few minutes, they both breathed in deeply as they stepped outside, as if released from a long ordeal.

Clearly relieved, Xian Mei, who had been watching the alleyway, hurried up to them. 'What did you find in there?'

'You don't wanna know,' muttered Sam. 'All quiet out here?'

Xian Mei nodded. 'I saw a couple of those things – a man and a woman – walk past the end of the alleyway, but they didn't see me.'

Purna looked up at the sky. All that remained of the night were a few shreds of inky cloud.

'Let's get this done quickly,' she said. 'It'll be full daylight soon.'

They hurried up the alleyway as fleet-footed as they could, dropping to a huddled crouch when the buildings to either side of them no longer provided cover. They scanned the main street in the hope of spotting a suitable vehicle. They had already discussed

114

what they should be looking for before setting off. Ideally they needed something like a delivery truck – something nippy and mobile, but large enough to carry plenty of provisions and stout enough to withstand attack. They had decided the best thing to do would be to target a vehicle that clearly belonged to a specific retail outlet rather than one that might just have been parked randomly on the street. That way it was more likely that they would find the keys inside the building that it served.

'There,' said Sam, pointing to his left. On the opposite side of the street, maybe a hundred and fifty metres away, was a surf shop called Wave Your Worries Goodbye. The shop sign above a display window full of surf gear and wetsuits was red, the name painted in calligraphy-type letters on a silver surfboard. Parked out front was a red van bearing the same logo.

'Wave your worries goodbye,' murmured Purna. 'Very appropriate.'

'I like to think of it as an omen,' said Sam.

From their vantage point they could see a couple of hundred metres along the street in either direction. At this moment only two of the infected were visible – a white guy of medium build in his early thirties wearing a black E Street Band tour T-shirt and cut-off jeans, and a pretty dark-haired girl of about eighteen in white shorts and a floral-print vest. The girl had brightly coloured plastic bangles on her wrists and a small shoulder bag on a long thin strap jouncing perkily on her hip. The man's hands and face were slathered in blood. The girl was chewing on what looked like a human liver, burying her face in it and snuffling like a pig.

'Those were the two I saw earlier,' whispered Xian Mei.

'If we're quick they'll hopefully be the only two we'll have to contend with,' said Purna.

Quickly she outlined her plan, and Sam and Xian Mei nodded their agreement. Without further preamble she said, 'Let's go.' Then the three of them stood up and began to run across the street.

They had covered almost half the distance before they were spotted. It was the girl who saw them first, her head snapping up as if she had caught their scent on the air. She let loose a snarling roar, dropped the lump of meat she was holding and started running towards them, the bag looped around her shoulder flying behind her.

She converged with them when they were around ten metres from the van. Ignoring Purna, who was in the lead, she targeted Sam.

'I got it!' he shouted, slowing just enough to raise the flare pistol and fire at the girl. The flare exploded against her chest in a flash of light, blackening her clothes. She screeched in rage and staggered slightly, but didn't go down. 'Fuck!' Sam shouted and veered to meet her head on, swinging the machete. When she reached for him, he hacked at her arm, almost severing it with one blow and knocking her off-balance. As she stumbled, her badly wounded arm gushing blood, he raised the machete again, stepping to one side so he could get a good swing at her head.

The first blow buried itself deep in the side of her skull, lopping off the top part of her ear. As she fell, he wrenched the machete free and followed up with two more savage blows, silencing her for ever. The adrenalin was pounding in his ears and so he didn't immediately register that Xian Mei was screaming for help. When he did, he turned to see her on the ground, the male zombie clinging to her kicking right leg, trying to bite it.

Her machete was lying several metres away from her, and she was simultaneously trying to scrabble towards it and avoid getting bitten. She pistoned her left leg out, hitting the zombie in the face with the sole of her foot and breaking his nose with a crunch. However, although the kick snapped his head back, it didn't loosen his grip on her leg. Hearing a crash, and registering in his peripheral vision that Purna was focused on kicking in the door of Wave Your Worries Goodbye, Sam ran across to Xian Mei, raising his machete once again.

He brought it down with all his force on the back of the zombie's head, cleaving its skull. The creature fell forward on to its face, its body spasming and jerking as its dying brain short-circuited. As it died in a spreading pool of its own blood, Xian Mei scooted backwards away from it and scrambled to her feet. Her right leg was scratched and a little bloody, but she seemed otherwise unharmed.

'You OK?' Sam asked.

'Fine,' she said, snatching up her machete.

The two of them glanced around, then hurried across to the van parked outside Wave Your Worries

Goodbye. Purna had succeeded in kicking the door open now and had gone inside.

Before Sam could even think about going in after her, she was running back out, left hand raised triumphantly, keys jangling on the loop of a keyring around her finger.

'You see anyone?' Sam asked.

She shook her head. 'Neither dead *nor* alive.' Then her eyes flickered beyond him and widened. 'Shit.'

Sam and Xian Mei turned to see a zombie running towards them. It was a fat, bald white man of about sixty, with a grey beard and fuzzy blue tattoos on his hairy arms. Unlike the other zombies they had seen, he was not drenched with the messy remains of a recent meal. The cause of his infection, however, was clear. His left leg was badly bitten and he was missing the thumb and forefinger of his left hand.

The man's face was as blue as a heart attack victim's and his pendulous belly swung beneath a yellow T-shirt bearing the legend *World's Greatest Lover*. His bottom half was clad only in a pair of black Speedos and he was wearing an open-toed sandal on his right foot; his other was bare.

Purna pressed a button on the key fob and the van chirruped and flashed its lights as its doors unlocked. They ran across to it and got in, Purna diving into the driver's seat, Sam and Xian Mei running around to the passenger door. Sam glanced at the approaching zombie as Xian Mei climbed into the van ahead of him. Though it was running as fast as it could, its steps were lumbering, its weight slowing it down. It made Sam think of an old lion that was getting too slow to hunt; he almost felt sorry for it.

The zombie was still ten metres short of them when the van pulled away. Watching it in the wing mirror, Sam saw it try to put on an extra spurt of speed but succeed only in tripping over and sprawling headlong in the dust.

Need to lose some weight, you fat fuck, he thought, then turned as Purna muttered, 'Hell.'

'What's wrong?' asked Xian Mei, who was sitting in the middle of the three front seats.

'We're almost out of gas,' Purna said. She raised her eyes Heavenwards. 'Thank you, God.'

'Bound to be a gas station around here someplace,' said Sam.

'There is,' said Xian Mei. 'There's one further along the main street, back the way we've just come.'

Without hesitation, Purna hit the brakes and turned the steering wheel, performing a neat U-turn. They were now heading back towards the fat, grey-bearded zombie, which appeared to be picking itself up almost ruefully, its bare legs and the front of its T-shirt covered in brown dust.

At their approach, the zombie held up its hands and lurched into their path, like a drunken late-night reveller trying to hail a cab. Purna gave a casual jerk on the steering wheel to bypass it, but in a desperate attempt to satisfy its hunger it flung itself at the van. There was a heavy thump and the van shuddered slightly as the zombie impacted with the side of it and bounced off. Once again glancing into his wing mirror as they sped away, Sam saw the zombie, its shattered arm now hanging at a bizarre angle, pick itself up from a spatter of its own blood and stagger hopelessly after them.

He had barely faced front again when two more of the infected appeared. One, a skinny, short-skirted black woman with spectacular legs, who had clearly been for a night on the town and had decided to head home a little too late, came running out of the open door of a nearby bar. The other, a white boy of about seven wearing nothing but a pair of green shorts, was crouched in the gutter on the other side of the road, devouring what might have been a dead cat, but he jumped to his feet at their approach.

With the zombies heading at them from separate directions, it was impossible to avoid hitting both of them. An expression of calculating grimness on her face, Purna took the path of least resistance, veering to her left just as the boy took a running leap towards them.

Caught in mid-air, the boy smashed into the van and all but disintegrated like a flimsy bag of meat – which, in effect, is what he was. For a few seconds the windscreen was coated in a thick spray of red and Purna was driving blind. Then, calmly, she flicked on the windscreen wipers and tugged the indicator lever towards her, activating the water jets. Sam sat back with a groan as the wipers swept the majority of the mess away, shocked by the fact that the boy's violent death hadn't affected him more than it had. What was it the psychologists called it? Combat fatigue?

With Xian Mei directing them, they reached the gas station without further incident. Opening the passenger door, Sam said, 'I'll fill her up. You guys watch out for more of those things.'

The girls nodded and Sam flipped open the cap on the side of the van, and unhooked the gas hose. For a second after squeezing the trigger he felt sure the pump would either be locked or run dry. But to his relief the gas started to flow.

The tank was almost full when he happened to glance up and saw a face watching him through a small dusty window in the closed side door of the body shop attached to the gas station. As soon as he established eye contact with it, the face disappeared with a wide-eyed expression of alarm.

'Hey!' he shouted.

Purna opened the driver's door and stuck her head out. 'You OK?'

'There's someone in there,' Sam said, nodding towards the body shop. 'A regular person, I mean.'

'They look friendly?' Purna asked.

'They looked scared,' said Sam. '*She* looked scared. It was a girl. Twenty years old, maybe younger.'

'I'll check it out,' Xian Mei called, getting out of the van and walking across to the body shop. She knocked on the door. 'Hello, anyone in there?' When no one answered, she said, 'We just wondered if you needed any help? We're not going to hurt you.'

After a few seconds there was a click and the door opened, albeit no more than a few inches. A girl's voice, young and nervous, said, 'What do you want?'

'We're just getting some gas,' replied Xian Mei. 'We'll pay you for it if you want. Are you OK in there?'

There was a pause and then the girl said, 'My papa's hurt.'

Sam and Xian Mei exchanged glances. 'Hurt how?' asked Xian Mei. 'Is there anything we can do?'

There was a further pause and then the door opened a bit more to reveal a slender, almost frail young girl, who peered out at them with wide dark eyes, like a timid animal uncertain whether to emerge from its burrow.

'Hi,' said Xian Mei with a sudden warm smile which transformed her face. 'What's your name?'

'Jin,' said the girl.

'Hi, Jin. I'm Xian Mei, that's Sam and our driver's called Purna.'

Jin looked at Xian Mei and then at Sam. 'How come you're not like the others?' she asked.

'The infected, you mean?' said Sam, and shrugged. 'We don't know. We're just not.'

'Infected?' Jin asked.

'There's a virus,' explained Xian Mei. 'It . . . affects people's minds, sends them crazy.'

'One of the crazy people hurt my papa,' Jin said.

Sam tried not to look alarmed. 'Hurt him how?'

'She bit him. She tried to kill him.' Jin swallowed. 'My papa had to shoot her.'

To his shame, the first question that leaped into Sam's head was to ask Jin what kind of gun her father owned. Resisting the urge, he asked instead, 'And how's your papa now?'

'He's sick,' Jin said. Hesitantly she asked, 'Can you help him?'

'We can try,' said Sam. 'You want to show me where he is?'

After another moment's hesitation the girl nodded and led the way inside.

'Let Purna know what's going on,' Sam muttered to Xian Mei, and followed Jin through the door and into the cool gloom of the body shop. There were tools on racks against the walls, a hydraulic pulley system overhead to lift heavy car parts and a small office space in the corner. The place smelled of oil, grease and metal. Jin led him over to an open door in the left-hand wall.

'This is where we live,' she said simply. 'Papa's through here.'

They passed through a short hallway with a thread-bare carpet and into a small sitting room at the back of the house. There wasn't much in there but a small colour TV perched on a wooden fruit box, a bookcase which mostly contained *Reader's Digest* editions of classic novels and a ratty grey sofa with matching armchair.

There were also lots of framed family photographs on the walls – some of Jin on her own at various ages, or with her parents, smiling and happy. Sam wondered what had become of the pretty woman in the photographs who, from the resemblance, was clearly Jin's mother. He turned his attention to the man lying on the sofa with a blanket over his legs. He was evidently the same man in the photographs, but the difference between the smiling images on the walls and the flesh-and-blood figure on the sofa could not have been more marked.

Jin's father was sweating and feverish, his face a ghastly grey, his eyes ringed with dark flesh and rolling in his sockets. He was breathing stertorously and there was a bad smell about him, a smell of sickness and fear. His left arm was heavily bandaged from elbow to wrist, and on the floor beside the sofa was a bowl of water with a white cloth floating in it.

'I cleaned and disinfected the wound, and gave him some painkillers, and I've been trying to keep him cool,' said Jin. 'But he's getting worse. He's been delirious for the past hour and he's had a couple of seizures. I tried calling for an ambulance, but all the phones are dead.'

'How long ago he get bit?' Sam asked.

'About . . . four, five hours.'

'And this woman who attacked him? It wasn't . . . ?' Instead of finishing his question, Sam glanced up at the family portraits.

Jin shook her head vigorously. 'No. My mama died when I was twelve. Anaplastic large-cell lymphoma.' When Sam raised his eyebrows she said, 'I'm a nurse. Just about to qualify anyway.'

'Good for you,' Sam said distractedly. He was thinking hard, wondering what to do, what to suggest. He knew that if Jin stayed here with her father he would eventually turn, just like the others, and attack her. Indicating the man's bandaged arm, he asked, 'So how exactly did it happen?'

'He heard a noise in the night, thought someone was messing with the gas pumps. When he saw the woman he thought she was drunk or maybe ill. He went out to ask if she was OK and she just attacked him. Papa said she was like a wild animal. He said if he hadn't shot her she would've killed him.'

'So where's this woman now?'

Jin shook her head. 'I don't know. Papa said he was sure he'd killed her, but when we looked out later she'd gone.'

Sam was silent for a moment, and then he said, 'Listen, Jin, there ain't no easy way to say this. Your papa's ill, *really* ill I mean, and he ain't gonna get better. This thing he's got, there's no cure for it. Pretty soon he'll turn, like the woman that attacked him, and he'll attack you too.'

Jin shook her head almost angrily. 'No! He would never do that!'

'He won't be able to stop himself. Believe me, I've seen it. You can't do nothing to help him. All you can do now is help yourself.'

'What are you saying?' Jin's face was stony.

Sam took a deep breath. 'You gotta get away from here. You gotta come with us.'

She recoiled, almost as if he had tried to strike her. 'I'm not leaving him!'

'You got to, if you want to live.'

'No!'

'He's right,' croaked a voice from the sofa.

Surprised, Sam looked down at Jin's father. Moments before, the man had been delirious but now, temporarily at least, the fever had abated and he seemed alert and lucid.

'Papa!' Jin exclaimed delightedly, and cast Sam an accusatory look. 'You see. He's getting better.'

'No,' said Jin's father, his voice so weak it was barely there, 'I'm not.'

Jin knelt beside her father and took his hand. 'I'm

not leaving you, Papa. You *will* get better. I'll *make* you well.'

Jin's father shook his head and winced, even that simple movement seeming to cause him pain.

'You *must* go,' he said. 'If you don't ... then I'll do something terrible, I know it ... I'm having such thoughts, my beautiful Jin ... such awful thoughts ... You are not safe here ...'

His eyes drifted closed. Jin clung to her father's hand, shaking her head, tears running down her face. After a moment the man's eyes flickered open again.

'Leave me some medicine ... and lock me in ... Help will eventually come ... I know it ... But in the meantime ... you must go ...' His eyes shifted to focus on Sam. 'What's your name?'

'Sam, sir.'

'Sam ... a good name ...' He swallowed. 'Sam, do you promise to look after my little girl?'

'Yes, sir,' Sam said gravely. 'I promise.'

A ghost of a smile played around Jin's father's lips. 'Thank you,' he whispered.

Gently Sam placed a hand on Jin's arm. 'We should go.'

Sobbing, Jin lifted her father's hand and kissed it. 'I'll come back for you, Papa. I promise.'

Chapter 8

CHIMES OF DOOM

'I hear church bells.'

It was the first time anyone had spoken for a couple of minutes. Jin's arrival had disrupted the status quo more than Sam had anticipated. He'd thought she would be warmly welcomed once he'd explained the situation, but although she hadn't made it explicit, Purna had given Sam the impression that she regarded him as a soft touch, who would have to be discouraged from picking up every waif and stray he came across. She cheered up when she saw the shotgun and ammunition that Jin's father had insisted they take with them, but had regarded Jin with exasperated disbelief when the girl had refused the offer of a machete on the grounds that she was a 'pacifist'.

'No such thing any more,' Purna said curtly. 'Not if you want to survive.'

Jin looked apologetic. 'Sorry, but there's no way I could bring myself to harm a living creature.'

'The infected aren't *living*,' Purna retorted. 'They're just people-shaped repositories of rage and hunger.'

'All the same,' said Jin, folding her arms as if she

127

was afraid Purna would try to *force* the weapon into her hands.

Scathingly Purna said, 'With that attitude you won't last a day.'

'We'll see, won't we?' said Jin, but it was not a defiant response; on the contrary, she looked intimidated, victimized.

Purna shook her head. 'No, we won't see. Because we can't afford to carry passengers.'

'Hey, who died and made *you* queen of shit-storm island?' Sam responded angrily.

Purna scowled at him. 'I know it's tough, Sam, but that's the way it is. It's kill or be killed. And if you or Xian Mei are looking out for Miss Goody Two-Shoes here as well as yourselves, your attention will be split and that'll lead to mistakes. And in this groovy new world, one mistake and suddenly you're human hamburger.'

'So what are you saying?' said Xian Mei calmly. 'That we should throw Jin out on the street and let her fend for herself?'

Jin looked alarmed, but Sam raised a hand to reassure her. 'Hey, don't worry. 'Cos that *ain't* gonna happen.'

'Course I'm not suggesting that,' Purna replied, scowling. 'I'm just saying that Jin's got to change her values, and quickly, because cosy little indulgences like pacifism are just not valid any more.'

'Maybe I don't have to fight because I have other skills I can contribute,' Jin said gamely.

'Yeah? Like what?'

'Well . . . I'm a nurse. I know how to treat wounds

and injuries. Plus I'm a pretty good mechanic. I've helped Papa in the body shop enough times to know my way around an engine.'

Sam nodded approvingly. 'You can't say that ain't gonna come in useful,' he said to Purna.

She raised her eyebrows but stayed silent, refusing to commit herself either way, and as if taking their cue from her the four of them descended into a simmering silence.

At Xian Mei's suggestion they were taking a round-about route back to the beach, following the coast road which took them close to the outskirts of Moresby's slum district. Although the virus had spread from the city into the far more salubrious environs of Banoi's resort area, Xian Mei had opined that it was worth taking a gamble on the fact that the infected would be sticking to the population centres, where there would be greater numbers of the living for them to feast upon. So far her theory had proved correct and the infected had been conspicuous by their absence. Now, though, the sound of church bells had thrown them a curve ball, and within minutes had prompted a fresh debate.

'They're coming from Moresby church,' said Xian Mei in response to Sam's observation.

'We should check it out,' Jin piped up.

Purna, in the driving seat, shook her head. 'No way.'

'But there might be people in trouble. Why else would they ring the bells unless it was a cry for help?'

When Purna didn't reply, Sam said, 'She's right.'

Purna glanced at him. 'So what if she is?'

'If people are in trouble, then we should try to help them,' Jin said obstinately.

Purna wore the expression of someone who was surrounded by idiots. '*Everyone's* in trouble – everyone alive, that is. Or hadn't you noticed?'

'Is that a reason not to try to help one another?' Jin said.

'Yes it is, because we can't help *everyone*,' said Purna scathingly.

'I'm not suggesting we should. But that doesn't mean we shouldn't try to help the ones we know about.' When Purna kept on driving, Jin added, 'If we ignore people in need, then doesn't that make us just as bad as the virus itself? Worse even?'

'She's got a point,' said Xian Mei.

'Fuck!' shouted Purna, and slammed on the brakes so suddenly that all three of her passengers were jolted forward, gasping as their seatbelts locked painfully across their chests.

'What's your problem?' said Sam.

'Well, I don't know,' said Purna. 'Maybe it's just that I'm not heavily into suicide missions.'

'Don't you think you're overreacting?' Xian Mei said.

Purna glared at her. 'Oh, you think? You want me to drive into a heavy population centre which we've been led to believe is swarming with the infected, and you honestly can't understand why I regard that action as a mite foolhardy?'

'People are in trouble,' said Jin.

Purna closed her eyes briefly. 'If you say that one more time I may punch you unconscious.'

Calmly Xian Mei said, 'Moresby church is less than a mile from here. And it's on a hill above the city. We can get there without having to go down into the streets at all.'

'And you think those bells won't have attracted the infected from miles around?' Purna said.

Sam shrugged. 'We can't say for sure that sound really registers with them. I mean, the TV in that old lady's house didn't seem to attract them.'

'Apart from the fact that the old woman had been gutted,' Purna pointed out.

'Which means *one* of them got in, sure. But maybe they got a sixth sense for fresh blood or a beating heart.'

'Why don't we vote on it?' Jin suggested, and raised a hand. 'I vote we check it out.'

'Me too,' said Sam. When Purna shook her head in disgust, he added, 'If people're in trouble I can't just ignore it. Maybe that makes me a dumb fuck, but at least I'll die with a clear conscience.'

'I vote we check it out too,' said Xian Mei, and pulled an apologetic face. 'Sorry, Purna.'

Purna sighed but said, 'I want it on record that I think this is a crazy idea – but I suppose I'll abide by the majority decision.' Putting the truck into gear, she asked, 'So how do I get to this damn church?'

The bells grew louder as they approached, and Sam couldn't help but think of a line from an old song, something about chimes of doom. Following Xian Mei's instructions they took a right on to what seemed little more than a leafy track through a patch of jungle that rose steadily uphill, the road so pitted and uneven that Purna had to slow the van to a crawl at times.

'No chance of a quick getaway here,' she remarked tartly.

No one said anything, and a few minutes later the road opened out into a dusty clearing dominated on the far side by a pair of imposing black iron gates. Slowing to a halt, Purna said, 'So what now?'

Xian Mei looked momentarily hesitant. 'Now we get out and walk, I guess.'

Purna looked at her. 'Are you kidding me?'

'It's only a few hundred metres through the grave-yard. Look, you can see the spire of the church from here.'

She leaned forward in her seat, pointing upwards. The others leaned forward too. At the top of the wind-screen, rising above the trees beyond the gates, they could just make out a dark spire topped by a crucifix standing out starkly against the pale dawn sky.

'A few hundred metres,' Purna repeated heavily. Beyond the gates were gravel walkways divided by occasional flights of wooden steps. On a regular Sunday, worshippers ascending the hill would no doubt feel they were plodding towards heaven, but right now it looked like nothing more than a potentially lethal obstacle course. 'Isn't there an access road we can use? What about deliveries?'

Jin shook her head. 'Anything the church needs is carried up from here. They've always managed before now.'

'Before now they didn't have the undead to contend with,' Purna remarked.

Sam unclipped his seatbelt. 'Come on, let's get this thing done.'

Because Purna had handled one before, and because the other three felt secretly guilty at involving her in a situation of potential and unnecessary danger, it was decided that the Australian girl would carry the shotgun. Sam and Xian Mei had a flare pistol and a machete each, and after a couple of minutes of heated debate, Jin was persuaded to carry a crowbar to – if need be – 'defend herself with'.

Despite the presence of dozens of sun-bleached grave markers straggling uphill and leaning every which way, the route up to Moresby church was more like a tropical garden than a typical graveyard. In fact, there were several routes to choose from, each one winding through clumps of palm trees and thick vegetation. The sun had burst over the horizon now and was creeping steadily higher in the sky, the insects and birds launching gustily into their dawn chorus as the day grew brighter and hotter. Purna looked around warily, remarking that everyone should be extra vigilant, as the sound of insects, birds and bells would almost certainly be enough to mask the approach of the infected. She had barely finished speaking when a zombie erupted out of the bushes about eight metres ahead of them, blocking their path.

It was a big, heavily tattooed guy with facial piercings and green hair. He was slathered in blood, some of it fresh, especially around his mouth, but much of it black and stiff on his white Kurt Cobain T-shirt and ripped jeans. Jin screamed as he ran at them, snarling like a particularly ferocious guard dog. Almost unhurriedly, Purna raised the shotgun and pulled the trigger, the blast hitting him square in the jaw and all but tearing his face away.

He went down so heavily that Sam fancied he felt the ground shake beneath his feet.

'This is *not* a good idea,' said Purna.

'Maybe you're right,' Sam conceded reluctantly. He turned, and was shocked to see three more of the infected break cover behind them, emerging from the bushes and trees flanking the gate. There was a middle-aged man and woman – they might even have been husband and wife – dressed in the loud shirts and shorts of the typical western holidaymaker, and a younger, bearded man wearing khaki shorts, whose naked upper torso was covered in bite-marks.

The trio of zombies ran at them, their faces bestial. The woman stumbled and fell, but picked herself up immediately, her chubby knees scuffed and bloodied. Purna raised the shotgun again and took out the bearded guy who was drawing ahead of the older man, but succeeded only in wounding him. Quickly assessing their odds, knowing that she wouldn't have time to reload before the zombies were on them, she gestured towards the church and shouted, 'Run!'

Although he didn't like turning his back on the snarling trio behind them, Sam knew that – for now at least – discretion was the better part of valour. Even so, he deliberately dropped to the back of the group, urging Xian Mei and especially Jin ahead of him. Fortunately he and his companions were younger and fitter than the animated cadavers chasing them and they quickly drew away from their pursuers. The only dangers with moving so quickly, of course, was that they were more prone to losing their footing and they didn't have time to assess

134

their surroundings or the terrain ahead of them.

This drawback almost proved Purna's undoing when another of the infected leaped from the clump of bushes she was running past and hit her side on, knocking her over. The shotgun flew from her hands as she fell, the zombie on top of her, its hands and teeth already trying to tear at her body. It was a teenage boy, a ghetto kid, his clothes frayed and threadbare, almost colourless from having been washed too many times. As he and Purna hit the ground, the impact knocked them apart, but the boy was up quickly and flying at her again.

Taken by surprise and momentarily stunned, Purna could only flail at him, yelling in anger and pain as he bit into the side of her arm. Sam ran forward to help her, already raising his machete, but it was Jin and Xian Mei, ahead of him, who reached Purna first. Acting instinctively, Jin raised the crowbar she was carrying and brought it down on the boy's back. Although it barely injured him, it was enough, at least, to distract him for a moment. His head snapped up and round, his face a screeching mask of white eyes and bared, blood-slicked teeth. Pushing Jin un-ceremoniously out of the way, Xian Mei sprang forward and decapitated him with one sweeping blow of the machete.

As the head flew into the bushes, the boy's body crumpled, his hands grotesquely clenching and unclenching. Hearing snarls and heavy breathing behind him, Sam whirled round. The delay had enabled the middle-aged couple and the wounded man to catch up with them. Sam raised the flare pistol and fired it directly into the middle-aged man's twisted, bespectacled face. His head flared like a struck match, his hair igniting. As he staggered to one side, Sam jumped forward and finished him off with the machete.

Xian Mei, meanwhile, was dealing with the bearded man. Leaping with athletic grace, she shot out her foot in a high kick which connected with his solar plexus. He stumbled backwards, his left arm hanging uselessly where Purna had almost severed it at the shoulder with the shotgun blast, and collided with the woman, both of them going down like skittles. Instantly Xian Mei and Sam ran forward, bloodied machetes raised, and hacked into their skulls, destroying their brains.

As abruptly as the violence had begun it was over, leaving them with nothing but the shocking aftermath of battle. Sam and Xian Mei stood side by side for a moment, panting and spattered with blood, while behind them Purna clambered gingerly to her feet and limped across to pick up the shotgun she had dropped. As she deftly reloaded despite her bitten hand, Jin, standing alone, dropped the crowbar with a clatter and began to shake and sob. Closing the cartridge chamber of the gun with a click, Purna moved forward and put her arm round Jin's thin shoulders.

'Hey,' she said gently, 'you did good. You saved my life.'

Jin looked at the carnage around her. 'That was . . . horrible,' she whispered.

Purna nodded. 'Yes it was. But it's all over now and they're at peace.'

Suddenly Sam raised his head. 'Hey, listen up every-one.'

Despite the constant clang of bells, they heard a rustling and grunting, coming from somewhere in the undergrowth, moving in their direction. It was not close to them, but not too far away either.

'Let's move,' said Purna. 'But keep alert. Eyes and ears everywhere.'

They moved swiftly uphill, Xian Mei in the lead, Purna limping along with the shotgun and Jin, who was still shaking, just in front of Sam. Closer to the church the vegetation died back a little and they were able to see the building, perched on the side of the hill and overlooking the city below, in all its glory.

In truth, however, despite its imposing location the building itself was not in the best shape. The roof was missing tiles, and many of the interlocking wooden planks that comprised its walls had either warped or rotted. In some places the damage was so bad it had been patched up with tin or corrugated iron, which itself had now gone rusty. Looking at the dilapidated building, it struck Sam that it didn't seem very defend-able. If enough zombies made a concerted effort to get in, they would – he was sure of it.

As they moved across the open patch of scrubby ground towards the sun-scoured but stout-looking main doors of the church, another of the infected crawled out from behind a tombstone and began dragging itself along the ground towards them. This one was an overweight man in his forties wearing a soiled and ripped policeman's uniform. Half of his face had been torn away and his right leg was a ragged, bleeding stump. Jin put a hand over her mouth and looked away as Xian Mei strode determinedly forward. Standing over the crawling zombie, but taking care not to come within range of its frantically grasping hands, she said, 'Sorry.' Then she raised her machete and ruthlessly brought it down.

The others waited for her to rejoin them before walking up to the church. Purna bashed on the door with the barrel of the shotgun. 'Hey!' she shouted. 'You in there!'

'We came to see if you needed help!' called Xian Mei.

They waited less than ten seconds and then one of the two doors creaked slowly open. Purna stepped back, half-raising the shotgun warily. A man's face appeared, his skin the colour of teak, his close-cropped hair and neat moustache white and grizzled.

'Friends or foes?' he enquired in a deep, gentle, almost melodious voice.

'Friends, we hope,' said Xian Mei.

'I hope so too,' said the man and pulled the door further open. 'Not that we refuse entry to anyone here. Come in.'

The four of them trooped inside and the old man closed and locked the door behind them.

'Name's Ed,' he said. 'Ed Lacey.'

Purna introduced herself and the rest of them. 'You're not native to these parts,' she noted.

'I'm from Florida. Was on holiday with my wife, Maya. Some holiday, huh?'

In spite of everything, Sam grinned. The man's gentle humour was a welcome tonic after what they had been through. 'Not exactly the paradise we were hoping for either.'

Ed laughed softly, then raised a hand and crooked a finger. 'C'mon, I'll introduce you to the others.'

The interior of the church was as shabby as the exterior – chunks of plaster missing from the walls, many of the pews broken or water-damaged. At the far end, huddled on rickety wooden chairs around a large crucifix that towered above the raised pulpit, were around thirty people. Most looked like shell-shocked parishioners who had fled here, seeking sanctuary, from the overcrowded slums of Moresby directly below. However, a few of the group were clearly more affluent, among them a smattering of white-faced western holidaymakers, who had somehow managed, whether by accident or design, to find their way here.

Looking around and nodding greetings at people as Ed named them, Sam noted that the ages of the group members ranged from less than one (a tired-looking bony-shouldered mother who couldn't have been more than seventeen was breast-feeding a fidgeting, fractious baby) to a half-dozen men and women in their seventies or possibly eighties. One man who was younger than that – sixty maybe – was lying full-length on a pew, bolstered by hassocks and cushions. He was an overweight white man (though his face at the moment was the colour of beetroot), and he was breathing in ratcheting gasps, a clenched fist resting on his chest and his fleshy features knotted in pain.

An equally overweight white woman in a floral summer dress was perched next to him on a stool, clutching his free hand and murmuring platitudes. For the first time Ed Lacey's face clouded with concern. 'That there's Mr and Mrs Owen,' he said. 'Mr Owen ain't too well.'

'What's wrong with him?' asked Purna a little sharply. Sam knew what she was thinking. If Mr Owens' condition was caused by a zombie bite then they were all in danger.

Ed read the meaning behind her question immediately. 'It ain't what you think. It's his heart, his wife says.'

Overhearing them, Mrs Owen turned her head. She seemed too preoccupied with her husband's illness to show any reaction to their bloodied state or the weapons they were carrying.

'He needs his pills,' she said. 'But they're back at the hotel.'

'What kind of pills are they?' asked Jin.

'They're called Nadolol. They're—'

'I know. Beta blockers, prescribed for the treatment of angina pectoris. Is that what your husband suffers from?'

'Yes,' said the woman, surprised. 'Are you a doctor?'

'No,' said Jin, 'I'm a nurse. How bad is he?'

'Very bad. He needs his pills regularly. If he doesn't get them . . .' The woman's voice choked off and she shook her head. When she next spoke they could all hear the flutter of fear in her voice. '. . . well, I don't know what might happen.'

Jin turned to the others. Quietly she said, 'We have to try and get this man his medication.'

Purna frowned. 'How?'

'There's a pharmacy on the high street. They should have some Nadolol there.'

Lowering her voice, Purna said, 'We can't go all the way back there. Taking a detour to come here almost got us killed.'

Hovering just behind them, Ed reached out and touched Purna on the arm. 'Mind if I say something?'

Purna turned with a frown, but raised her eyebrows to indicate he should continue.

'Maybe we can resolve this situation to our mutual benefit,' Ed said.

Purna's frown deepened. 'How?'

'Come with me. There's a couple people I think you should meet.'

He led Purna and Jin away from the main group by the pulpit and across to a moth-eaten red curtain in the far corner. He lifted this aside to reveal a door, which he pushed open. Beyond the door the continuing sound of church bells grew instantly louder. Ed led them through a small sacristy and then through another door into a stone chamber containing nothing but a flight of circular stone steps. As they ascended the steps the church bells became so loud they could barely hear themselves think. Eventually they emerged into a stone-floored bell tower, where two people, both very different in age and build but wearing identical expressions of grim determination, were tugging at long black bell pulls. Ed raised a hand, but it was a redundant gesture. As soon as they caught sight of Purna and Jin, the couple ceased their bell-ringing as if by mutual consent.

One of the bell-ringers, a wizened, wiry woman in a

141

nun's habit, scuttled forward with a beaming smile and took Purna's hand. At the top of her voice she shouted above the slowing but still-clanging peal of the bells, 'Has He sent you to find us?'

At first Purna didn't know what she meant, but then she realized. 'I don't know about that. We followed the sound of the bells.'

The little nun seemed pleased with her answer. 'Of course you did.'

Ed leaned forward and said, 'I think we and these people might be able to help each other. Can we talk downstairs?'

The nun nodded and they all descended to the sacristy. The second bell-ringer, a tall, handsome broad-shouldered man with caramel-coloured skin, brought up the rear. Quickly Ed made the introductions, then explained and summed up the situation.

'We need medication for Mr Owen, and we also need food and water for everyone, and a way to defend ourselves until help arrives. I'm guessing you people would welcome the chance to get your hands on some better weapons too, to help you do whatever you're doing?'

'We're getting off the island,' Purna said firmly. 'I think you should too.'

Ed shook his head. 'There are too many of us, and some of us aren't as . . . well, as physically adept as you young people. No, we'll sit it out here until they send in the cavalry.'

'What if they don't?' said Jin.

Unease flickered briefly over Ed's face, then he said confidently, 'They will. They always do.'

The nun, whom Ed had introduced as Sister Helen, had been sitting throughout the conversation with an almost beatific smile on her face. Purna now turned to her and asked, 'What do you think, Sister Helen?'

'About what, my child?'

'Well, it's evident from what I've heard that a lot of the people here look up to you, that they regard you as their spiritual leader. Do you think you should wait here for help or try to help yourselves?'

Beaming, Sister Helen said, 'Oh, there's no help to be found anywhere, except ultimately from God.'

Purna looked confused. 'I'm sorry, I don't follow.'

Sister Helen leaned forward and gently took her hand. 'There is no escape for anyone, my child, not in this life. God's wrath is upon us all. This is His judgement.'

Purna licked her lips, glanced at the others. 'I'm sorry, I don't believe that. To me, that just sounds like giving up, accepting the inevitable. And I'm not a giving-up sort of person.'

She expected an argument, perhaps even recriminations, but Sister Helen simply spread her hands. 'That is your prerogative, my child.'

Again Purna glanced around, focusing on Ed. 'So what's the deal here?'

'The deal is that this church is a sanctuary, that Sister Helen is kind enough to take in anyone who wants shelter or protection. Personally she believes that this is the Apocalypse, that we can do nothing more useful than pray and wait out the inevitable, but – and forgive me for saying this, Sister – not all of us feel the same way. Personally I respect Sister Helen's beliefs, and I can truly say that my wife Maya and I will be eternally grateful for her kindness, but I happen to think there's a way out of this – or that even if there isn't, then that don't mean we should quit trying to find one. So here's my proposal: if you guys head back into town to pick up some medication for Mr Owen and enough provisions to keep us going for the next few days, and weapons to defend ourselves with, if needs be, then we'll show you a way to get better weapons for yourselves – guns, maybe even explosives.'

'How?' Purna asked.

Ed indicated the tall handsome man, who had so far said barely a word. 'Dani here and his brother, Pedro, run a business that sets up security systems for companies and individuals on Banoi – electric fences, CCTV, internal coded locking systems, you name it. And it just so happens that one of their clients is the police, and that a few years ago Dani and Pedro installed a weapons vault in the resort station on the main street.'

Dani nodded. His voice was soft and deep, his English good but strongly accented. 'I have security codes in here.' He tapped his head. 'Inside vault is plenty of weapon for all. If Sister Helen says is OK, I come with you.'

They all looked at Sister Helen, who said smilingly, 'Oh, we all have free will. I cannot possibly speak for Him.'

Dani looked at Purna and nodded slowly. 'Then I come with you,' he said.

Chapter 9

LOW-LIFE

'Holy crap.'

Sam's tone was almost reverential. The sight that greeted them as they turned the corner on to the main resort street was both terrifying and awe-inspiring.

The infected were everywhere. In a hideously grotesque parody of consumerism, they were shuffling up and down the long main street as if window shopping. Some of them were even wandering aimlessly in and out of the stores and bars and restaurants, presumably looking for food.

If anyone *was* still alive in the buildings, however, they were keeping well hidden. There were a few eviscerated bodies, or parts of bodies, strewn about like roadkill, which Sam guessed must belong to people either lucky or unlucky enough to have been so badly torn apart that there was no chance of them coming back, but there was no sign of anyone actually *alive* – no survivors sitting on roofs with 'Help' signs, or peering out of upper-floor windows.

As for the infected themselves, they were made up almost entirely of holidaymakers and resort staff.

Many were dressed in nightwear or brightly coloured holiday clothes; some were wearing the uniforms of hotel staff or retail assistants. They were of all ages and colours and creeds, and they almost all bore the evidence of bites or other, more serious wounds. Sam could see one old man constantly stumbling on his own intestines, slick pink loops of which were hanging out of a rent in his stomach and trailing around his feet like a tangle of dead snakes. Other zombies were missing limbs or feet or hands; some, unable to walk, were dragging themselves along, their fingernails torn and bleeding. Yet others were missing parts of their face – one man had had his entire lower jaw torn away and his fat, blackening tongue was plastered to his throat like a feeding leech. The majority of them were smeared with the remains of recent meals, hands and faces caked in drying blood and clots of raw meat.

So far, despite the noise of the van's engine, Purna, Sam and the others had been ignored – further evidence that Sam's theory was correct and that the infected only responded to what they could eat, blanking out everything else.

'You reckon they can smell us in here?' Sam said as the van idled at the intersection.

Purna shrugged. 'Maybe they don't need to smell us. Maybe if they just catch sight of us, that little "food" sign will ping in their heads.'

'So where *is* this police station?' Sam asked, half turning to Dani, who was crouched in the back of the van, hands curled around the headrests of the front seats to stop him being shaken about too much.

'About half-mile that way,' Dani replied, pointing

left along the main drag. 'Big white building. We park at bottom of steps and run up. There is ... er ...' He mimed pressing buttons.

'Keypad?' suggested Xian Mei.

'Yes. Keypad outside door. Four-number code.'

'You'd better tell us what it is,' said Purna. 'Just in case of unexpected developments.'

Dani nodded. 'Is four-two-seven-four.'

'Four-two-seven-four,' repeated Purna. 'Everyone got that?'

Sam, Jin and Xian Mei all nodded.

'OK. Let's do this.'

They had already discussed the plan – get the guns first, then drive round the back of the main super-market to the delivery warehouse, where it would hopefully be quieter. Jin had explained there was a pharmacy outlet within the supermarket itself, which had a prescriptions counter, so with luck they would be able to get Mr Owen's Nadolol there. If not, they would have to make a separate trip to the bigger phar-macy, which was further up towards their resort hotel. Purna remarked sourly that at this rate they'd do so much backtracking that eventually they'd end up in their hotel rooms.

She eased off the brake and edged forward slowly, the silver-grey van nudging into the main street. It struck Sam that the van was kind of like a shark, cruis-ing slowly through the shallows of a sea packed with holidaymakers – except in this case the tourists, and not the shark, were the predators. The infected milled about in front of them, ignoring the van and each other. They even ignored the van when it bumped gently against them, nudging them out of the way.

They had crawled maybe a hundred metres without incident when they encountered a girl in a white Christian Dior T-shirt and denim shorts standing directly in front of them. The girl would have been pretty if it wasn't for her glazed and milky eyes, and the red gruel of blood and offal clotted in her shoulder-length blonde hair. She was just standing there, her head tilted vaguely upwards, as if distracted by something in the sky whilst out for a morning's shopping. As the van glided towards her, engine rumbling softly, she lowered her head with a slow, almost creaky movement and stared through the windscreen straight at them.

At least, she seemed to. Sam held his breath as her dead eyes regarded him unflinchingly. Beside him, Jin and Xian Mei, crushed into the middle seat together, were rigid, barely daring to move. Speaking quietly through compressed lips, Jin asked nervously, 'You think she sees us?'

'I don't know,' murmured Purna, moving her hands as slowly as possible as she eased the van to a halt.

The vehicle came to rest with its front grille only an inch or so from the girl's sun-bronzed thighs. The girl continued to stare at them for several more seconds, mouth half-open, face slack. Then she took a stumbling step forward, bumped into the front of the van and veered off in a different direction. Sam breathed a sigh of relief.

'Man, that was—' he began.

He jumped in shock as something slammed into the passenger window, inches from his face. He turned to see the girl's suddenly enraged, screeching face, her dead eyes glaring into his own. She was scrabbling at the glass with hooked fingers, leaving smeary marks.

'Shit,' said Purna as other zombies began to turn towards them, alerted by the commotion.

Swiftly, but without panic, she put the van into gear and depressed the accelerator. It slid forward as a dozen or more of the infected converged on them from all sides. The blonde-haired girl's hands squealed down the outside of the window, leaving greasy imprints, and then she was gone. The van's forward momentum left most of the initial group of suddenly alerted zombies in its wake, but already others were turning in their direction as if a psychic signal was sizzling through their reanimated brains like a mental Mexican Wave.

'Hold on!' Purna shouted as the van picked up speed. The infected were running at them from all directions now, in such numbers that in a matter of seconds it was going to prove impossible to avoid hitting them.

Jin screamed as the first collision jolted them in their seats. A corpulent, dark-haired woman in her early thirties was knocked backwards with such force that she all but flattened a small boy in Batman pyjamas who was running up behind her. The van rocked from side to side as the infected began to throw themselves at it like human battering rams. Most of them bounced off, though one – a young man in a checked shirt – managed to leap up on to the bonnet, where he skittered like Bambi on ice for a couple of seconds, screaming in at them through the windscreen, before tumbling off and going under the wheels. The van gave a tremendous lurch as it drove over him and Sam clung to the door handle, convinced for a horrible second they were going to tip over. Fortunately the van righted itself with a crunching jolt, surging ahead as all four wheels regained the road. It slewed from side to side, Purna trying to manoeuvre a way through the throng as more zombies thumped and battered at the van's bodywork. There was another crunch, then another, as two more of the infected were smashed out of the way. Sam gritted his teeth and wondered how much punishment the van could take before it gave up the ghost. If it stalled or crashed they were fucked. They'd be like meatballs in a can, waiting to be plucked out and devoured.

It was difficult at times for Purna to see beyond the screeching faces and scrabbling hands, but somehow she kept going, her face set and determined, her hands and feet deft on the controls. The windscreen and side windows were smeared with blood, but luckily the glass had so far survived intact. Sam wondered briefly how crumpled and dented the van's bodywork was – not that it mattered, as long as it held – and how much further it was to the police station. As if he could read Sam's thoughts, Dani, who had been clinging on for dear life to avoid being thrown around in the back like a shirt in a tumble dryer, jammed his face between two of the front seats and gasped, 'Police station just up here. Two hundred metres on right.'

Because the infected were not cunning or organized enough to arrange an ambush and so had simply run at them from all directions, Purna had now managed to break through the first wave of attackers and surge ahead. However, although the chasing pack was currently falling further behind, they were still too close for comfort. Close enough, at least, to be on them before they'd have time to park the van, get out, run up the steps to the police station and punch in the code to open the doors.

'We need to draw them away,' Sam said.

'Already ahead of you,' replied Purna, glancing in her wing mirror.

Instead of speeding up, she slowed down a little, allowing the infected to get closer, but not close enough to catch up. Ignoring the white building that Dani had pointed out to them, she kept going, heading along the street for another hundred metres or so before taking a right at the intersection. Checking that the infected were still following, she took the next right and hit the accelerator. By the time she had completed a circuit that brought them back on to the main street, most of their pursuers had been left far behind. The instant the van screeched to a halt at the bottom of the white stone steps outside the police station, Purna and Sam threw open their doors. Two seconds later, all five of them were running up the steps towards the main door.

Although many of the infected had been lured away, there were still enough of them wandering around to cause trouble. The moment Purna, Sam and the rest emerged from the van, zombies began to swarm towards them, like wasps attracted to a picnic. Xian Mei and Jin ran up the steps with Dani while Purna and Sam turned to fight a rearguard action. Calmly Purna picked off the closest and most agile zombies with the shotgun, swiftly and unfussily reloading after each double blast, while Sam held the stragglers at bay with his flare pistol, distracting them by igniting their clothes or hair.

'We're in,' Xian Mei shouted a few seconds later. Abandoning their positions, Purna and Sam turned and bounded up the steps, taking them three at a time. Xian Mei was waiting anxiously at the top, holding the door of the station open with one hand whilst urging them on with the other. Seconds later, with the infected just metres behind them, Sam and Purna reached her. All three of them slipped into the building, Sam, at the rear, slamming the door behind them.

They stood for a moment, recovering their composure and their breath. They could hear the infected outside, not exactly pounding on the door, but blundering against it, as if unable to work out why there was suddenly a barrier between themselves and their meal. The police station was a modern, clinical building, the vestibule area with its reception desk, low sofas and potted plants more like the waiting room of a private hospital than a law enforcement agency. The cop shops back in Sam's old New Orleans neighbourhood had been run-down grimy places with wire mesh over the bullet-proof glass in the windows and a constant procession of low-life streaming in and out. Sam guessed that the cops here in the resort area of Banoi, however, had a much easier time of it. The worst they probably had to contend with were traffic violations, the odd public order offence, maybe an occasional bout of shoplifting. He doubted the cells – if they even had them – were ever full and that before today there had ever been much (if any) call to break out the heavy artillery. It was clear, from the fact the station appeared to be deserted, that the local authorities had been totally ill-equipped to deal with the events of the past twenty-four hours. The only cop they had seen had been the one in the grave-yard – infected and mutilated, his right leg nothing but a bleeding stump.

Beyond the vestibule area was a corridor on their left, which led deeper into the building, and a staircase on their right. 'Weapons this way,' said Dani, pointing to the staircase. They ascended two flights to the floor above and passed through a set of double doors into a corridor leading to an open-plan office which con-tained eight desks, a drinks machine and several filing cabinets. They were crossing the office when three dark shapes – one on either side of them and one directly in front – rose up like shadows, guns in their hands.

Immediately Purna started to raise the shotgun, but the man to their left barked out, 'Try it and you're dead.'

She froze, as if assessing her chances, then reluctantly lowered the weapon.

'Put the gun on the floor,' the man said. 'The rest of you, drop your weapons too.'

When they had complied, Sam slowly raised his hands, showing the men his palms. 'Easy, guys,' he said. 'We don't want no trouble.'

'So what *do* you want?' said the man directly in front

of them. He was weaselly, twitchy, with a sparse beard and pockmarked cheeks. He looked pale and ill, like a junkie in need of a fix. In his hand was a chunky silver handgun, which he was pointing at them side-on.

Before anyone else could answer, Dani said, 'We here to get more guns.'

The man who had first spoken sniggered. In contrast to his skinny colleague, he was powerfully built and clean-shaven, his skin a light shade of brown. His features were heavy, pugnacious, and he had a tattoo of what looked like an eagle on the left side of his neck, the tips of its outstretched wings stretching across his cheeks like the shadow of a hand. He had more tattoos on his bare arms and was pointing a hunting rifle at them.

'Then you've come to the wrong place,' he said. 'There's no guns here.'

'Yes,' said Dani. 'I know code.'

Loudly Purna said, 'So why are you guys here?'

The weasel ignored her. Staring at Dani with narrowed eyes he said, 'What do you mean, you know the code?'

Dani licked his lips nervously, realizing too late, that he had said too much. Deliberately the weasel moved his arm so his gun was pointing directly at Jin's face.

'Tell me now or the pretty girl loses her head.'

Dani's eyes widened and his mouth opened and closed, but he was clearly too scared to speak. In a steady, almost casual voice, Purna said, 'Dani installed the security systems here. He knows the code to gain access to the armoury.'

The third man whooped. He was older and heavier-set than the others, his hair thinning and his eyes small and piggy in his fleshy face. He had large sweat stains under the arms of his brown T-shirt, and like the tattooed man he was holding a hunting rifle.

'Looks like we hit the jackpot!' he cried.

'What do *you* need guns for?' Xian Mei said. 'You've already got them.'

'Best currency there is right now,' the weaselly man said. 'Guns. Ammunition. We got those, we can bed ourselves in here till all that shit out there blows over.'

'Oh yeah? And what about food?' asked Purna.

The weaselly man looked uncertain. Then over-confidently he said, 'We'll find enough to keep us going. Place this size, there's bound to be plenty.'

Purna shook her head. 'This is a police station, not a restaurant. If you're thinking of bedding in here and waiting for help to arrive, then you're going to need provisions.'

'How about we send you to get us some?' proposed the tattooed man.

Purna turned slowly and looked at him. 'How about we do a deal?' she countered.

The weasel sneered. 'We don't do deals.'

'Then you're idiots,' said Purna calmly, looking him straight in the eye. 'We're not your enemies. Those things out there are your enemies. Think about it for a minute. Fighting is a waste of time and energy. There are plenty of resources for everyone, and we're in a position to help each other out here.' She paused. 'So – this is the deal. We get you food, you allow us access to the armoury. Food for guns – and plenty of both for

155

everyone. Once we've both got what we want we go our separate ways. That sound reasonable to you?'

The weasel stared at Purna for a moment, then glanced at his colleagues. 'How do we know you won't just run out on us?' he asked finally.

'We want guns,' said Purna simply. 'One isn't enough.'

'You look hard enough, you can find guns anywhere,' said the tattooed man.

'We ain't got time to go lookin',' said Sam.

The weasel thought about it, then eventually he nodded. 'OK. But you get the guns *after* you get back, not before. And just so's we know you won't run out on us, we keep two of you here. As insurance. Him and her.'

He gestured casually with his gun at Jin and Dani.

Purna shook her head. 'That's unacceptable.'

'That's the deal,' said the weasel. 'Take it or leave it. But if you leave it, I reckon that'll be bad news for you.'

He grinned, and looking into his eyes Purna knew exactly what he meant. But she tried not to show her anger or frustration; for now the weasel and his cronies were holding all the aces.

'I'll be OK,' Jin said bravely.

Dani nodded. 'I look after her.'

Purna glanced at Sam and Xian Mei. Sam raised his eyebrows. Xian Mei's face was stony.

Sighing, Purna shrugged. 'Guess we don't have much of a choice,' she said.

Chapter 10

AN ACT OF LOVE

'Be careful.'

They approached the door cautiously, Sam in the lead. They could see that it had been separated from its hinges by a crowbar or something similar and then shoved roughly back into position. On the door a sign read: STAFF ENTRANCE ONLY. Situated on the far left of the huge back wall of the supermarket, the door was almost unnoticeable next to the big metal roll-up doors of the loading bay, which were five times higher and wider. It was here, adjacent to the currently empty staff car park, that trucks delivered goods in bulk to the warehouse. And it was here that Xian Mei had suggested they try to gain access to the building.

Getting to this point had actually proved easier than any of them had anticipated. Rather than hanging out by the offices and municipal buildings that seemed to dominate the far end of the long main street, most of the infected had wandered away by the time Purna, Sam and Xian Mei were ready to exit the police station, and were congregating en masse at the other end, where the retail outlets were. Maybe it was some kind of long-buried memory that drew them to that area, thought Sam, or maybe it was simply that that was where the majority of their food was – or at least had been. He guessed that, like the old woman with the loud TV, a lot of people must live in houses or apartments above or behind their business premises. Where the majority of those people were now was anyone's guess. He liked to think that some of them had got away, or even that they were still holed up in their homes with plenty of provisions to hand. But he suspected the real truth was that they had either been ripped apart and devoured by the infected, or had become part of the massed and still growing ranks of the walking dead.

Whatever the motivations of the infected, in this instance they had given Sam, Purna and Xian Mei a relatively easy ride. Sprinting from the door of the police station to the van, they had only had to take out a couple of slavering, snarling attackers instead of an entire horde of them. And on the short drive round to the back of the supermarket, only one zombie had got in their way – a girl of about ten in a pink dress, who had flown through the air after being hit by the van and had clattered to the pavement like a broken doll. Glancing in the side mirror as they sped away, Sam had seen the girl lurch to her feet and shuffle point-lessly after them, despite sustaining what appeared to be multiple fractures.

Thankfully, the area at the back of the supermarket had been even more sparsely populated. In the almost-empty car park, which was enclosed by thick hedges, they had come across only three of the infected. One, an old black woman, who had been down on her hands and knees, her face buried in the torn-open belly of a headless corpse, had ignored them completely as they drove past. The other two – a long-haired guy in a Led Zeppelin T-shirt and a thin woman in blood-spattered spectacles, who looked like an archetypal librarian or prim schoolmistress – had run at them from opposite directions the instant they opened the van doors.

Purna's first shot at the long-haired guy had been a bad one for her; the blast had gone low, taking away most of his left hand, but barely slowing him down. The second shot, by which time he was less than ten metres away, had ripped off the top of his head. He had kept running for maybe two steps, and then, as though realizing what had happened to him, had collapsed like a felled bull.

By this time, however, the schoolmistress was on them and targeting Xian Mei. As she leaped like a panther, her teeth bared and fingers hooked into claws, Xian Mei spun and side-stepped, bringing the machete round in an upwards sweep. It was such a perfect stroke that it separated the woman's head from her shoulders with almost surgical precision, her now lifeless body continuing to fly forward before thumping to the ground and skidding along the tarmac. Her severed head, meanwhile, spun over and over in such a high, wide arc that it bounced on the roof of the van and looped away out of sight before eventually hitting the ground with a wet crunch.

Now, having despatched their attackers, they were moving towards the 'Staff Entrance' door. It was Xian Mei who noticed that someone had taken the door off

159

its hinges, and she who warned Sam to be careful.

Sam turned and glanced at her briefly, flashing a wide but nervous grin. 'Careful is my middle name,' he murmured, and reached out to pull the door open.

It came free with a splintering creak, listing slightly. Sam steadied it, at the same time peering into the gloom of the high-ceilinged warehouse beyond. He could see nothing but rows of tall metal shelves stacked with boxes. There were no sounds of movement, no sign of anything shifting in the shadows.

'All clear,' he said, glancing at Purna, who was standing with the shotgun raised, alert as ever. She nodded and they moved as one into the warehouse, their eyes darting everywhere.

Immediately they became aware of the low buzzing of flies and a faintly unpleasant smell. They edged to the left, where both seemed to be coming from. They crept from the top of one aisle to the next, halting to peer around the end of each row of shelves. Eventually, after checking out five aisles and finding nothing, Sam peered around the corner of the next row along and instantly drew back. 'There's something there,' he whispered.

'What?' asked Purna.

'I can't make it out. It's too dark.'

Cautiously the three of them peered around the corner. Sure enough, about halfway along the aisle, was a bulky dark shape. From their position it looked like a crumpled tarpaulin or a collapsed tent. The lazy drone of flies was louder here, and they could even see flies looping and hovering above the shape, like flecks of static in the gloom.

'It's something dead,' said Xian Mei. 'An animal maybe.'

Sam broke cover, machete in one hand, flare pistol in the other. 'Let's check it out.'

They crept along the aisle towards the shape. It didn't move. It was only when they were a few metres away that Sam realized what it was.

'Aw, man,' he muttered.

It wasn't a single shape, but several – several bodies, in fact. It looked like a family: a man and a woman in their mid-thirties, a girl of maybe six or seven, and a boy wearing nothing but a nappy and a white T-shirt, who could have been no older than three.

They hadn't been killed or eaten by zombies, but shot through the head. The man, who looked as though he might originally have come from China or Vietnam, was lying on his back, half across the woman, a stubby black handgun in a pool of blood on the floor by his outstretched right hand. Both the children and the woman appeared to have been shot through the backs of their skulls, the bullets having erupted out of their faces. The man's exit wound, however, was in the top of his head, suggesting that he had put the gun in his mouth and angled it upwards towards his brain before pulling the trigger.

Xian Mei looked at the carnage sadly, wafting at the flies that buzzed above the corpses. 'This was an act of love,' she said.

Sam turned his head away, sickened. 'That don't mean it ain't fucked up.'

Purna stepped forward and bent to pick up the gun, glutinous threads of blood remaining attached to it for

161

a couple of seconds before snapping. 'Waste not, want not,' she said, handing Sam the man's gun and her own. 'Hold these a second, will you?'

She squatted down and began to go through the dead man's pockets.

'What are you doing?' asked Xian Mei.

'Looking for ammunition,' replied Purna. There was a metallic jingle and she nodded in satisfaction. Holding up a handful of loose cartridges, she said, 'It's not much, but it's better than nothing.'

Sam had been spattered with a lot of zombie blood over the past few hours, but feeling the cold, sticky, almost jelly-like blood of the dead man that coated one side of the gun was worse somehow. Grimacing, he wiped as much of it as he could on the side of a cardboard box on one of the metal shelves. Then he took the cartridges from Purna and loaded the gun, making sure the safety was on before slipping it into his jacket pocket.

They spent the next half-hour checking out the shelves in the warehouse, selecting provisions and stacking up boxes to the left of the loading-bay doors. They went mainly for bottled water and non-perishable goods that could be eaten cold if necessary – tinned food, crackers, biscuits. They also grabbed themselves a few essential toiletries – soap, shampoo, toilet paper, toothbrushes, toothpaste. When they had chosen what they needed from the warehouse, they moved deeper into the building, towards the double doors at the back of the room that led on to the shop floor.

The right-hand door opened easily and they slipped

through into the public part of the supermarket. The neatly stacked shelves, silent aisles, unmanned check-outs, stacks of baskets and rows of trolleys were currently bathing under a softly glowing half-light, everything set out and ready for another day's trading. Standing there and looking around, it suddenly struck Sam that it was a day that would never come. He couldn't imagine when life would return to normal here on Banoi – or, indeed, if it ever would. Certainly it seemed likely that long before then the fresh fruit and vegetables would have withered or turned to gloop, and the bread and cakes would have gone green and rotten in their cellophane packets. The meat, too, would decay, and before long the entire building – like many other buildings on Banoi – would start to stink like a charnel house. The sheer horror of that prospect all at once threatened to overwhelm him, making him feel breathless and sick.

'You OK?' asked Purna, frowning.

Sam pulled himself together with an effort and gave a curt nod. 'I'm cool,' he muttered.

Xian Mei pointed off to the right. 'The pharmacy counter is over there. Aisle two.'

Purna nodded. 'OK. Let's take this slowly.'

They moved forward, Sam's rubber-soled shoes squeaking slightly on the polished floor. There was the faint hum of fluorescent lighting overhead but no other sound. Xian Mei had suggested that as well as looking for Mr Owen's Nadolol, they should also stock up on basic medical supplies, dietary supplements and vitamin pills. She grabbed a metal basket from a rack, which provided an almost comical contrast to the blood-smeared machete in her other hand. When they reached the pharmacy section, Xian Mei rounded the counter while Sam and Purna kept watch. Swiftly the Chinese girl scanned the shelves and began filling her basket with vitamins, painkillers and other over-the-counter medication.

'There's no Nadolol here,' she said. 'If they have any it'll be in the back.' She crossed to a white door at the back of the counter and tried the handle. 'Locked. Though I think I could probably kick it open.'

Purna nodded. 'Go for it.'

Xian Mei stood back, centred herself, then kicked out at the door. She did it twice more in quick succession, the flat of her foot impacting just to the right of the handle. In the silent, high-ceilinged room, the sound boomed and echoed, causing Sam to grit his teeth. On the fourth kick there was a crunch and the door flew open.

Xian Mei entered the tiny, shelf-filled room and emerged within fifteen seconds, holding up a number of white boxes. 'Success,' she said – and then her eyes abruptly widened. '*Sam, look out!*'

Sam turned just as an enormously fat man in a gore-spattered green T-shirt burst from the cover of a nearby aisle and crashed into him. Both he and his attacker went down in a heap, Sam smashing his head against the bottom of the counter. The gun flew out of his hand and skidded away across the floor. Dazed, he could barely defend himself as the zombie snarled and snapped like a rabid dog, baring its teeth and lunging forward in an effort to tear out his throat.

Unable to risk shooting the zombie for fear of hitting

Sam, Purna flipped the shotgun around and smashed the butt of it into the side of the creature's head. Its cheekbone broke with a brittle crunch and its head snapped back, but it was only a momentary respite. Eyes fluttering, Sam raised his hands to keep the creature's teeth from his face, howling in pain as it bit into the side of his wrist. Purna hit the zombie again, catching it just behind the ear, but again the blow seemed to have little effect.

Xian Mei vaulted over the counter and joined in the fight. She hacked at the zombie's back with her machete, opening terrible wounds which gushed with foul-smelling, partly congealed blood. Purna, mean-while, rammed the stock of the shotgun between Sam and the creature, trying to prise the zombie off him, or at least prevent it from tearing out his throat. Composing herself, Xian Mei took aim and then brought the machete down with precision, slicing through the back of the zombie's neck and severing its spinal cord. The creature began to thrash and convulse, its limbs jerking spasmodically. Putting aside their weapons and working together for a moment, Purna and Xian Mei were able to haul the creature off Sam. It lay on its back, its mouth opening and closing, like a fish washed up on the shore. Xian Mei picked up her machete, stepped forward and beheaded the creature with two blows. The rage faded from its eyes and it stopped moving.

Semi-conscious, Sam writhed and muttered, his eye-lids fluttering. His wrist poured with blood where the zombie had bitten into it, and while Purna stood guard with the shotgun, Xian Mei grabbed some more bandages and antiseptic ointment from a shelf to supplement the ones she had already put in her basket and quickly patched him up. By the time she had finished, he was coming round, rubbing his head and wanting to know what had happened.

'Tell you later,' said Purna. 'You OK to walk?'

'I think so.'

'Here's your gun.' She thrust it at him almost brusquely. Scowling, she said, 'From now on, we keep our wits about us at all times.'

They took the rest of what they needed and hurried back through the double doors into the warehouse. Xian Mei knew that Purna was angry with herself as much as anything; because of a split-second's distraction back there, Sam had almost died. The Australian girl strode through the warehouse as if defying anyone to mess with her, and across to the broken staff entrance door, which they had pulled back into place as they entered. Pushing the door open, she checked outside, then said, 'Right, open the loading bay doors. I'll get the van.'

Two minutes later Purna had backed the van into the warehouse. She and Sam quickly filled it with boxes while Xian Mei stood guard. The car park was quiet and they were able to complete the task without interruption. Climbing into the van, Sam said, 'How much of this stuff we giving to those guys?'

'Just enough to carry in one trip,' Purna said. 'Somehow I don't think the infected will stand by and watch us unloading box after box, do you?'

'What if they decide they want more?' said Xian Mei.

'Then they'll have to come out and get it themselves.'

They drove out of the car park and back round to the main street. The situation was pretty much the same as before, the infected congregating largely at the far end. As they parked at the foot of the steps outside the police station, a naked man in his early twenties wandered in front of them, his legs, buttocks and torso covered in bites. They watched him silently until he was about thirty metres away, then Purna unclipped her seatbelt and climbed over the front seats into the back of the van. She passed over two boxes of canned goods and a 12-litre plastic-wrapped pack of bottled water, before climbing over the seats into the front again.

'We take one of these each, run up the steps and let ourselves in. Sam, once we're inside, don't let the guys know you've got a gun – just in case.'

He nodded.

'Everyone remember the code number?' Sam asked.

'Four-two-seven-four,' Xian Mei replied without hesitation.

They looked out of the windows and in the mirrors, checking every direction to ensure none of the infected was close enough to surprise them. Then Purna said, 'Go.'

Throwing open the doors, they jumped out of the van and ran up the steps. With one hand curled around the provisions tucked under their arms and the other clutching their weapons, they felt weighed down, encumbered. The naked man spun towards them immediately, like a radar dish picking up a signal, and broke into a shambling run. Sam turned halfway up the steps, but paused a moment, not wishing to waste his shot. He allowed the man to get within five metres of him before pulling the trigger. The bullet hit the man in the jaw, shearing half his face away and spinning him round in a clumsy pirouette. He rolled down the steps, but at the bottom he picked himself up and doggedly started climbing them again. Two more of the infected were now homing in on the steps behind him, but Xian Mei had reached the door and, after putting her box of food down on the floor, tapped in the four-number code.

To her horror the red light failed to change to green. Thinking she must have done it wrong, she tried again, forcing herself to concentrate, knowing that all their lives depended on it.

Once more the red light remained constant.

'It's not working!' she shouted.

Purna put down her own box of food and stepped forward, face set. 'Let me try.'

Although she was certain she had done it right, Xian Mei knew this was no time to argue. She stepped back and allowed Purna access to the keypad. A few feet away Sam pulled the trigger of his gun and out of the corner of her eye Xian Mei saw the naked man's head become a crimson spray. As the zombie pitched backwards down the steps, Purna punched in the four-number code. It gave Xian Mei no satisfaction to see the light remain stubbornly red.

'Shit,' Purna muttered and stepped away from the door. She turned to assess the situation, raising the shotgun.

Two zombies were coming up the steps towards them, an old man and a teenage girl. The old man was shambling, dragging his left leg behind him; the girl was running, almost scampering, lips drawn back in a snarl, the metal braces on her teeth clogged with blackening meat. Further away, other zombies seemed to be receiving the signal that there was fresh meat to be had here, and were turning round, sniffing the air, homing in.

Clinically, Purna took the girl out, the shotgun blast hitting her right in the centre of her face, reducing her features to pulp.

A few steps below her, Sam glanced round. 'What's going on?'

'Those bastards must have changed the entry code,' Purna said.

'How they do that?'

'They've got Dani, remember?'

'Shit!'

'We'd better get back to the van and rethink this,' Purna said.

'What about the food?' asked Xian Mei.

'Leave it.'

They were halfway back down the steps when a chunk of stone exploded less than a metre away from Sam's foot. He stared at it uncomprehendingly for a split-second and then something whacked into the pavement below, causing a mini-eruption of stone chips.

'Get down!' Purna yelled.

Sam ducked instinctively. 'What the fuck?'

'They're firing at us,' she said, dropping to a crouch,

spinning round and pulling the trigger of the shotgun all in the same movement. As the shotgun blast hit the building and Purna hastily reloaded, Sam was aware of Xian Mei, bent almost double, leaping down the steps to his left.

'Go,' Purna said. 'I'll cover you.'

Knowing – as Xian Mei had done before him – that there was no debating the matter, he ran down the steps, catching up with Xian Mei at the bottom just as she straightened up and fired her flare pistol at a zombie that was still fifteen metres away, but approaching rapidly enough that it would have reached them before they had chance to open the van doors and scramble inside.

The front of the zombie's shirt burst into flame and a sheet of fire rose up and engulfed its head. It began to stagger around, arms waving like a kid playing blind man's bluff, as its face browned and sizzled like barbecue meat.

The other zombies were still far enough away for them not to be an immediate problem. Keeping an eye on the burning zombie, Sam pulled open the passenger door of the van and shouted, 'Get in.'

Throwing her machete into the foot well, Xian Mei dived across the front seat and scrambled upright. Sam climbed in after her, then immediately turned, pointing his gun up at the police station. The oldest of the three guys was at one of the upstairs windows, albeit trying to keep out of sight, the barrel of his hunting rifle resting on the sill. Purna was crouched down, trying to use the steps as cover. Although the nearest of the infected was still twenty metres away from her, they were closing in from all sides.

'Come on, Purna!' Sam shouted, and fired a bullet towards the upper window of the police station to demonstrate that he was now in a position to cover *her*.

She needed no second bidding. Breaking cover, she ran across to the van, Sam scooting along the seat to give her room to dive in and slam the door shut behind her.

As she was doing it, the door of the police station opened and the tattooed guy ran out, keeping low, and quickly dragged the discarded boxes of food and the pack of water bottles inside. Seeing him, Purna wound down the driver's window a few inches and stuck the barrel of the shotgun out, but before she could fire he was back inside the building and had closed the door behind him.

'Bastards,' she muttered.

'What—' Xian Mei began. But before she could complete her question the gloating voice of the scrawny man called out from an upstairs window.

'Hey, thanks for the food, guys. We're real sorry that we're no longer in a position to offer you anything in return. Oh, you can have your boy back, though. We've finished with him.' There was movement at the window and the dead or unconscious body of Dani was dropped out. He hit the ground head-first, his limbs splaying in all directions. The men in the building cackled and whooped as though this was the funniest thing they had ever seen.

'Think we'll keep the girl, though,' the scrawny man said after a moment. 'We need us a little *recreation*.' He sniggered again, then shouted, 'You

171

folks take care now. Make sure the zombies don't get you.'

The window slammed shut – and their sight of the building was blotted out by a middle-aged man with thinning hair and a punctured eyeball, who lurched into view and snarled in at them through the driver's side window. Without hesitation, Purna pulled the trigger of the shotgun and his head exploded in a gory confusion of blood, bone, flesh and brain. Yanking the gun back into the van, Purna wound up the window and turned on the engine. With zombies moving in rapidly, she drove away.

Chapter 11

GOING UNDERGROUND

'I think I might know a way.'

Purna and Sam looked at Xian Mei. Once again they had parked in the car park at the back of the super-market, having needed to find somewhere quiet where they could talk over what to do. In the back of his mind Sam had been worried that Purna might take the hard line, dismissing Jin as a casualty of war and pro-claiming that, though the situation was regrettable, it was not worth risking all their lives simply to rescue a girl who was not even prepared to handle a weapon.

However, he had underestimated her. Unless she had some ulterior motive (the stash of weapons in the armoury maybe?), she wasn't entirely the hard-nosed pragmatist he had taken her for. True, she had told them earlier that she had joined the police force because she wanted to help people who couldn't help themselves, but Sam had assumed her noble aspirations had waned in the wake of her dismissal from the force and the general disillusionment with life that she had suffered since. It was good, therefore, to see her so outraged, so impassioned, so concerned for Jin's fate.

'We've got to get her out of there,' she had said. 'If those fucking animals harm her I'll never forgive myself.'

When Xian Mei said she thought she might know a way to get into the police station, Purna leaned forward eagerly. 'How?'

'In the hotel where I worked,' Xian Mei said, 'there was an old sewer outlet in the basement laundry. Someone told me that the tunnels ran right under the main street, and that at one time you could gain access to every building from below if you wanted to.'

'At one time?' repeated Purna. 'You mean you can't any more?'

Xian Mei shrugged. 'I don't know. I'm not an expert. But this is the *old* sewer system we're talking about. I guess whoever's in charge of these things eventually decided it was unsanitary to have sewage constantly flowing directly underneath people's homes and either diverted the flow or built an entirely new system. It could be that the old tunnels are impassable now. They could have been blocked up or the access to certain buildings might have been sealed. There have been a lot of renovations to some of the buildings over the years. Extensions, new walls and floors, maybe even new foundations in some cases . . .'

'It's worth a try, though,' Purna said. 'The vulnerable parts of buildings are always either above or below. And unless you can climb walls like Spiderman or you've got access to a helicopter . . .'

She let her words hang in the air. Sam nodded. 'Let's do it.'

'We might be able to gain access from the

supermarket,' Xian Mei said. 'We should look for the lowest point.'

It took them less than five minutes to find what they were looking for. The warehouse floor was concrete but inside the supermarket itself they found a fire exit tucked away behind the frozen foods section. Beyond this was a short corridor leading to a door that led outside and a set of stone steps to a basement area, which had not been used in a long time, except as a dumping ground for some old and rusting shelf fixtures. A couple of minutes' searching resulted in the discovery of a circular iron manhole cover in the corner of the stone floor, crusted with moss and gunge.

Sam tried to lift it, but it was fixed solid. 'We need something to lever it up,' he said.

Xian Mei walked over to the shelf fixtures and dragged out a metre-long V-shaped metal bracket. 'What about this?'

'Perfect,' said Sam. 'There any more of those in there?'

Xian Mei found another two and they set to work, first scraping away as much of the slime and moss as they could from around the rim of the manhole cover, then ramming the metal edges of the brackets into the thin gap between cover and floor and applying their collective weight to the other ends.

After ten seconds, there was a creaking groan and the manhole cover started to rise. As the gap widened, they rammed their brackets in further to gain more purchase, and suddenly the cover tilted up and over like a hinged lid, clanging to the ground with such force that Xian Mei had to jump out of the way to prevent her foot getting crushed.

They all recoiled from the fetid smell that rolled up from the hole in the floor.

'Jeez!' Sam exclaimed, clamping a hand over his nose and mouth. 'You think any of those things are down there?'

'Don't see how they'd get down there, or why they'd want to,' said Purna. 'They only tend to go where the fresh meat is.'

They peered into the hole, but it was pitch-black. 'Anyone got a flashlight?' asked Sam.

Purna pulled a face and shook her head. 'They'll probably have them in the store upstairs. Damn, I should have thought of that.'

'Don't beat yourself up about it,' Sam said. 'You can't think of everything. I'll go get one. Be right back.'

'Don't say that,' said Purna.

Sam raised his eyebrows. 'Why not?'

'Because that's what they always say in horror movies just before . . .' She made a sharp *crrrk* sound and drew a finger swiftly across her throat.

Sam grinned and disappeared. Two minutes later he was back, preceded by the circular shining disc of a heavy-duty flashlight.

'Quiet as the grave up there,' he said, and again flashed his teeth in a grin. 'Guess I shouldn't say that either, huh?'

He shone the flashlight into the hole, to reveal a circular stone tube like the inside of a well, the walls covered in green-black slime. Despite the light it was too dark for them to see all the way to the bottom. Iron rungs were set into the wall, and Sam dropped to his knees, reached down and gripped the first one to test how strong it was.

'Seems OK,' he said.

He went first, stopping every now and then to shine the beam of the flashlight down into the darkness. It was awkward descending with their weapons, especially as the rungs were slippery with slime, but they managed somehow. The deeper they went, the colder it became, the air heavy with the stench of rotting vegetation. Eventually Purna said, 'I hear water.'

Her voice echoed hollowly off the walls. When the echoes had died away, they all heard the sound of rushing water below. They continued their descent, the sound getting louder, until at last Sam called, 'We're nearly there.'

'What can you see?' Purna asked.

'Moving water. Not much else. Wait, there's a kind of ridge at the side, like a raised path. Looks kind of narrow.'

'But passable?'

'Yeah, I think so.'

A minute later they were standing at the bottom of the ladder, catching their breath. They were standing in a square stone tunnel on a slippery, wet, narrow sidewalk, beside which oil-black water flowed like a river, glittering and rippling under the flashlight beam.

The tunnel stretched straight and unbroken in both directions. Pointing against the flow, Sam said, 'I guess we go this way?'

Purna nodded and they started to walk, their feet splatting in puddles of water.

'It don't smell like sewage,' said Sam.

'I don't think it is,' said Purna, 'but I wouldn't wash your face in it.'

'I'm not sure it's supposed to be flooded like this,' said Xian Mei. 'It could be because of rising sea levels. There are lots of internal waterways and swamplands on Banoi and they all link to the ocean. These tunnels may have just taken some of that extra water on board.'

'You mean this is sea water?' said Sam.

Xian Mei shrugged. 'Well, that's my theory.'

'Damn,' Sam said. 'Shoulda brought my fishing rod.'

Walking along in single file, they lapsed into silence, the flashlight beam slithering and jerking ahead of them. Passing another of the vertical shafts which linked the disused sewer tunnels to the surface, Xian Mei said, 'There are five buildings between the supermarket and the police station, so the sixth shaft we come to should be the one we want.'

They walked on, passing another shaft and then another. Suddenly Sam stopped.

'What's wrong?' Purna asked.

'Thought I saw something in the water.'

'Like what?'

'I dunno. Something surfaced, then went back under with a splash.'

'A fish?'

'Maybe. Or perhaps just a log or something.'

'I wouldn't worry,' said Purna. 'I don't think the infected can swim.'

Sam nodded, and was about to set off again when something erupted from the water a few metres ahead of them. In the flashlight beam he saw a pair of wide-open jaws edged with pointed teeth, and an enormous grey-pink gullet.

Purna had shoved Sam aside and fired both shotgun barrels into the elongated mouth before he had registered it was a crocodile. The bullets tore into it, shredding its tongue and the underside of its upper jaw, turning the inside of its pink mouth a sudden and startling red.

The massive creature – at least five metres long from snout to tail – twisted in mid-air, like a vast fish caught in a net, so close to them that Sam could have reached out and touched its ridged prehistoric hide. Then it crashed back down into the water, sending up a wave that surged over the narrow sidewalk and drenched them from head to toe. Sam watched as the creature submerged, slipping beneath the now-churning black water like an enemy submarine. He was both awestruck and more terrified than he had ever been in his life. For a few seconds he could neither move nor speak.

Then Purna shoved him in the back. 'Get going,' she said.

Sam forced his legs into action, stumbling ahead of her.

'Is it dead? Did you kill it?' Xian Mei panted from the rear of the group.

'No idea,' replied Purna. 'And I'm not hanging around to find out.'

By the time they reached the sixth shaft they were

still shaking with shock and a raw, primal terror that the creature might attack again. Even Purna was finding it difficult to hold the shotgun steady as she turned briefly to scan the black water behind them.

'You go first,' Xian Mei said to Sam. 'I don't think either Purna or I will be able to push up a manhole cover from underneath.'

Sam nodded and began to climb, not knowing whether he'd be able to do it himself. While he knew it was true that neither of the girls possessed his brute strength, he wouldn't have fancied taking on either of them in a fight. With the image of the crocodile still looming large in his mind, he was relieved a few seconds later to hear first Xian Mei and then Purna start to ascend behind him.

At least fucking crocodiles can't use ladders, he thought.

The climb seemed twice as long as the descent, and by the time he reached the top of the shaft Sam's muscles were trembling with fatigue. He paused a moment, sweat running down his face. His arm was throbbing where the zombie in the supermarket had bitten him, and so was the back of his head where he'd hit it on the side of the counter. Ideally he could have done with something to eat and drink, maybe some painkillers and a few hours' sleep to recharge his batteries. He knew, however, that he wasn't going to get any of that any time soon. Instead he was somehow going to have to dredge up the energy to launch an attack on the heavily armed low-lifes who had killed Dani and taken Jin hostage. This time yesterday he hadn't even *met* any of the people currently in the building above him or clinging to the ladder below. Now it seemed they occupied his whole life.

Wrapping his left arm round the topmost iron rung set into the wall of the shaft, Sam took several deep breaths in an effort to stop himself feeling dizzy, then tilted his head back as he directed the flashlight beam upwards. He saw a circular indentation directly above his head where a manhole cover should be, but the manhole cover wasn't there. Instead, laid across the top of the hole was what looked like wood.

Floorboards, he thought, his spirits sinking. In the intervening years, someone must have laid a wooden floor over the original stone flags. Transferring the flashlight to his left hand, he adjusted his position to reach up and push at the underside of the wooden floor. He expected there to be no give whatsoever, and was astonished when the wood rose easily above his hand.

It took him a moment to realize it wasn't a wooden floor above him after all, but a trap door – or, more likely, a trap door set into a wooden floor. He allowed the door to settle back into place and briefly told the girls what he had found.

'Can you open it?' Purna asked.

'I think so.'

Sam pushed again and the trap door rose. When it had risen to the extent of his outstretched arm, he climbed up and out, attempting as he did so not to drop the flashlight or impale himself on the machete which he had tucked into the belt of his jeans. He half-expected to find himself surrounded by guys pointing guns at his face, but instead he emerged into what seemed to be a janitor's office. There was a sink, a mop and bucket, various tools and cleaning implements on shelves, and an armchair with a newspaper folded on the seat.

He turned to help the girls out and then lowered the trap door back into place. Purna crossed the room and put her ear to the door. 'I can't hear anything,' she said.

'Could be this ain't even the right building,' Sam said.

She puffed out her cheeks at the prospect and Sam knew that, despite her focus and drive, she was as fatigued as he was. 'Let's see, shall we?' she said.

Once she and Sam were in position, Purna nodded and Xian Mei plucked open the door. Purna and Sam stepped out quickly, turning in opposite directions, guns poised. However, the corridor they stepped into was dark and quiet, and although a brief examination revealed the floor to contain little more than a staff locker room and shower block, it was obvious from the stickers on the lockers and the wording on a staff shift chart on the wall that they were in the right place. As if further proof were needed, at the far end of the corridor was a reinforced fire door with a keypad on the wall beside it, above which a sign read CELLS 1–12. Idly Purna tapped in the four-digit security code – 4274 – that had failed to open the main door earlier, and was not surprised to find it failed to open this one either. Retracing her steps, she pushed open a set of double doors on to a stairwell and the three of them cautiously and silently began to ascend.

The sign on the wall next to the double doors of the floor above read G. Although that presumably stood for 'Ground', Purna guessed that because of the steps outside, which led up to the main door, it was more likely to be the floor above this one where they had first entered the building, and the one above that where they had encountered the three men. She whispered as much to Sam and Xian Mei and they nodded their agreement. The trio ascended another flight, and then another, whereupon Purna crossed to the double doors and peered through the reinforced glass panel set into it. Recognizing the corridor leading to the open-plan office where the men had ambushed them, she turned to check that Sam and Xian Mei were ready, then pushed the door open a few inches.

She slipped through the gap quietly, checking left and right. The door to the office was about three metres to her right on the opposite wall of the corridor. Purna crossed the corridor swiftly, turned to flatten herself against the wall and sidled along it to the door. She waited until Sam and Xian Mei were beside her, then she peered around the edge of the glass door.

She saw the men immediately. They had cleared one of the desks and were sitting around it, playing cards. She saw Jin too. The girl was huddled against the opposite wall, hands and feet tied, face bruised and streaked with tears. Purna saw the oldest of the three men, the one with piggy eyes who had fired at them out of the upstairs window, raise his head and call something across to Jin, his voice rough and mean. Jin cowered, lowering her head, and the other men laughed. Trying not to let her anger cloud her judgement, Purna saw that the older man and the tattooed man had replaced their hunting rifles with Heckler and Koch MP5 submachine guns, presumably from the police armoury. The weapons were propped against their chairs, within easy reach should the need arise. Because the scrawny man was on the far side of the table, Purna couldn't see where his weapon was, or whether he had replaced his original handgun with something else. She drew her head back and told Sam and Xian Mei what she had seen and how she thought they should handle the situation. Again, and without hesitation, both nodded their agreement.

Purna took a slow deep breath, composing herself, then nodded. The three of them stepped away from the wall, moving into position. Purna nodded once more, then strode forward and kicked the door open, raising the shotgun as it flew back. Before the men with their backs to her had even turned round, she barked, 'All of you, raise your hands! Do it now!'

She didn't glance round to see if Sam and Xian Mei had moved into position on either side of her; she trusted them to have followed her instructions. She was focused only on the three men, on what they would do with their hands.

When the tattooed man twisted and reached for his gun, Purna shot him.

She did it without hesitation, blasting a hole in his back. There wasn't a coin-sized wound and a trickle of blood like on the TV. Instead, a chunk of flesh tore away from between his shoulder blades, shattering his spine and causing blood to gush from him like a punctured water bag. He collapsed forward, his face smashing against the edge of the desk as his chair tipped over. When, a split-second later, the older man jumped up and clawed vainly for his gun, which had already toppled to the floor because he had stupidly knocked it over when he had moved his seat, Sam shot him in the stomach.

The scrawny man, meanwhile, snatched a handgun off the table beside him. The handgun had been hidden from view by the older man's body, and the scrawny man actually managed to raise it an inch or two before a flare, fired by Xian Mei, exploded in his face. He screamed and went over backwards, but still managed to squeeze the trigger of his gun as he fell, the bullet dislodging a chunk of plaster from the ceiling. To ensure he wouldn't be able to get off another lucky shot, Purna adjusted her aim, tilted the shotgun down and to the left slightly, and shot him through the heart.

The echoes of the gun battle seemed to reverberate in Sam's ears for far longer than they should have done. It was only when they finally began to abate that Sam realized the room wasn't as silent as he had thought. Huddled against the wall, Jin was sobbing hysterically, her hands covering her face, and the man Sam had shot was whimpering and clutching his stomach, his hands and shirt slick with blood.

As Xian Mei went over to comfort Jin, Purna walked forward, cursorily examining the two dead men and then looking dispassionately down at the wounded man at her feet.

'Please . . .' he whispered. 'Please . . .'

'Sorry,' Purna said, her voice flat and dead, 'but there's nothing we can do for you. You can either lie here and die slowly in pain, or we can make it quick.'

The man's eyes widened. 'No . . .' he whispered. 'You can take me with you . . . Please . . .'

Purna shook her head. 'We can't carry you and you're too badly wounded to walk. Sorry, but that's just the way it is.'

'Please . . .' the man whispered again, his world suddenly reduced to nothing but a desperate desire to survive and a terrible fear of death. 'Please . . . please . . .'

Purna sighed and slowly, wearily began to load her shotgun.

'No,' Sam said, walking towards her.

She looked up at him, her face expressionless.

'No,' he repeated, reaching out and putting a hand on her arm. 'It ain't fair you should do this. Not again. It's someone else's turn.'

She stared into his face, her eyes so deep and penetrating that Sam couldn't help but think she could see all the way down into his soul. He turned away from her gaze, but was still aware of her eyes on him, and of the weight of the gun in his hand.

'It's my turn,' he said quietly.

Chapter 12

MYSTERY MAN

'Open up. It's us.'

Purna and Xian Mei scanned the area like border guards, while Jin waited in the van and Sam thumped the door of the lifeguard station with his clenched fist. It was almost noon now and the sun was at its peak.

From here Banoi looked beautiful. To their left the stretch of powder-white beach edged a sparkling blue crystal sea, while to their right the lush vegetation rose towards mountains whose summits glowed a soft purple where they met the bright and cloudless sky. A warm breeze blew in from the west, kissing their skin and tempering the heat of the sun, and despite the chaos in town, the only sounds that disrupted the midday tranquility were the languid calls of exotic birds.

If not for the individual parts of a dismembered body scattered in bloody profusion further along the beach, it might almost have been possible to believe that the events of the past twelve hours were nothing but a terrible nightmare. Sam was about to thump on the door again when Logan's voice replied, 'Who's "us"?'

Sam rolled his eyes. 'Stop messing about, man. It's dangerous out here.'

There was the heavy chunk of disengaging locks and the door opened. Grinning, Logan said, 'Sorry, no hawkers, no traders and definitely no blood-drenched zombie killers.'

Sam matched his grin with a tired one of his own and said enticingly, 'We got Twinkies.'

'Oh well, that's different,' Logan said, and pulled the door wide.

The four of them trooped in, Purna immediately discarding her weapon – no longer the shotgun, but an HK G36 assault rifle appropriated from the police armoury – and slumping into one of the seats around the table. Jin shuffled in like an old woman with her head down, Xian Mei's free hand (in her other she was also carrying an HK G36 assault rifle) round the younger girl's shoulders. Sam, who had stood aside to let the women in before him, walked over to the table and dropped a big bag of pastries and cakes on to it.

'We brought breakfast,' he said. 'They were all out of skinny muffins, so if anyone's on a diet, tough shit.'

'You, my man, have got class,' Logan replied, closing and locking the door. 'Hey, Sinamoi,' he called. 'How 'bout some coffee for our guests?'

Sinamoi was hunched over the radio, headphones on, twiddling dials, but at Logan's words he looked up and grinned. 'Sure. I make coffee.'

As Sinamoi bustled about, Purna squinted tiredly up at Logan. '*You* look better.'

188

'You don't,' he replied cheerily. 'Added to which – if I could just raise a little personal hygiene issue here – you guys *stink*.'

Sam sniffed his sleeve and recoiled. 'That's not us, that's zombie.'

Logan shook his head. 'It'll never catch on.' Pointedly he looked at his watch. 'So what took you so long? I was beginning to think you'd abandoned me and I was going to have to live out the rest of my days in this two-bit shack with no one but Sinamoi for company – hey, no offence, man,' he called across to the lifeguard, who grinned yet again and raised his hand in acknowledgement.

Over cake and coffee, Sam, with Purna and Xian Mei butting in at regular intervals, told Logan their story. When he got to the part where they had encountered Jin, Logan gave a crooked smile and said softly, 'I wondered when they were going to get round to you.'

Jin didn't reply. She didn't even raise her head.

'Don't say a whole lot, do you?' Logan muttered.

Xian Mei said quickly, 'She's been through a bad time.'

To everyone's surprise, Jin suddenly looked up, her eyes black and glittering. In a voice shaking not only with trauma, but also with barely suppressed rage, she said, 'I was raped by three men. They killed the man who was trying to protect me, and then they beat me and raped me. And they kept beating me and raping me until I passed out.'

Silence followed her words. Logan looked away, shaking his head.

'Shit, man ... that's ... shit. I mean ... that's

189

fucking awful, man . . . sorry . . .' he mumbled.

Jin took a shuddering breath and said, 'I used to have faith in people, you know? And faith in God too. Even after Mama died, I thought . . . I thought that the good in the world was stronger than the bad, and that eventually evil would be vanquished. But now –' she shook her head – 'that sounds so . . . so pathetic . . .' Her voice tailed off and she lowered her head again. Xian Mei reached out and gently stroked her back.

Sam grimaced and carried on with the story, his voice a low rumble. He told Logan about killing the men in the police station and rescuing Jin, about stocking up on weapons from the armoury, then going back to the church and delivering provisions and medicine and weapons to Sister Helen's rag-tag group of survivors.

'It seemed weird taking guns to a church,' Sam said, 'but in a way those guys are fighting God's war, I guess . . . fighting against the demons.'

'The infected aren't demons,' said Xian Mei. 'They're victims, like everyone else.'

Sam shook his head. 'That's not what I meant. That thing that's got inside those people – *that's* the demon. The people themselves . . . well, they're dead. They're just shells.'

'No such things as demons,' muttered Purna. 'What's got inside them is just a virus, that's all. A germ. There's nothing *biblical* about it. It's not evil. Only people are evil.'

Sam shrugged. 'Well, I guess that depends on what you believe.'

The expression on Purna's face suggested she was

prepared to take the argument further. To prevent her from doing so, Xian Mei said quickly, 'So what about you, Logan? Has anything happened here?'

Logan raised his eyebrows. 'Apart from the clam bake and the beach volleyball tournament, you mean? Yeah, our mystery man's tried to get in touch a couple times. Reception was so bad, though, he didn't make a whole lot of sense. Said something about the satellite transmitters being down and some fucking offshore storm causing radio interference. You ask me, it's here where the fucking storm is.'

'He say anything else?' asked Purna.

'Only that he'd try to call back around noon today.' He glanced at his watch. 'Hey, which I guess is about now.'

They all looked at the radio expectantly, but it remained silent. They had to wait another fifteen minutes before it crackled into life.

Instantly Sinamoi scuttled across and put on the headphones. He twiddled dials and knobs, trying to get the best reception. At first the voice trying to get through was so engulfed in static they couldn't make out what it was saying. A few more tweaks from Sinamoi and all at once it came through loud and clear.

'Hello,' it was saying. 'Hello, can anyone hear me?'

Logan nodded at the chunky old microphone on its stand, his raised eyebrows forming a question, and Sinamoi nodded. Talking into the microphone whilst simultaneously carrying it over to the table, its long lead trailing behind it, Logan said, 'Hearing you loud and clear. Well . . . clear*ish* anyway.'

'Who is with you?' asked the voice. 'Is everyone safe?'

Logan glanced around. 'Yep, the gang's all here.'

'And everyone is safe? No one has been infected by the virus?'

'Well, it's pretty hard to tell with Sam,' Logan said, earning himself a finger and a grin in response, 'but . . . yeah, they all seem pretty healthy.'

'How come you don't already know?' Purna said challengingly. 'I thought you were monitoring us? Last time you called you seemed pretty aware of our movements.'

'Nothing sinister in that,' the voice reassured her. 'We simply have some extremely powerful monitoring equipment here. We're able to intercept satellite signals from anywhere on the island, including CCTV footage. Unfortunately the satellite transmitters are behaving somewhat erratically at present. Adverse atmospheric conditions, I'm told.'

'And where's "here" exactly?' Purna asked.

'Please,' the voice said, 'as I explained before, our windows of opportunity for speaking to one another are so limited that you must refrain from asking quest—'

'Fuck that,' interrupted Purna. 'You expect us to trust you for no reason? To follow your instructions blindly?'

'I'm trying to *help* you,' the voice said.

'Yeah, that's what *you* say,' muttered Sam.

'See, the thing is, we've been talking,' Purna said, 'and we're maybe not as stupid as you'd like to believe.'

'I don't think you're stupid at all,' said the voice smoothly. 'On the contrary, I believe you to be intelligent, resourceful individuals. That's why I think you have a chance to escape from this mayhem – and that's why I'm prepared to help you.'

'Bull*shit*,' said Sam with feeling.

'Sam's right,' said Purna. 'You don't want to help us because we *deserve* it for being so *resourceful*. You want to help us because we're *immune*.'

There was a moment's silence. Purna looked round at the others, a quietly triumphant look on her face.

'Nothing to say?' she asked.

The owner of the voice sighed – or perhaps it was simply a surge of static – and eventually replied, 'All right. I admit there is some truth to what you say—'

In a rare burst of anger Xian Mei suddenly blurted, 'You caused this! You or whoever you're working for! You *manufactured* this situation! And you threw us into the mix just to see what would happen!'

'No!' the voice said, shocked. 'No, it wasn't like that at all.'

'So what *was* it like?' asked Sam.

'It's cards on the table time, *mystery man*,' said Purna. 'Why don't you start by telling us who you are?'

The pause was so long that at first Sam wondered whether the caller had rung off. Then at last he said, 'My name is Ryder White. I'm a colonel in the Banoi Island Defence Force. I'm currently speaking to you from Banoi prison.'

'That funky-looking place with the tower?' said Logan.

'That's right. My wife –' he cleared his throat – 'my wife is the prison doctor here.'

He paused again, as if composing himself.

'Go on,' said Purna.

'As I said previously,' White continued, 'the first full-blown victim of the virus was identified in the downtown area of Moresby around –' he did a quick calculation – 'fifteen hours ago now. However, we have reason to believe that the contagion became active in the population at least twenty-four hours previous to that, that carriers were – unbeknownst to them – infecting everyone they came into contact with. Many of the resort's maintenance staff – cleaners, gardeners, janitors – commute between the city and the resort every day. The maintenance staff at the prison are similarly recruited from that area of the city . . .'

He paused again. Purna was the first to make the leap. 'So you're saying the virus has spread to the prison?'

'I'm afraid so.' White's voice was hollow. Once again there was a pause and then he said, 'My wife has been infected.'

'Shit,' said Sam. 'Sorry to hear that, man.'

'Me too,' said Purna curtly. 'But that still doesn't explain why you want to help us.'

'Or how you knew about us in the first place,' said Xian Mei.

'As I told you, our monitoring equipment here is sophisticated and powerful enough to intercept satellite signals. We are also . . . ah . . . able at times to intercept certain sensitive information from elsewhere.'

'Computer hacking,' said Logan, snorting laughter. 'You a dirty hacker, Mr White?'

Almost primly White said, 'I would prefer not to go into details, if you don't mind.'

Logan laughed again. Sam asked, 'So what is this information?'

'I think I can guess,' said Xian Mei. 'It was information about us, wasn't it? About our immunity to the virus?'

'Yes,' said White simply.

'And where did the information come from?' asked Purna.

White hesitated, and then said, 'Even in these circumstances, I'm afraid some information is *too* sensitive to impart, and therefore must remain secret. Suffice to say that my desire to help you is a purely selfish one.'

'You want to find out whether our immunity can help your wife?' said Purna.

'Restore her, yes.'

'How you gonna do that?' asked Sam. 'You ain't gonna experiment on us, are you?'

White laughed. 'Of course not. We have fairly modest medical facilities here, but enough resources to at least analyse your blood.'

'You're hoping to develop an antidote?' said Purna.

White sighed once again. 'It's a long shot, admittedly, but . . . yes.'

There was silence for a moment as they all thought through what White had told them. Eventually Purna said, 'But doesn't the virus kill before it reanimates? That's what you told us.'

'That's true, yes.'

'So ... not wishing to be blunt, but doesn't that mean your wife's already dead? That even if you manage to cure her of the virus she still won't survive?'

'I'm hoping not,' said White. 'The virus in my wife's blood was identified at an early stage of its gestation. At the moment we're managing to slow down its progression rate with drugs. But obviously time is running out. I realize I'm clutching at straws here, but the quicker you can get to the prison the better chance Dana has of surviving.'

'OK,' said Sam. 'So let's say we buy this. How do we get to you?'

'You have to go further inland,' said White. 'Deeper into the jungle. Keep following the road that runs closest to the river and eventually you'll come to a village. Once you're there, ask for a man called Mowen. He has a boat and knows the waterways of Banoi like the back of his hand. He can bring you across to the prison. He knows how to negotiate the minefield.'

'Hang on,' said Logan. 'What minefield?'

'The sea between Banoi and the prison is laid with mines. But Mowen knows the way through. You can trust him.'

'And what if we need to contact you at any point?' said Purna.

White hesitated, then said, 'I'll text you a secure number you can reach me on. If you manage to get a signal, that is.'

Purna looked at Sam and raised her eyebrows, as if

silently asking him what he thought. Sam's answering expression seemed to say: *Sounds OK, I guess.*

'So?' White asked. 'Will you come?'

Purna licked her lips.

'We'll think about it,' she said eventually.

Chapter 13

INTO THE TREES

'I used to think shooting zombies would be fun, but this is fucking grim, man.'

'You want to swap places, let me take over for a while?' asked Sam.

Logan looked tempted, but he shook his head. 'Guess not. You've done your bit for now. Never thought I'd end up saying this, but I reckon I gotta take my share of the responsibility.'

After leaving Sinamoi some provisions and a couple of guns, Sam, Purna, Xian Mei, Logan and Jin had thanked the lifeguard for all he had done for them and said their goodbyes. Initially Logan had tried to persuade Sinamoi to come along too, but he had elected to stay behind. Quietly Xian Mei had asked Jin if she wanted to stay with him, but the girl had shaken her head.

'I thought you might prefer to be close to your father,' Xian Mei said.

'What's the point?' replied Jin bluntly. 'He's dead.'

Xian Mei had been shocked at the finality of Jin's words. 'You can't know that for certain.'

'The world is cruel,' Jin said, her face expressionless. 'There's no longer any hope for any of us.'

Xian Mei had been troubled by how much the younger girl's outlook had changed by her new-found nihilism. When they had first encountered her she had been compassionate, hopeful, eager to help people, but in the space of a few hours her faith and optimism had been shattered, her world torn apart.

'Maybe this man, Ryder White, will help us find an antidote,' Xian Mei reassured her. 'Maybe then we can help your father.'

'Papa will be gone by then,' Jin said. 'This virus is without mercy.'

To get to the road that would take them into the jungle, they had had to pass again through the resort area, which meant negotiating at least part of the highly populated main street. Purna had hoped they would be able to do what they had almost done last time – crawl through undetected. However, it was not to be. Either the infected were able to retain recent memories or Sam, Purna and the rest had simply been unlucky enough on this occasion to have been instantly spotted.

Whatever the reason, as soon as the van nosed into view at the intersection leading on to the high street, the infected began to turn, almost in unison, in their direction.

'Fuck!' said Logan, who was witnessing the infected en masse for the first time. 'I see our problem's gotten a whole lot bigger since last night.'

'We're going to have to shoot our way through this

time,' said Purna, 'otherwise we'll be swamped. Logan, Xian Mei, you ready?'

They nodded, each raising their assault rifle, as Purna pressed the buttons set into the driver's door that automatically lowered the two front windows. As soon as there was enough of a gap, Logan and Xian Mei poked the barrels of their rifles through and started firing.

The automatic weapons cut a swathe through the zombies closing in on both sides. Chunks of bloody flesh and bone and shredded clothing filled the air like grotesque confetti as the first wave of the marauding dead went down and were casually trampled by the ravenous hordes behind them.

Purna, meanwhile, floored the accelerator, surging forward, using the vehicle as a battering ram. Zombies were thrown aside or knocked to the ground and crushed beneath the wheels. A few of them made it on to the van's hood and one – a lanky teenage boy with long greasy hair and a face full of acne – managed to scramble up on to the roof. He stayed there for a full minute or more, before a particularly violent jolt sent him spinning off into the crowd like a stage diver at a rock concert.

Eventually, however, they were through the worst of it, and Purna was able to take her foot off the accelerator. The windows and bodywork of the van were splattered with already-congealing blood. Logan and Xian Mei drew in their weapons and Purna closed the windows.

Sam, sitting on a stack of boxes in the back, noticed that Logan was shaking a little.

'You OK, man?' he asked quietly.

Logan nodded. 'Just adrenalin. I'll be fine in a minute.' He took a deep breath. 'Jesus, I have never seen anything like that before. That was totally . . .'

'Insane?' Sam suggested.

'Insane,' agreed Logan.

As they left the resort area behind, the road narrowed and the lush tropical vegetation that covered eighty per cent of the island began to press in on both sides. Dazzling birds of paradise gossiped in the treetops, and at one point they rounded a corner and startled a group of macaque monkeys, who were relaxing on the dusty road like fans soaking up the sun at a music festival.

As civilization became ever more distant, a silence settled over them – partly self-reflection, partly weariness, partly a sense of delayed shock at the abruptness with which the world had irrevocably changed. In the back of the van, sitting among their accumulated booty of weapons and provisions, Sam closed his eyes, all at once overcome by a great rolling wave of lethargy. Soothed by the rumbling of the engine, he felt his thoughts breaking up, the harsh images of the past few hours softening and receding. Blackness rose to meet him and he slipped gratefully beneath its surface.

It seemed no time at all before someone was prodding him awake.

'Huh?' he said, uncertain for a moment where he was. 'Wass happenin'?'

'I think we're here,' said Xian Mei, her voice hushed as if in reverence.

'Already?' muttered Sam.

'You been out for two hours, man,' said Logan. 'Regular Sleeping Beauty.'

Sam rubbed vigorously at his face with both hands to wake himself up and stretched to relieve the stiffness in his back. Turning his head to peer between the front seats and out through the windscreen, he saw that the jungle had been cut right back on both sides of the road, and the wide and dusty clearing was flanked by a haphazard collection of houses. Most of the houses were stout, wood-framed, one-storey buildings, though a number had been erected on stilt-like timber pilings, either for reasons of status or as a preventative measure against the intrusion of snakes and poisonous insects. The walls were insulated with dried packed mud, which was pale grey, almost white in colour, and the roofs were thatched with thick sheaves of grass baked yellow and dry by the sun.

Untethered goats and wild fowl wandered nonchalantly among children and adults performing a variety of tasks in the open air. Sam saw women weaving or grinding corn or washing clothes. He saw men mending or making various household implements; one even tinkering with an ancient rattletrap of a motorcycle. As they drove past, nearly everyone stopped what they were doing and turned to look at them. Most of the people were wearing a rag-tag collection of western clothes that looked as though they had been donated by some charity or other. However, a few – mainly women – wore flowing, brightly coloured garments, which they had clearly either made themselves or bought locally.

The overall impression was of a people on the cusp

of modern society, a community with one foot in the technological age and one still firmly planted in ancient tribal traditions.

'So how do we find this Mowen guy?' asked Logan.

'I suggest we ask someone,' Purna replied.

'Why don't we try here?' said Xian Mei, pointing at a building coming up on their left.

It was a ramshackle wooden homestead with steps leading up to a long canopied porch. It reminded Sam of some of the houses built way out on the bayou back home, houses reputed to be populated by voodoo priests and priestesses, and surrounded by constantly dripping trees which loomed from 'gator-infested swamplands. This particular building, however, had a sun-bleached sign that simply read STORE dangling on rusty chains from its wooden canopy. Another sign – this one metal and screwed to the door – was emblazoned with the proud boast WE SELL COCA-COLA.

Purna shrugged and pulled up next to a pale blue flatbed truck that looked as if it might have been new back in the 1950s. The five of them climbed out, stretching and groaning, still uncomfortably aware that they were being candidly and silently assessed by the local population, but trying to ignore it.

Logan sidled up to Sam. 'Hey, man, ever feel like a virgin at a rapist convention?'

'Hush up,' Sam hissed, glancing anxiously across at Jin.

Realizing what he had said, Logan clapped a hand to his mouth. 'Sorry, man, I forgot,' he mumbled.

They trooped up the steps into the store, Purna in the lead. Though he knew it wouldn't have exactly made a great impression, Sam felt a little nervous about leaving their weapons in the van.

The interior of the store was surprisingly well stocked. There were tinned goods, boxes of over-ripe fruit, various dried meats beneath a sheet of transparent plastic to keep the flies off, and an upright drinks cooler, which did indeed contain cans of Coca-Cola, as well as Sprite, 7-Up and lemon Fanta. There was even a creaky old paperback spinner stuffed with dog-eared books that looked as though they had been transported here from the 1970s. Flipping through it briefly, Logan recognized authors his parents used to read – Harold Robbins, Nevil Shute – as well as a novel *he* had read in high school (possibly the *only* novel he had read in high school), *The Wolfen* by Whitley Strieber.

Standing behind the counter was a gangly old black man with a halo of white hair and a thick fuzzy beard. His arms were so thin that they made his work-calloused hands look huge. He watched them warily, saying nothing. Purna smiled and walked up to him.

'Hi,' she said. 'You speak English?'

The old man simply stared at her.

'We're looking for someone,' said Xian Mei. 'A man called Mowen. You know him?'

The old man frowned a little.

'Mo-wen,' repeated Logan, drawing out the name, emphasizing each syllable. He held up his hands and grinned. 'It's OK. We're friendly.'

'Don't do that, man,' muttered Sam. 'Makes you look even more of a psycho than you already do.'

To their surprise, Jin suddenly stepped forward and spoke a few words to the old man in a language they didn't understand. The old man responded with a few words of his own, then turned and stuck his head around a ratty blue curtain covering an opening at the back of the counter.

He shouted a word that sounded like, 'Afreela.'

'What's he doing?' said Logan.

His question was answered a moment later by the appearance of a boy of twelve or thirteen. The family resemblance was obvious. The boy was as gangly as the old man and the bone structure of his face gave him the same pinched nose, hollow cheeks and strong jaw. The boy tensed as soon as he saw the new arrivals, his eyes becoming wide and wary. The old man spoke a few rapid words to him, one of which was 'Mowen'. The boy gave a brief nod, sidled cautiously around the counter, then darted out of the shop, as if he expected to be challenged or pursued.

Jin spoke a few more words to the old man and he grunted in response.

'What did you say?' asked Purna.

'I told him we'd wait outside.'

'Tell him we're not here to cause trouble,' said Purna.

'I already did. I don't think he believes me.'

Logan bought sodas and they stood in the shade of the front porch, drinking them while they waited for the boy to return with Mowen.

'Why are they all fucking staring at us?' Logan said nervously, glancing up at the large number of local people who were still sitting or standing around nearby, watching the newcomers with a kind of dead-pan curiosity.

'Have you *seen* what we look like?' said Sam. 'Have you *seen* what the van looks like?'

Logan frowned and stared round at Sam and the others, then at their mode of transport, as if seeing them all with fresh eyes. He realized that to someone who had no idea what had been going down, the crumpled, dented, blood-covered van and their equally gore-stained appearance must have been a pretty alarming sight. The five of them and their trusty vehicle looked as if they had just emerged from a medieval battlefield.

'See what you mean,' said Logan, and then nodded at Sam, a twinkle in his eye. 'You're talking about that dumb bandanna, right?'

Not for the first time Sam showed him the finger. Logan laughed.

It was twenty minutes before the boy returned with a tall, rangy black man in his early thirties. The boy jabbered a few words to the man and then cast a fearful look in their direction, before skirting round them in a big circle and scuttling back into the shop.

'Hey, kid,' Logan called after him, 'we ain't gonna hurt you. We're not as bad as we ... aw, what's the use?'

'He think you cursed,' said the man who had accompanied the kid, his voice heavily accented. 'They *all* think you cursed.' The man's eyes were hidden behind mirror shades, and his head was a mass of black dreadlocks that cascaded over his shoulders. He wore boots, combat pants and a sleeveless T-shirt, and carried a rifle on a strap over his shoulder.

'But you don't?' Purna said.

The man pursed his lips, as if partly amused, partly insulted. 'I a civilized man. I know better.' He flicked his head at Purna, as though throwing out a question. 'You want speak to me?'

Purna nodded. 'A man called Ryder White sent us to find you. He told us you have a boat, and that you would take us off the island and over to the prison.'

Mowen may not have thought them cursed, but he regarded them with the same candour as the rest of the villagers. Though they couldn't see his eyes, the movements of his head suggested his gaze was moving unhurriedly from one to the next, as if he was assessing their individual strengths and weaknesses.

Finally he said, 'Why you want to leave island?'

'Paradise is a little too green for us, man,' said Logan.

Purna flashed a frown at him, a silent warning that now was not the time for levity. 'There is a sickness,' she said. 'It's affecting everybody. Turning them ... crazy.' She demonstrated by swirling her hands around beside her head.

Mowen seemed unimpressed. 'I know of sickness. Very bad for business.'

'What *is* your business?' asked Sam.

Mowen turned casually to look at him, his face implacable. 'I buy things. I sell things.' He paused, then added as an afterthought, 'I help many people.'

'Can you help us?' asked Purna.

Mowen shrugged. 'Why I should help you?'

'Because Ryder White said you would,' said Purna firmly.

Mowen's lips gave a dismissive twitch, as if that

207

argument held no sway with him. 'Is too dangerous. Nothing in it for me.'

Purna looked thoughtful for a moment, as if deciding what she should tell him. Eventually she said, 'You say this sickness is bad for your business?'

Mowen nodded.

'If we get to the prison,' she continued, 'there's a chance we can stop this sickness. Cure it.'

'Why you go to prison?' Mowen said. 'Why you not go to place in jungle?'

Purna blinked. '*What* place in the jungle?'

Mowen waved a hand vaguely. 'Is deep. Near Kuruni village. Is doctor there. Is place of . . . how you say . . . science?'

'Like a laboratory?' suggested Xian Mei.

'Laboratory, yes. Doctor there . . . *he* start this.'

'You're saying there's a laboratory in the jungle, and that the doctor there *started* this virus? This sickness?' said Sam.

Mowen nodded as if it was obvious.

'How do you know this?' said Purna.

Mowen grimaced as if she was being naïve. '*I* know. *Everyone* know.'

Purna stared at him. 'Wait a minute,' she said, holding up a hand. 'Don't move.'

She turned and walked a couple of dozen paces away from the group, pulling her cell phone from her pocket. The signal was not great, but hopefully it would be good enough. She keyed in the number Ryder White had texted them all a little earlier.

After just one ring, White's clipped voice said, 'Yes?'

208

As concisely as possible Purna told him what Mowen had said.

Excitedly, White asked, 'Will he take you there?'

'He seems reluctant. He wants to know what's in it for him.'

'Tell him I'll pay him whatever he wants. He's done jobs for me in the past and he knows he can trust me to keep my word. Time may be running out, but money's something I'm *not* short of.'

'It could be a dead end,' said Purna.

'Or it could be exactly what I need – what we *all* need. It's just too good a lead to ignore, despite the extra time involved.'

'OK,' Purna said. 'How is your wife, by the way?'

'Deteriorating. But stable enough for now. Listen, keep in touch, OK? Let me know what's going on.'

'If I can,' said Purna, and broke the connection.

Chapter 14

MAD SCIENTIST

The journey to the laboratory would take almost three hours.

Because they hadn't all needed to go, and because none of them were happy about leaving the van unguarded, it had been decided that Xian Mei would stay behind with Jin.

Mowen's boat was a small ex-army tug. He had negotiated the waterways skilfully, standing proud astride his vessel like a pirate captain on the High Seas. Occasionally he had flipped his rifle off his shoulder to fire at what Logan had at first thought were drifting logs. 'Friendly looking fuckers, aren't they?'

'Crocodile,' Mowen had explained. 'I shoot so they stay scared. If scared they not attack.'

At times the waterways had been nothing but dark, narrow swampy channels through dense green tunnels of vines and creepers; at others the banks had widened out and the overhanging treetops above them had separated like sliding shutters to admit a vast blue vista of sky. Mowen had been happy for

Purna, Sam and Logan to bring their weapons along, and in fact seemed reasonably laid back about the entire venture, despite his initial reticence. Purna had been watching him closely the whole time, eyes narrowed, as if she didn't really trust him.

For his part, although he felt a little unsettled about venturing into unknown territory, Sam was just glad to get a break from the relentless rage and hunger of the infected. And although he had initially thought Logan a bitter, over-pampered douche-bag, he was now glad of the guy's company. In a strange way, what had happened had actually been good for Logan, or at least had shown him in a more favourable light. Deprived of the drugs and alcohol he had evidently started to become dependent upon since his accident, and given something other than his own woes to worry about, the ex-football star had proven himself to be a witty and likeable companion. He could be relied on to keep people's spirits up with a quip or an irreverent comment when things got too heavy. Sam thought that even Purna liked having Logan around, though the Australian girl was hard to read – harder even, in many ways, than Mowen, despite the trader's mirror shades and uncertain grasp of the English language.

Eventually they had come to a small jetty in the middle of the jungle, where Mowen had tied the boat up.

'Now we walk,' he'd said, gesturing off into the jungle.

'How far?' Purna had asked.

Mowen shrugged. 'One hour maybe.'

211

At Mowen's recommendation, they had each brought a rucksack of provisions, which they hoisted on to their backs, and a machete to hack their way through the jungle. Mowen had led the way at a brisk pace, occasionally pointing out hazards for them to avoid – snakes, spiders, plants that would sting or scratch or otherwise irritate their skin. It was not long before Sam and Logan had been dripping with sweat and even Purna's flawless brown skin had gleamed with a light sheen of perspiration. Only Mowen ahead of them had seemed relatively unaffected, though as Sam used his soggy bandanna to wipe sweat away from his forehead for perhaps the twentieth time, he had eventually been gratified to see a small damp triangle forming on the back of Mowen's T-shirt, between his shoulder blades.

It had seemed considerably more than an hour's walk before they had finally reached the 'laboratory'. What surprised Sam most about it was the way it appeared, with no prior warning. One minute they were tramping through thick jungle, hacking encroaching vegetation out of the way, and the next they had stopped at the edge of a clearing where a good half-acre or more of trees and bushes had simply been excised, as if by a devastatingly corrosive energy beam from a passing alien spacecraft.

The 'laboratory' comprised a jumble of ugly grey prefab buildings surrounded on all sides by an unbroken, three-metre tall security fence. Armed guards, dressed in black combat fatigues and black baseball caps despite the heat, patrolled the perimeter. Attached to each of the guard's baseball caps was a headset and microphone. Concealed behind bushes at the clearing's edge, Mowen, Purna, Sam and Logan spent a minute or so observing proceedings. Logan made a wry comment about the apparent friendliness – or lack of it – of the guards, but no one replied. Instead Mowen raised a hand and whispered, 'You wait here one moment.'

'Why? What are you going to do?' asked Purna suspiciously.

'I talk to them,' Mowen said and tapped his chest with the flat of his hand. 'They know me.'

Before anyone could respond he stood up and walked out of the bushes. Immediately half a dozen AK 47s swung up and around to cover him, but Mowen seemed unconcerned. He simply raised his hands and strolled forward, and after a few seconds all but two of the guns were lowered. Purna, Sam and Logan looked on as the guards silently watched Mowen approach. The trader walked right up to the fence and started talking to one of the two guards who still had his gun raised.

'What's he saying?' hissed Sam.

'I don't know,' said Purna, clearly not liking the fact. 'I can't hear.'

The muttered conversation continued for maybe another thirty seconds, then the guard turned away and they saw him speaking earnestly into his microphone. Eventually he returned to Mowen to relay what instructions he had been given – whereupon Mowen turned and made a beckoning gesture.

'Come out,' he shouted. 'Is OK.'

It was clear from Purna's face that she was not

happy with the situation, but she stood up and walked out into the clearing.

'Well, here goes nothin',' Logan muttered to Sam, as the two of them rose and followed her.

Immediately the guns, which had been lowered when the guards had recognized Mowen, now snapped up again. 'Hands up!' one of the guards shouted, a swarthy-looking man with a thick black moustache. The three of them complied, though as they walked forward Purna muttered out of the corner of her mouth, 'They better not ask us to give up our weapons.'

Sam wasn't entirely sure what she meant by that statement. Did she mean she would rather go down fighting than be rendered defenceless? He hoped not.

Registering the mistrust on Purna's face, Mowen made a placatory gesture with his hands and said, 'Is OK. Is cool.' He turned to exchange a staccato burst of conversation with the moustached guard and then turned back and said, 'You can put hands down.'

They lowered their hands, but Purna still looked mistrustful, her movements considered and cautious, the muscles in her arms and legs tight with tension. Her eyes darted left and right, taking in every tiny movement of the armed men on the other side of the fence. She reminded Sam of a big cat, a puma or a panther, wary of its human captors, or perhaps even of those trying to give it back its liberty.

The moustached guard gestured with his gun that they should move to the right. Sam wondered why, and then saw there was a gate about ten metres in that direction. Beyond the gate a caged tunnel led to another gate. They were ushered through one at a time, Purna first, then Sam, then Logan. The moustached guard pointed at Purna's gun and said something she didn't understand. She shook her head and turned to Mowen, who was still standing on the other side of the fence.

'Tell him we're not giving up our weapons,' she said. 'They're all we've got out here.'

Obediently Mowen complied, and again a burst of conversation rattled between the two men. Then the moustached guard shrugged, and Mowen turned to Purna.

'He say OK. But you keep them on back. You not touch them.'

'We won't touch them unless we have to,' muttered Purna.

Logan was the last to be ushered through the caged tunnel. When he realized the guard was locking the gate behind him, he turned to Mowen. 'You not coming with us?'

'I wait here. You honoured guests. I . . . ?' He shrugged and laughed.

'I don't like this,' Purna murmured as the moustached guard indicated they should follow him and another four flanked them, two on each side. 'Something's happening that we don't know about.'

'Just take it easy,' said Sam. 'If they were gonna do anythin' bad they'd have done it by now.'

'Not necessarily,' she replied. 'We're immune, remember. That makes us valuable.'

'Yeah, but *they* don't know we're immune,' said Logan.

215

'Don't they?' she muttered darkly.

They were led to a door in the wall of one of the grey buildings, where the moustached guard pressed a button and spoke into a metal grille beside it. After a moment there was a buzz and the door clicked open. The moustached guard led them down a bare, narrow corridor, and from there through an interconnected series of functional low-ceilinged rooms. They reminded Logan of the claustrophobic Antarctic base in one of his favourite movies, *The Thing*.

Eventually they passed through another door and found themselves in a well-appointed laboratory, almost the entirety of one wall of which was dominated by stacks of cramped cages containing a variety of animals – monkeys, wallabies, rats. Running round the other three walls was a waist-high counter cluttered with items of gleaming hi-tech equipment and several computer consoles, on each of whose screens were displayed graphs or diagrams or simply tables of fluctuating data.

Examining the readings on a piece of equipment that looked to Sam like some kind of over-elaborate cappuccino machine was a wiry man in his thirties with close-cropped sandy hair. Although he was wearing a white lab coat, he didn't match Sam's idea of a mad scientist at all. He'd been expecting someone older, with wild hair and maybe a pair of spectacles perched on his forehead. This guy, however, looked more like a mountaineer or a marathon runner. When they entered the room, he turned sharply to look at them, his eyes so startlingly pale and blue that for a moment he looked almost other-worldly.

Then he smiled and bustled across, hand outstretched.

'Welcome! Welcome! I'm Dr West. How nice to have visitors. Way out here it happens so rarely.'

Of the three of them, Sam was the one who automatically put out his hand. The scientist's grip was surprisingly strong as he shook it.

'What's with all the animals?' Logan asked.

For a moment West's smile faltered and he glanced at the moustached security guard.

'Something wrong?' asked Purna.

'I was informed that you came here with Mowen? And that you had important information about a recent virus outbreak in the city?'

'That's pretty much it,' said Sam. 'So?'

West looked at Logan, his eyes piercing. 'So why ask me about the animals?'

Perplexed, Logan shrugged. 'Just askin', that's all. Hey, it's no biggie. You don't have to answer if you don't want to.'

West's face and body remained tense for a couple more seconds and then he relaxed, his shoulders slumping.

'Forgive me,' he said. 'I thought for a moment you had got in here under false pretences.'

'What false pretences would those be?' asked Purna.

West glanced at the caged animals almost guiltily. 'Well ... the nature of my research doesn't always meet with ... shall we say "universal approval"?'

'You're a vivisectionist?' said Purna coldly.

West winced. 'Please. That's such an emotive word.'

'What would you call it?'

217

'I'm a research scientist. I'm currently engaged on a programme of cosmetic testing.'

'On animals?' said Sam.

'Would you rather I used human beings?' snapped West.

Sam shrugged. Animal experimentation wasn't something he approved of exactly, but neither did he feel strongly enough about the subject to engage the doctor in a moral debate. 'Hey, you gotta do what you gotta do,' he mumbled. 'Stuff's gotta be tested some-how, I guess.'

'Exactly,' said West. 'Though try telling that to the animal activists.' Perhaps realizing he was getting a little too emotional, he made an obvious effort to relax, and eventually managed a tight, somewhat twisted smile. 'That's why we're right out here in the . . . ah . . . boondocks, as it were.'

'Is that the only reason?' asked Purna.

West's expression was now one of polite puzzle-ment. 'What do you mean?'

'This virus we came to talk to you about,' said Purna. 'There are people out there who claim you're responsible for it.'

West laughed. 'Do they now? Well, that's a new one, I must say.'

'It was Mowen himself who claimed it originated from here. He told us it was common knowledge among the local people.'

'The mad scientist lurking in his jungle hideaway, unleashing all manner of monstrosities on the world?' West said, and laughed again, longer and harder this time. 'I'm afraid the local people are a superstitious

218

lot. They don't trust anything they don't understand.'

'You know *something* about the virus, though, don't you?' pressed Purna, her tone remaining just this side of accusatory. 'Otherwise why would you have been so willing to see us?'

'Perhaps it's just that I crave company. It does get *terribly* lonely out here, you know.'

Purna smiled tightly. 'Do you honestly think we're that stupid, Dr West?'

Another disarming laugh. 'Of course not. I was curious, that's all. Why would the three of you come all the way out here to talk about a virus endemic to the local tribesmen? It struck me as odd that you would even know about such a thing. And then, of course, there is your appearance.' He gestured towards them. 'Raoul informed me that you looked as though you had just emerged from a pitched battle. And he was right.'

Purna stared at him hard and long. 'You *really* don't know what's been happening?'

'Communication networks are unreliable out here at the best of times. These past twenty-four hours they have been non-existent.'

'Oh, man, are you in for a shock,' said Logan.

West frowned. 'Why? What *has* happened?'

Sam looked at his companions and blew out a long weary breath. 'Who's gonna start?'

They spent the next thirty minutes filling West in on the grim events of the past twenty-four hours. The scientist reacted with horror and shock, but he didn't seem *quite* as surprised as they might have expected. When Purna questioned him on this, he said, 'I confess,

I was aware of the virus, and was concerned that it *would* eventually spread into the wider population. But I must say, what you've just described is way beyond any worst-case scenario I might have envisaged. When I first came here six months ago, a delegation from the Kuruni – that's the local tribe – asked me to examine a man who was suffering from the virus. From what I could gather, the Kuruni have been afflicted with it for generations, and have come almost to accept it. It's a cumulative illness that can strike at any time during a tribesman's – or woman's – adult life, and it eventually leads to dementia and death. However, what the Kuruni seemed to be telling me was that recently the nature of the virus had changed, and that somehow the villagers who were dying from it were then *returning* from the dead as . . . I don't know . . . demons? Evil spirits? To be honest, I took a great deal of what they were saying with a pinch of salt; I simply assumed they were hysterically interpreting the symptoms of extreme dementia as some kind of . . . supernatural mumbo jumbo. Anyway, I examined the man's blood and discovered that his symptoms were reminiscent of Kuru, a prion disease that affects the brain. To put it in its most basic terms, it's like a human version of mad cow disease, and it is believed to be caused by cannibalism.'

'Cannibalism?' repeated Logan.

West nodded. 'The Kuruni are cannibals, have been for generations.' He hesitated, then said, 'Although I managed to separate and identify the virus, what particularly disturbed me about it was that it was not only highly contagious, but it was also unstable, constantly mutating. However, the puzzling thing was why – given that the virus was so contagious – the entire Kuruni population had not long ago been wiped out by it.'

'They had a natural immunity, you mean?' asked Purna.

'Not all of them, but a significant proportion of them, yes.'

'Like us,' said Sam.

'So what's to stop you taking a sample of our blood and whipping up a quick vaccine here and now?' asked Logan.

West smiled. 'Maybe I could – if I had a stable form of the virus. The thing is, though, your immunity may be simply an anomaly, something that works for you, but doesn't necessarily work for everybody.'

'So what would you need to maximize your chances of creating an effective vaccine?' asked Purna.

West said, 'Ideally a blood sample from an immune Kuruni villager, in which the genetic signifier would be dominant and therefore unmistakeable, plus a sample of the stable form of the virus.'

'A stable form?' said Logan. 'What does *that* mean?'

'It means one that hasn't reached the stage where it's constantly mutating.'

'From someone who died a while ago, you mean?' said Purna.

West nodded.

'So when you say "a while ago",' said Sam, 'how long ago we talking here exactly?'

West shrugged. 'A year. Maybe two to be certain.'

Sam looked nonplussed. 'So you need a blood

sample from an immune villager, *plus* a blood sample from some dude who died of the virus two years ago?'

'The stable form of the virus doesn't have to be a blood sample,' said West. 'Any DNA sample would do.'

'Oh, why didn't you *say* so?' said Sam with heavy irony. 'That's *easy*. All you have to do is dig some dude up and chop off his finger or somethin'.'

'So if we can get you these things,' said Purna, 'you'd be willing to develop a vaccine?'

'I'd be willing to *try*, of course,' replied West, 'but there would be no guarantee I'd be successful.'

'But how long would it take?' Purna asked. 'Doesn't it usually involve months of lab work to come up with these things?'

'It can do,' West replied, wafting a hand vaguely, 'but it all depends on the nature of the infection. And I *have* already done some groundwork, remember. We *may* strike lucky – if you can bring me what I need.'

'Hey, wait a minute,' said Sam. 'How come *we're* doing this? The doctor here's friendly with these guys.'

West shook his head. 'I'm not really, you know. I may have befriended a few of the Kuruni people, but the majority are hostile. Plus I'm not immune to the virus like you are. I was extremely fortunate not to contract it from the infected Kuruni man I examined. Luckily for me, the virus was not in its later, most contagious phase at the time, and my contact with the patient was minimal, not to mention conducted under the strictest of laboratory conditions. It was only afterwards, when I realized what I had been dealing

222

with, that it struck me what a lucky escape I'd had.'

'So let me get this straight,' said Sam to Purna. 'You're wanting us to go deeper into the jungle to look for a village of mean motherfucking cannibals, so that we can ask them for some blood and for permission to not only *dig up* their dead relatives, but to *chop little bits* off 'em.'

'Put like that, you make it sound so bad,' said Logan.

Purna smiled grimly. 'What's the problem? We've got guns, haven't we?'

'Well, whoop-di-do,' said Sam.

Chapter 15

HEART OF DARKNESS

'We stop here. Now you walk.'

West had instructed Raoul, the moustached guard, to lend them one of four open-top jeeps parked in a smaller clearing just north of the research centre. Mowen had told Purna, Sam and Logan that the route to the Kuruni village had been formed over the centuries by the passage of feet, not vehicles, and that it would therefore be narrow and uneven, but passable. When Purna had asked for directions to the village, Mowen had surprised her by saying there were many paths, and that they would quickly get lost without him.

'But it's too dangerous for you to come with us,' Purna said. 'There's sickness in the village.'

Mowen grinned and patted his chest. 'I not get sick,' he told her.

At first she wondered whether he was immune like the rest of them, but when, after a stop–start journey during which they had had to get out of the jeep a dozen times to hack a path through the dense vegetation, he cut the engine and instructed them to walk, she realized he meant he had no intention of getting too close to the action.

'How far is it?' she asked.

He raised his hands as if the distance was negligible. 'Less than one hour.'

'And you'll be here when we get back?'

He nodded. 'Yes. I wait.'

Purna hesitated, and Sam knew she was debating whether to issue a warning about what would happen to him if he let them down. However, in the end she simply said, 'OK. Thanks, Mowen. See you later.'

They began to walk, flies and mosquitoes buzzing around them, their journey accompanied by the ever-present chorus of birds and insects. Although Sam was pretty sure they'd hear if one of the infected came crashing towards them through the undergrowth, he wondered how aware he, Purna and Logan would be if the regular cannibals started to stalk them. This was their natural habitat, after all, and for all Purna's training and athleticism the three of them were little more than prey out here. Their guns might give them a certain amount of reassurance and authority, but Sam couldn't help but think it was a false comfort. He'd seen those old Tarzan movies as a kid and knew how easy it would really be to bring them all down. A bunch of curare-tipped blowpipe darts in the backs of their necks, and that would be it.

Something else that concerned him was the time factor. With the sun still high overhead, it was easy to forget that it was now late afternoon. Sooner rather than later, therefore, it would start to get dark. If it took an hour to walk to the Kuruni village and an hour to get back, it would be early evening before they rejoined Mowen at the jeep, by which time the sun would be sinking rapidly towards the horizon.

Although Sam really didn't like the thought of being stuck out in the jungle at night, he kept his fears to himself. There was no point expressing them until the possibility became a reality. He hoped everything would work out OK, in which case they could bed down at the research centre tonight, head back to Mowen's village with the vaccine in the morning, then get the trader to take them all out to the prison. With any luck, by lunchtime tomorrow they would be sitting in a chopper and heading away from this fucked-up place.

The first indication they were nearing the village was when they heard the faint jabber of raised voices beyond the screen of vegetation ahead. Purna glanced back, gesturing at Sam and Logan to move quietly, then crept forward, her body bent in a crouch.

For a minute or more the sounds rose and fell, as if carried by the faint warm breeze that intermittently rustled the leaves of the plants around them. Then they began to consolidate, to acquire substance. Now, although none of them could understand the words being spoken, Purna, Sam and Logan could tell the voices were full of fear and urgency, and that under-pinning them were the familiar heart-sinking snarls and moans of the infected.

When the quality of the light lancing through the gaps between the fleshy overlap of leaves became more piercing and less green, they knew they were reaching the edge of the jungle. Purna glanced back once again, perhaps simply to reassure herself her companions were still closeby, then she bent down and carefully parted the leaves with both hands so they could all peer through them.

More by luck than judgement, the gap she had made framed a perfect tableau of what was happening in the village. At the end of a long, dusty street lined with conical hive-like huts of mud and grass, was a cluster of mature trees, which marked the boundary between the far side of the village and the continuation of the jungle. Perched in the branches of the trees were at least a dozen people, the shadows cast by the fleshy-leaved branches reducing them to little more than bobbing-headed silhouettes. Their voices, calling to each other, could clearly be heard. They were quarrelling voices, full of anxiety and anger; voices bordering on, and occasionally spilling over into, panic.

The reason for their distress was obvious. Gathered at the base of the trees, reaching up to scrabble and claw at the trunks, or simply at the air, were dozens of the infected. They were clambering over one another in an effort to get closer to their potential prey, though fortunately they seemed unable to coordinate their thoughts enough to climb the trees themselves. However, without help it would surely only be a matter of time before what now appeared to be the minority of Kuruni people still unaffected by the virus succumbed to thirst or hunger or simple fatigue and fell into the clutches of the ravenous hordes below. From the evidence it appeared that events here had suddenly and shockingly come to a head, and that

227

after years, perhaps centuries, of living with the virus, the balance of the scales had tipped and the dead – perhaps through sheer weight of numbers – had instigated some kind of bloody, albeit mindless, coup.

Aside from the few villagers who had had the luck and foresight to head for the only safe direction – straight up, into the trees – it was obvious that the Kuruni tribe had been decimated by the attack. Between the edge of the jungle where Purna, Sam and Logan were crouching, and the trees providing temporary sanctuary for the survivors at the far end, was a scene that resembled the aftermath of an explosion. Dozens of mutilated bodies were lying in pools of blood along the dusty street, many of them missing limbs, or with their flesh stripped down to the bone or their stomachs ripped open and their entrails exposed to view. Most were permanently and merci-fully dead, their remains crusted with fat and feasting flies, though there were a few that had been resur-rected by the virus and were now wriggling pitifully in the dirt, trying desperately to re-animate bodies that were damaged beyond repair.

Sam swallowed, his mouth dry, his mind reeling at the sight of this fresh atrocity.

'Fuck me,' Logan whispered. 'Guess we're a little late, huh?'

'We still have to help those people,' whispered Purna. 'We can't just leave them up there.'

'I hear ya,' Sam whispered. 'But how?'

Purna was silent for a moment, her eyes restless as she took note of the terrain ahead and their available resources. Eventually she said, 'I've got an idea.'

'Make it a good one,' replied Logan.

She outlined her plan to them, pointing out the land-marks she was referring to. When she had finished Logan laughed quietly. It was an incredulous laugh rather than a happy one.

'You're fucking crazy, you know that?'

A brief smile fluttered at her lips. 'That's why you love me.' She tapped Logan's backpack. 'Lucky we brought plenty of ammo with us.' After a couple of deep breaths she said, 'Ready?'

'No,' said Logan. 'But let's do it anyway.'

'OK. On the count of three. One. Two. *Three!*'

Readying their weapons, they broke cover, each of them running as fast as they could. Purna and Logan to the right, Sam to the left, like a SWAT team spread-ing out to cover the area. They were halfway to each of their individual destinations when they were spotted. Sam, the pounding of his heart filling his ears, was aware of heads turning in his direction, shapes peeling away from the crush of semi-naked bodies crowding around the trees at the far end of the village and lurching towards him. When several of the infected let out blood-curdling shrieks in unison, prior to breaking into shambling, long-legged sprints, the shock was almost enough to make him lose his footing. A jolt went through his body, powerful as electricity, and he felt himself stumble, his right knee crumpling at the sudden unexpected weight. *No*, he told himself, and the sheer terror of what would happen to him if he went down was enough to keep him going. He turned and let off a few shots, felling the most rapidly advancing of the zombies, before darting between two huts. Just beyond them was the tree Purna had pointed out to him, and Sam saw immediately that she had chosen well. Swinging the rifle over his shoulder on its adjustable strap, he leaped at the lowest branches of the tree and began to haul himself up. He found his hand-holds and lifted his right leg to a higher branch, and was just about to lift his left foot too when it was seized from below. He looked down to see a woman, her eyes glaring and yellow, her face demonic with rage, clutching his blood-stained Reebok in both hands. Then he felt pain as her head darted forward and she sank her teeth right through his jeans and into his calf.

'*Fuck!*' he yelled, the bright white shock of the pain enough to give him a surge of adrenalin. He wrenched his left leg upwards with such force that his foot popped clean out of its shoe, leaving it clutched in the zombie's hands. The zombie regarded the empty shoe almost comically for a second, then allowed it to drop to the ground. By the time she raised her head and clawed up towards Sam, he was out of her reach.

He found a branch wide enough and strong enough to take his weight and lay across it for a moment, leaning back on his backpack, panting and shaking. Below him, through a shifting canopy of leaves, he could see zombies already congregating, snarling in what he fancied was frustration, their bloodied fingers scrabbling ineffectually at the tree trunk.

He might have lost a shoe, but at least he hadn't lost his gun or his pack full of ammo – or, indeed, his life. His calf where he'd been bitten was stinging like fuck, though, enough to make him feel ill and faint. He wrapped his arms around the branch he was draped across and clung on desperately, fearful for a moment that he might pass out and plunge to the ground below. His forehead was oozing sweat and his heart was like muffled but persistent thunder in his ears. It took several seconds before he realized that someone was shouting his name.

He looked up groggily. At first his vision was nothing but a confusion of waving leaves and blinding flashes of sunlight. The sound penetrated the fug in his mind, enabled him to get his bearings, and eventually he shuffled upright and through a gap in the branches saw Logan sitting high up in his own tree about thirty metres away, behind a bunch of huts on the far side of the clearing.

'Hey!' Sam shouted, his voice thick and a little slurred.

'Fuck, man,' Logan yelled back, sounding pissed off, 'what you been doing? Taking a nap?'

'Kinda,' shouted Sam. 'I got bit. Think I phased out for a moment.'

'You OK?' shouted Purna, the direction of her voice enabling Sam to pinpoint her half way up a tree forty metres to Logan's left.

'I'll live,' replied Sam, and then almost laughed at the irony of his statement.

'Yeah, but will the poor bastard who bit you?' shouted Logan. 'Oh, hang on. I forgot. That's something he doesn't have to worry about.'

'It wasn't a he, it was a she,' shouted Sam. 'And she took my fucking shoe.'

231

'I'm jealous,' Logan replied. 'What *is* the secret of your success with the ladies, man?'

'I guess you either got it or you ain't,' Sam yelled back.

Their loud exchange had at least caused the survivors at the far end of the village to stop bickering. Sam imagined them all perched up in the branches of their trees, shocked into silence at this unexpected intrusion into their village. One thing they ought to be grateful for, however, was the fact that the majority of the infected, perhaps realizing that their prey was inaccessible for now, were drifting towards the new arrivals, presumably in the hope of easier pickings. If so, then they were going to be disappointed – if zombies could be disappointed, that was.

'OK, let's do this,' Purna shouted from across the clearing. 'You ready, Sam?'

Sam unslung his rifle, raised it to his shoulder and pointed it down at the ground. 'Ready.'

'Ladies and gentlemen,' Logan announced loudly, 'we are just about to make a hell of a fucking noise. I apologize for any inconvenience that this may cause.'

Then they started firing.

'Operation Fish in a Barrel' Purna had called it, a name that was nothing but apt. Sam felt almost guilty as he sat in his tree, firing down at the milling hordes below. Oblivious to fear and danger, the infected didn't run or seek cover; they simply stood there, allowing themselves to be picked off. For over five minutes, Sam, Purna and Logan kept firing and reloading, pumping round after round into the hungry dead, shattering skulls and destroying brains with the

232

same clinical determination they might show if they were eradicating a nest of ants.

By the time it was over, the ground beneath Sam's tree was a thick lake of blood, a swamp of pulped and fallen flesh. The stink that rose from it made him feel sick, and already he was wondering how he could possibly avoid having to wade through it when he climbed down. After so much activity the gun was hot in his hands and the shockwaves of the hundreds of rounds he had fired rippled through his body like a never-ending echo. He felt his hearing had gone into trauma, his jaw ached from having been clenched so tightly, and the double pulse in his temples seemed to prompt an answering beat from the bite-wound in his calf.

Aside from the throbbing of his own body, for several minutes after the shooting was over Sam experienced nothing but a deep, almost profound silence. He suspected that, like him, Purna and Logan were sitting quietly, alone with their thoughts, perhaps trying to come to terms with the oddly heightened reality of what they had just done, or attempting to make sense of the conflicting emotions of exhilaration and self-loathing battling for supremacy in their heads. Sam felt enervated, but at the same time so alert it was like a caffeine buzz. He felt heavy and weight-less, centred and scattered, light and dark. Time seemed meaningless, and at the same time he was almost achingly aware of every passing second. He closed his eyes for a moment, and when he opened them again it felt like the world had changed.

At last, slowly, he climbed down from the tree.

When he reached the lowest branch, he shimmied along until it started to bend, and then he jumped. Despite clearing the base of the tree by a good five metres, he still landed at the very edge of the killing ground, his shoeless foot landing in blood that had the consistency of cold, partly set jelly. Grimacing, he trudged out on to the dusty main street, leaving a trail of red footprints behind him.

As if by mutual consent, Purna and Logan emerged from between huts on the other side of the street at exactly the same moment and they all walked towards each other, like outlaws meeting for a noon show-down. No one said anything, though the looks that passed between them seemed to convey how they were feeling far more eloquently than words. As one they turned and walked towards the cluster of trees at the far end of the village, and as they got closer the survivors began to drop to the ground, one by one, like strange fruit.

Most prominent among them was a man with long matted hair, whose dark-skinned body was painted in swirling red and white shapes. He wore a crocodile-skin cape and when he walked the bone ornamentation adorning his wrists, ankles and neck jangled ominously. Showing no fear, he marched up to the three visitors to his village, drawing a ceremonial dagger from his belt as he did so. Purna tensed and half raised her gun, but the man halted a couple of metres from them, placed the dagger on his palm with the blade pointing towards his own chest and dropped to his knees. He tilted his upper body forward as though in supplication, his forehead all but touching the dusty ground, and stretched out his right hand, offering them the dagger.

Logan looked at Purna. 'I think that means he likes you,' he said.

Chapter 16

THE LIVING DEAD GIRL

'Koritoia-Ope.'

Purna slowly repeated the name and the witch doctor nodded delightedly. Despite his fearsome appearance he had been an amiable enough companion. They had been walking for several hours now, heading ever upwards. For the first three hours they had been hacking their way through thick jungle, but now they had risen beyond the treeline and were ascending the dusty, upward-sloping trail of a jagged-peaked mountain. Sam couldn't decide whether he preferred struggling through dense vegetation, where at least the ground was level and they were sheltered from the sun, or toiling uphill, where they were unencumbered by trailing vines and ankle-entangling plants, but where they had to contend with the mercilessly beating sun.

At least they had set off at dawn, which meant that the sun had not been at its height. Even so, long before they reached their destination sweat was rolling down Sam's face and his freshly laundered T-shirt was plastered to his body. The hiking boots that West had lent him (he hadn't even bothered trying to locate his lost Reebok in the charnel pit of zombie remains at the bottom of the tree) were pinching a little, but he could cope with that. And at least, for once, he didn't stink of zombie blood – which was always a bonus.

After making the acquaintance of the surviving Kuruni villagers yesterday, Purna, Sam and Logan had persuaded them – through a combination of gestures and basic vocabulary – to accompany them back through the jungle to where Mowen was waiting with the jeep. After getting over his initial surprise, Mowen had spoken to the witch doctor and, although their two tribal languages had not been entirely compatible, had at least been able to make him understand why the four of them had come to the village and what it was they needed. Perhaps in exchange for saving their lives, or simply because he had witnessed first-hand how frighteningly out of control the virus had become, the witch doctor – Koritoia-Ope – had eventually agreed to lead his people to the research centre and allow West to take blood samples from them in an effort to develop a vaccine. Furthermore he had agreed to take a party up to the sacred Kuruni burial site early the following morning, so they could get a sample of the stable form of the virus.

Sam had never before appreciated the sheer bliss to be found in what he had always thought of as the simple things in life – taking a shower, putting on clean clothes, eating a good meal, sleeping in a comfortable bed. It might have been only twenty-four hours since the outbreak of the virus had reached pandemic proportions, but by the time they arrived back at the research centre and he was finally able to enjoy a bit of downtime. He felt like he'd been fighting and running for days.

It was agreed that he and Purna would accompany Koritoia-Ope to the burial site at dawn the next day, while Logan and Mowen would monitor proceedings at the research centre and keep Ryder White up to date with developments. At first Logan had offered to go with Purna to give Sam more time to get over his latest zombie bite, but Sam had insisted that he'd rather be doing something than hanging around – and besides, although he didn't say so, he was pretty sure that Logan's knee would not be able to stand up to what Mowen had told them would be almost a full day's hike there and back over pretty tough terrain.

It was obvious that the same thought was in the back of Logan's mind too. Shrugging he had said, 'Well, if you *really* want to go, man, far be it from me to spoil your fun. I'm more than happy to hang around here all day. Hanging around is what I'm good at. And if I get bored I can always pass the doc a test tube or something.'

By the time they finally arrived at the burial site, Sam was beginning to regret telling Logan that he'd rather be doing something than nothing. It was still only 10 a.m., but the reflection of the sun on the pale ground was enough to make him wish he'd thought to ask Mowen if he could borrow his shades, and every outcrop of rock he touched with his hands or brushed against with his leg was red hot. He was relieved when Koritoia-Ope stopped and pointed at a carved stone arch jutting from the mouth of the cave, which was stoppered by a boulder just as tall and at least three times as wide as Sam himself.

The witch doctor unleashed a stream of words, nodding and pointing to emphasize what he was saying.

Purna nodded back at him. 'I think this is it,' she muttered to Sam.

Sam shrugged off his backpack and delved inside, grateful that he'd heeded Mowen's advice to bring plenty of water. Finding a full litre bottle he unscrewed the cap, gulped several mouthfuls and poured some over his head. He was almost surprised when the water didn't sizzle and evaporate on contact with his skin.

'Don't waste it,' said Purna. 'We've got the return journey to make yet, remember.'

'Yeah, I was thinking about that, and I figure I might catch the bus back,' said Sam.

Koritoia-Ope waited patiently while Sam and Purna rehydrated. Purna offered him the water bottle, but he simply looked at it with a mixture of suspicion, perplexity and contempt before shaking his head. Certainly he didn't seem to be affected by the heat; his skin appeared as dry and leathery now as when they had started out. Walking up to the boulder plugging the cave entrance, he made a pushing gesture with his hands.

'Great,' said Sam. 'Manual labour. Just what we need.'

'If you don't stop moaning I may be forced to break your nose,' Purna said mildly.

Sam laughed. 'Man, I bet you are one high-maintenance chick.'

'You better believe it.'

Shrugging off their backpacks and laying their guns carefully on top of them, Sam and Purna walked forward and placed their hands on the boulder. Once again the witch doctor made a pushing gesture.

'I think we get the general idea,' muttered Purna.

Gritting their teeth, Sam and Purna pushed as hard as they could. At first the rock seemed immovable, but eventually it shifted a little before settling again.

'I think we need to rock it,' Purna said.

'I been rocking it all my life,' replied Sam.

They tried again, coordinating their movements, giving the boulder a series of shoves rather than trying to shift it with one sustained effort. Sure enough, after ten seconds or so, the boulder began to rock backwards and forwards, just a little at first, and then more and more as it gained momentum. Finally, face sheened with sweat, Purna said, 'One more big one . . . Now!'

The two of them grunted and heaved, and the rock rolled aside before toppling over with a crash.

Released from the cave, a wave of air rolled out and over them, and although they welcomed its chilliness, Purna and Sam wrinkled their noses at its fetid odour. They turned to the witch doctor, who was chattering excitedly. Purna pointed at the dark cave opening. 'We can go in?' she asked.

Even though they were unsure whether Koritoia-Ope had understood the question, they took his answering nod as confirmation. Retrieving their guns and backpacks, they ventured inside, Sam first, Purna just behind him and the witch doctor bringing up the rear.

The interior of the cave was dank and cold and dark, the ground uneven. Indeed, immediately upon entering, there was a series of natural steps, which all but cut off the spill of daylight from outside and resulted in the floor level quickly dropping by several metres. Purna took a flashlight from her backpack and shone it around. The passage ahead was narrow and winding, the walls rising up from it in a curve. It made Sam think of that old story about Jonah in the belly of the whale.

'How far?' he asked the witch doctor, but the old man simply waved him on, the jangle of the bone bracelets on his wrist echoing eerily. They ventured forward, wary of stumbling and turning an ankle or worse on the slippery floor.

In fact, it wasn't long before the passage widened out into a huge cavern, the ceiling high above their heads and the walls lined with row upon row of alcoves hacked from the rock. In each of the alcoves had been laid a body, virtually all of which were now nothing more than exposed grey bones and mummified flesh, the bindings they had been lovingly wrapped in having perished to grey scraps as insubstantial as cobwebs.

Looking around, Sam said glumly, 'A couple of years, West said. But these guys look as if they've been dead for centuries.'

Koritoia-Ope, however, was already pushing past them, taking the lead, gesturing towards a black opening on the far side of the cavern. He spoke urgently, nodding all the while.

'This is obviously the oldest cavern,' Purna said. 'I

guess once this one was full, the Kuruni had to go deeper. That's where the fresher meat will be.'

'Nice,' said Sam.

They moved on, passing through the valve-like opening on the far side of the cavern into another narrow tunnel. Purna's flashlight beam slithered around the walls, highlighting the gleam of dampness and the black ridged shadows in a startling and somehow primal chiaroscuro.

After another fifty metres or so the tunnel widened into a second vast cavern, the walls of this one too resembling a vast hive for the dead. As Purna had guessed, the bodies were fresher here, as evidenced not only by the sight of them, but also the smell.

Sam felt his gorge rise and swallowed it down with an effort. Taking shallow breaths, he muttered, 'Let's get this done quick. It ain't nice in here.'

'Shh,' Purna said.

'What's up?'

She raised a hand. 'Just be quiet a minute.'

Sam stood still and listened, holding his breath. He could hear the steady drip of water, and something else too. A scratching sound.

'What's that? Rats?'

Purna's flashlight beam danced across to her left. 'It's coming from over there.'

As soon as she began to head in the direction she had indicated, Koritoia-Ope ran across and stepped angrily in front of her, blocking out her flashlight beam, shaking his head and waving his hands.

'What's with him?' said Sam.

Purna halted, looking at the agitated witch doctor

thoughtfully, but she didn't retreat. 'There's obviously something he doesn't want us to see.'

'Something alive, from the sound of it,' said Sam.

'Or some*one*,' she replied.

Koritoia-Ope stepped even closer to her, put his hands on her arms to steer her away. Purna shrugged him off.

'Get off me. What are you hiding?'

The witch doctor jabbered at her, his eyes flashing, his lips curling back to reveal teeth sharpened to points.

Stepping back from him, Purna raised her flashlight and shone it around his body on to the opposite wall. Between two rows of alcoves was an arched opening sealed not only by a stone slab but a boulder almost as big as the one at the mouth of the cave, which had been wedged up against the slab to keep it firmly in place.

'Hey!' Purna shouted, her voice echoing around the walls. 'Anyone in there?'

There was a renewed flurry of scratching.

'There *is* someone!' Purna said.

'Unless it's some kind of animal,' replied Sam.

'Knock if you can hear me,' Purna shouted.

There was a pause, and then a bout of weak but unmistakeable pounding from the other side of the slab.

Without hesitation, Purna swung her rifle from her shoulder and pointed it at Koritoia-Ope. 'Step back,' she said.

The witch doctor looked almost incredulously at the gun and started speaking again. Although they didn't know what he was saying, they could tell from his tone that he was pleading with them, trying to make them understand the folly of what they were doing.

'Back off,' Purna said more firmly, jerking the gun to indicate that he should move aside.

Koritoia-Ope looked furious. Clearly he thought she was doing something very foolish indeed. He began to rant at her again, waving his arms.

'I *said* . . . *Back. Off.*' She jabbed him with the barrel of the gun, forcing him to retreat a few steps.

Koritoia-Ope shook his head and controlled himself with an effort. When he next began to speak he did so quietly and earnestly, clearly trying to appeal to her reason.

'Sam, do you think you can roll that boulder away from the door?' she said.

'I can try,' said Sam. Hesitating, he added, 'You do think we're doing the right thing here, don't you?'

Purna flashed him a disbelieving look. 'Releasing someone who's been sealed behind a wall and left to die? You can't be serious?'

'Yeah, but what if it's like . . . a criminal or something? What if it's someone who's done something really bad?'

'That still doesn't mean they deserve this.'

'Or, OK, what if it's a custom or some kind of ritual we're messing with? You know, like the Aztecs? They had that whole Perfect Victim thing going on. Guys who *wanted* to be sacrificed to the gods, 'cos it was like this great honour.'

The pounding, though weakening now, was still continuing.

'I get the feeling that whoever's in there doesn't really want to be,' Purna said.

'OK,' Sam said, holding up his hands to concede the point. Watched by a horrified Koritoia-Ope, he walked forward and put his shoulder to the rock. Using all his strength, he heaved, and little by little was able to push the boulder away from the door. Without the boulder jamming it in place, the slab was easier to shift. It scraped, centimetre by centimetre, across the rocky ground until there was a gap big enough for someone to slip through.

Still keeping Koritoia-Ope covered with the rifle, Purna handed Sam the flashlight. He shone it into the gap between the slab and the doorframe, and his eyes widened.

'Holy shit!' he said.

Purna glanced at him. 'What do you see?'

'A girl,' said Sam. He held up his free hand in a calming gesture, clearly intended for the girl to see, and said, 'It's OK.'

'A Kuruni girl?' Purna asked.

'Maybe, but she's wearing normal clothes. Western clothes, I mean. She's been tied up and gagged.' Even as he was saying this, Sam was laying the flashlight aside, crouching down and reaching forward through the gap.

'It's OK,' Purna heard him say again, his voice slightly muffled. 'We're here to help. We ain't gonna hurt you.'

Next moment he was backing out of the gap with a young girl in his arms. She looked half-dead, her clothes torn and dirty, her face filthy and tear-streaked, her head lolling.

Gently Sam lay her down on the rock-strewn floor of the cavern and tried to untie the vines securing her wrists.

'Shit,' he said after a moment. 'This is impossible. You got a knife or somethin'?'

'In my backpack,' said Purna, one eye on the girl, one on the witch doctor.

Sam found the knife and returned to the girl. He cut away the gag around her mouth and then the vines securing her wrists and ankles. He winced at the ugly red weals caused by her constraints and hoped that the loss of circulation in her hands and feet hadn't caused her any permanent damage.

'You're OK,' he kept saying, 'you're safe now.'

Although she seemed dazed, the girl nodded.

'You understand what I'm saying?' said Sam, surprised.

'Yes,' whispered the girl.

'What's your name?'

'Yerema.'

'Hi, Yerema. I'm Sam and this here's—'

Before he could say Purna's name, there was a sudden shriek and Koritoia-Ope leaped forward. Taking advantage of Purna's momentary distraction caused by Yerema's confirmation that she could speak English, he shoved the Australian girl aside and snatched up a jagged fist-sized rock from the floor. Still shrieking, he kicked Sam hard in the side of the head with the flat of his foot, stunning him, and raised the rock, clearly intending to smash it down on the girl's head.

He was just about to deliver the first blow when two

246

shots rang out. Koritoia-Ope was hurled forward across the girl's body, ragged bullet holes opening in his back and gushing blood. The rock dropped from his hand and rolled harmlessly away into the darkness. For a few seconds there was silence.

Then Sam groaned and sat up, rubbing his head. A little dazed, he looked at the dead witch doctor sprawled across the terrified girl's body.

'Oh, good work,' he muttered.

'I had no choice,' said Purna tightly.

'You OK?' he asked Yerema.

The girl gave a single jerky nod.

Sam grabbed Koritoia-Ope's arm and hauled him off Yerema's body, then helped her to sit up. Turning his head to look at Purna he said, 'Let's just get that sample and get the hell out of here.'

Chapter 17

CAGED ANIMALS

'Hey, you're back! So how'd it go?'

Logan jumped up from his bunk as Sam walked in to the tiny room they were sharing at the research centre. Sam groaned, shrugged off his backpack and dumped it in the corner along with his gun.

'Don't ask,' he said, staggering over to his own bunk and collapsing on to it.

'Already did,' said Logan. 'So come on. Spill the beans.'

Sam's legs were humming with tiredness. He thought that if he closed his eyes he might sleep for a week. 'Well, we got the sample,' he muttered. 'Purna's giving it to West now. That's the good news.'

'Which means there's bad,' said Logan.

'Uh,' Sam grunted.

'"Uh"? What does "uh" mean? I know you've walked a million miles today, but if you don't tell me I'll just keep on asking till it drives you insane.'

Sam groaned again and shuffled halfway upright, folding his pillow to prop up his head. 'That witch doctor guy's dead,' he said.

'Shit! No way, man! What happened?'

'Purna shot him.'

Logan blinked. 'Oh-K. Any particular reason? He look at her funny or somethin'?'

Briefly Sam told Logan what had happened up at the burial site. When he had finished Logan asked, 'So who *is* this Yerema chick?'

'She was the witch doctor's daughter, if you can believe it,' said Sam. 'Her daddy was the one who sealed her in there.'

'Sounds like a hell of a family argument. She tell you why?'

'Some. Seems she decided she wanted to see the world and get an education, even though her daddy wanted her to stay home, become a wife and mother, follow the traditions, all that shit. They argued about it – a lot, I guess – till finally she just upped and left.'

'Ran away?'

'I guess so. Anyway, she told us that at first she thought she'd never be able to go back home, that if she did her daddy's vengeance would be terrible. But then once she'd been among "civilized" people for a while, and had seen how *reasonable* they could be – how they listened to you, and how sometimes, if you put over your argument well enough, you could get them to change their mind – she started to think that maybe her own people weren't as rigid and primitive as she'd thought, that maybe she *could* get her daddy to see her point of view, after all.'

'I'm guessing that was a big mistake,' said Logan.

Sam nodded. 'Not only did her daddy not listen to her, but he tried to drive the evil out of her by getting some of the guys in the village to torture and ritually rape her.'

'Jesus,' Logan said. 'That's fucking sick.'

Still nodding, Sam said, 'And the thing was, it looks like that's how all this shit started in the first place.'

'What do you mean?'

'The guys who raped Yerema? They got ill and died. But not only that – they *came back*. They were resurrected as the walking dead. Yerema said at first that her daddy saw this as a sign of forgiveness from the gods. He thought the gods were telling him the guys had been made immortal, and that they'd sent back their bodies so the rest of the village could eat their brains and become immortal too. So a whole lot of brain-eating went on, and a whole lot of people died and came back. Thing was, the Ope family and their close relatives *didn't* get sick. They contracted the virus, but it didn't change them; they just lived with it. Yerema's daddy thought this was because the gods had cursed them due to Yerema's running away an' all. So to appease them he offered her up as a sacrifice. He locked her in the tomb and left her there to die.'

'And then the plague began to spread all over the island,' said Logan.

'Pretty much. The Kuruni kept themselves to themselves most of the time, but they had occasional contact with the outside world. It must have started with a trader or something; maybe even one of the security guards here picked it up when the Kuruni came to call and took it back into the city with him.'

'Shit,' Logan said. 'Guess the girl must be feeling pretty bad knowing she's the cause of all this.'

Sam's brow wrinkled in a frown. 'It ain't her fault.'

'I know that,' Logan said. 'I just meant, if she hadn't come back to the village . . .' His voice tailed off and he smirked. 'Hey, you got the hots for her or something?'

'Give me a break,' Sam muttered. 'She's just a sweet kid is all. She don't deserve all the shit she's had to put up with.'

'Guess none of us do,' said Logan.

'Yeah, well, some of us create our own problems.'

'What's that supposed to mean?'

Sam's frown faded and he waved a hand, as if to dismiss his own comment. 'Nothing, man. I'm just tired. I was thinkin' of me more'n you. All this shit, it's made me realize how much we blame other people for our own fuck-ups. If I ever get out of this I'm really gonna straighten my life out, y'know?'

Logan nodded. 'You and me both, man.'

There was silence between them for a moment, then Sam said, 'So what's been going down here?'

Logan shrugged. 'Nothin' much. West's been analysing blood samples.'

'What about the people we rescued? They OK?'

'Not really.' Logan grimaced. 'West had to lock them up.'

Sam sat upright with a jolt. 'Why'd he do that?'

Logan hesitated, then said, 'Come see for yourself.'

Although Sam really didn't want to get vertical again, he followed Logan through the base until they came to the laboratory. West was there, talking to Purna.

'Where's Yerema?' asked Sam.

Purna turned to look at him. She looked drawn, but

she was holding it together pretty well. 'She's resting.'

'OK if I show Sam the patients?' asked Logan.

West waved a hand in a vaguely affirmative gesture. If anything, he looked more worn out than Purna did. 'No problem. But be careful.'

There was a second door on the far side of the laboratory, which until now had always remained closed. Logan punched a code into a keypad on the wall beside the door and the door opened. He led Sam down a short flight of steps and then along a dingy corridor to another door. This one too he opened by punching a number into a keypad.

'Heavy security,' said Sam.

'Yeah, except for the fact that the walls in this place are paper thin,' said Logan, rapping on the wall next to the door and producing a hollow sound that gave the impression it was constructed of nothing more substantial than thick cardboard.

Beyond the second door was a wider corridor, the left wall occupied by four cages, the bars of which stretched from floor to ceiling. Inside the cages was the handful of Kuruni people who had survived the massacre in their village. Although some were worse than others, they all looked in a pretty bad way. Curled up on mattresses on the floor, or slumped listlessly against the far wall, they were sweaty and feverish and hollow-eyed, some tossing and turning and muttering deliriously in their sleep, one or two even tensing and shuddering as if their bodies were being wracked by a series of small seizures.

'What's wrong with them?' asked Sam, though he was pretty sure he knew.

'They're displaying symptoms of the virus,' said Logan. 'It happened not long after they got here. Considering how contagious it is, and what eventually happens to the infected, it was thought it'd be safer to lock them up.'

Sam hated the thought of locking innocent people up like animals, but he nodded. 'Can't nothin' be done for them?'

'What *can* be done is *being* done. West's given them drugs to try to slow the infection down. If he develops a vaccine before it takes too much of a hold –' he gave a small, ironic whoop – 'party time.'

'What about West?' asked Sam. 'What's to stop *him* getting infected?'

Logan shrugged. 'Nothin', I guess. But maybe that's the best incentive he can have for developing a vaccine.'

Sam put his hands on the bars of the cage and leaned forward. He felt a wriggle of despair go through him. 'Shit, I thought these guys were survivors. I thought they were *immune*.'

'West says the virus is mutating all the time, constantly changing to find a way in under people's defences.'

'You make it sound like it's alive. Like it *thinks*,' said Sam.

'Maybe it does.'

'Bullshit!' Sam's response was unequivocal, but there was anxiety, even a hint of fear, in his eyes. 'If this thing's mutating all the time, what's to stop it eventually finding a way in under *our* defences?' he said.

Logan didn't answer immediately. Eventually he admitted, 'Beats me. But you gotta remember there's one big difference between us and them.' He nodded at the Kuruni.

'Which is?' asked Sam.

'They been chowing down on zombie brains for the last fuck knows how long. Closest I've got to that was the burger I ate in the airport motel the night before we flew out here.'

Sam and Logan retraced their steps back to the laboratory. When they got there, Purna turned to them and said, 'Dr West and I have been talking, and he says it's going to be at least twelve hours, but probably more like twenty-four, before he'll know whether it's possible to develop a vaccine. Therefore to save time I think we should head back to Mowen's village, pick up Jin and Xian Mei, and come back here in the morning. Then if Dr West *does* have a vaccine for us by then, we can head straight over to the prison island to meet White.'

'OK with me,' shrugged Logan.

'Me too,' said Sam with a sigh. 'So you spoken to White about this?'

Purna nodded, smiling a little as she said, 'I am nothing if not efficient. It was a terrible line, but I got the impression that White's wife was in a really bad way. By the time we get there it might already be too late.'

'Nothing we can do about that,' said Logan. 'We're all going as fast as we can. Can't hurry genius, eh, doc?'

West smiled faintly.

'So when you wanna go?' asked Sam.

'Well, Mowen says he's ready any time, so I suggest we grab a bite to eat and then head off. No time like the present, eh?' said Purna.

'Nope,' sighed Sam heavily. 'No time like the present.'

Chapter 18

NIGHT THOUGHTS

'Hey, you OK?'

Even though Sam's voice was soft, Jin still jumped, her head twisting round sharply. In the moonlight he could see the silvery gleam of tears on her cheeks, but he had already been aware of how upset she was; it was her crying that had woken him.

He was surprised the sound had penetrated his unconscious mind. He had been so tired when he had finally crashed out on a reed sleeping mat that he had thought it would take an earthquake at the very least to drag him out of his slumber. He guessed he had been more subconsciously alert than he had realized – must be a survival thing, he thought, something he had developed without knowing it over the past couple of days. He raised his hands slowly to show his intentions were harmless. When Jin didn't reply, he murmured, 'It's just . . . I heard you crying. Thought I'd come see if I could do anything.'

Jin sniffed, hitched in a breath. In a small cracked voice, she said, 'Sorry I woke you.'

'Hey, no problem,' said Sam. 'My back was kind of

aching anyway. That mat's not exactly big on the spinal support.'

This wasn't true, but Sam didn't want to make her feel any worse than she already did. When she remained silent, he glanced beyond her at the night sky. Unlike in the cities he was used to, the stars out here were incredibly bright, and the sky too was a deep, rich velvety blue, undiluted by the sodium glare from street lamps and neon signs.

'Beautiful night,' he said.

Jin made no comment.

'Hey, you want a soda or somethin'? I'm kinda thirsty. And Mowen said we could help ourselves.'

For a moment he was sure Jin would refuse, and then she gave a small tight nod. Sam re-entered the house and made his way through to the kitchen, the polished wooden floor pleasantly cool on the soles of his bare feet. Mowen's house was spacious and surprisingly homely. There were brightly coloured rugs on the floor and tribal art framed on the walls. The trader – Sam was convinced that some of that trade involved drugs and guns, as well as various other ill-gotten gains – obviously made a good living out of what he did. His house was one of the biggest in the village, and one of a minority that even had electricity.

Although Sam wouldn't exactly have *trusted* Mowen, the guy had proved a congenial enough host. No doubt motivated by the hefty financial recompense Ryder White had promised him, he had given all five of them a place to sleep, and had even cooked them a meal – a rice and sausage concoction that reminded

Sam of the jambalaya his mom made for him whenever he went home.

Entering the kitchen, he didn't bother turning on the light. Although everyone else was upstairs, he didn't want to risk waking them. He grabbed a couple of Cokes from the fridge and padded back through the house to the room where he had been sleeping. He crossed the room and slipped through the screen door on to the front porch. Jin was still sitting out on the wooden steps, a frail hunched shape in the darkness.

'Here you go,' Sam said, holding the can out to her.

She took it. 'Thanks.'

Sam indicated a space next to her on the steps. 'Mind if I sit down?'

She shrugged and he sat, popping open his can with a hiss. He gulped at the fizzy soda for a moment, relishing the sweetness, the way it made him feel instantly more alive.

'That's good,' he said, glancing at Jin, who was drinking from her own can in tiny sips.

Behind them moths the size of humming birds batted their plump dusty bodies against the softly buzzing porch light.

After a few moments of silence, Sam said, 'Weird to think how much things have changed in the past couple of days, huh? Pretty tough thing to come to terms with.'

Again, Jin gave a tiny jerk of a nod.

'It's bad enough for me, but I guess it's a hundred times worse for you, this being your home and all.'

Jin said nothing, but when Sam glanced at her he saw fresh tears spilling down her cheeks.

'Sorry,' he muttered. 'Didn't mean to upset you.'

'You didn't,' she snivelled.

'It's just –' he shrugged. 'I dunno . . . I just wanted to let you know that you're not alone. That I'm here for you – we *all* are. And that if you ever want to talk, you just have to say the word. OK?'

She sniffed and nodded.

'OK,' said Sam, and put a hand on the step beside him to push himself to his feet. 'Well, I guess I'll head back to bed and give you some space.'

He rose to his feet. She glanced up at him.

'I'd like to,' she said in a small voice.

'Huh?'

'I'd like to talk.'

'You sure?'

She hesitated, then nodded.

'Well, OK,' he said, lowering himself back down beside her. 'So what do you want to talk about?'

Jin took a long shuddering breath, and said, 'I've been thinking about Papa, and what he must be going through, and how . . . how unfair it all is.'

Sam nodded but stayed silent, not wanting to interrupt her.

'He's a good man,' Jin said. 'He's always been a good man. He looked after me when Mama died, and he always protected me, and yet because of this . . . this *sickness*, he's going to become like the rest of them out there. A monster, feasting on the flesh of the living . . .'

She tailed off, slumping forward, her head drooping into her hand, as if vocalizing the thought had proved too much for her. After a moment, however, she continued, 'I know good people get sick and die, or have

259

accidents, but this is just ... just *wrong*. It makes people into something disgusting, something to be feared. It *uses* people, and it ... it ...' She tailed off, unable to find the words to fully express the horror and revulsion she felt.

Sam had never had kids, had never even *thought* about having kids, but right now he wanted to put a fatherly arm round Jin, to give her the comfort and reassurance she so obviously needed. He thought about doing it and then decided that maybe it wouldn't be such a good idea. After what had happened to her with those three guys, she had (not surprisingly) become both jumpy and withdrawn, and was now no doubt wary and suspicious of people's motives towards her, especially motives that involved any kind of physical proximity. He didn't want to make things worse by doing something she might take the wrong way. So he just sat, a foot or so between them, and tried, stumblingly, to put his reassurance into words.

'I guess what you gotta remember is that those things ... the infected, I mean ... are not the people they once were. Those people are gone, dead ... and whatever makes us *us* –' he tapped his chest to emphasize his point – 'by which I mean our soul, or our essence, or whatever ... has shipped out, passed on, gone to wherever we go to when we die. And the things that are left ... the bodies ... they're just puppets for the virus. They ain't people. They're just things. They don't feel love or pain. They don't find things funny or beautiful or ugly. They're just ... hunger. That's all they are. Just hunger and primitive instinct. And if your papa becomes one of them . . . well, that ain't your papa any more. That's just something that's using your papa's skin like . . . like a set of clothes. Your papa's somewhere else. Somewhere good.'

Sam got the feeling that he hadn't expressed himself too well. He wanted to ask Jin if she understood what he was trying to say. But before he could, she said, 'I used to believe in goodness. I used to believe that although there was bad in the world, there was a God up in heaven who would eventually make things right, would eventually reward us. But now I feel stupid for being so . . . so naïve. I mean, what kind of God would allow such suffering? I know I'm being selfish. I know it's easy to keep believing in God when the bad stuff is happening to someone else. But . . . but it's still how I feel, and I can't help that. I used to have faith, and now it's gone . . .'

She began to sob again, long and hard this time. Helplessly Sam watched her, wanting to tell her not to cry, that everything would be all right, but knowing how false that would sound. Eventually he mumbled, 'Hey, you want a hug?' And then he added hastily, 'No pressure. It's just . . . well, it's hard to stand by and watch someone cry and not do anything about it, y'know.'

For a moment she didn't respond, then she nodded and leaned towards him. Sam put his arm round her shoulders, aware of how sparrow-like and delicate she was. He felt furious and sickened at the thought of the three guys in the police station taking advantage of her physical frailty, and at the thought of how terrified and helpless she must have been.

For a while they just sat there, Jin weeping, Sam wishing he could protect her from stuff that had already happened.

Eventually her sobs subsided and she became quieter, calmer. Sam was beginning to wonder whether she'd cried herself to sleep when she said, 'I don't think I'll ever get over what those men did to me.'

Not wishing to offer hollow platitudes, Sam said, 'Maybe you won't ever forget it, but one day you'll learn to live with it. These things just take time.'

'You don't know what it was like,' Jin said, a hint of sharpness creeping into her voice.

Sam shook his head. 'That's true. But I've read about women who've been through the same thing. And they all say there comes a time when you decide that you're not gonna let the bad guys ruin your life any more, that you're not gonna let them win. 'Cos they're not worth it, and you are.'

'They laughed when they were doing . . . what they did to me,' whispered Jin. 'They made me feel like nothing.'

'Try not to think about how they made you feel,' Sam said. 'Try not to believe it. It's *those* guys who're nothin', not you. What they think don't count.'

Jin lapsed into silence again. Then she whispered almost guiltily, 'I'm glad they're dead.'

'I'm glad too,' said Sam. 'People like that don't deserve to live.'

'Problem is,' said Jin. 'They're not *really* dead, are they?'

'They looked pretty dead to me,' Sam said softly.

'But if you mean you're worried they'll come back—'

'No, that's not it.' She sighed and said, 'I mean there's plenty more like them out there. Bad people. People who don't care how much they hurt other people. Who even *enjoy* hurting other people.'

'Yeah, they're out there,' Sam said. 'I'm not gonna insult you by saying they ain't. But what you gotta remember is that there's plenty good people too. A whole lot *more* good people than bad, in fact. Whatever we've seen these past couple days, there's still plenty of love out there in the world.'

'Not here, though,' she whispered.

'Hey, thanks,' said Sam with a smile.

'No, I don't mean that. I mean . . . love seems to be abandoning Banoi, and fear and hate is taking over.'

'Yeah,' said Sam softly. 'That's how it looks, all right.'

They sat in companionable silence for another thirty seconds or so, listening to the carefree chirrup of unseen night-bugs.

Then Sam asked, 'So, you coming with us tomorrow?'

There had been a kind of unspoken understanding that, after calling at the lab, all five of them would be heading over to the prison island with Mowen the following morning. But Sam had wondered earlier whether Jin was happy just to go along with the plan. Banoi was her home, after all. She had more of a stake in this place than the rest of them did.

She shrugged. 'I guess.'

'You thought about what you might do . . . after?'

She gave a small grunt. It might have been a

humourless laugh, but it could just as easily have been prompted by a stab of pain in her belly. 'How can I? Everything I have – *had* – is here. Out there –' she waved a hand to indicate the wider world – 'I might as well just not exist.'

'Well, like I say,' mumbled Sam, 'you ain't alone. We'll look out for you – me, Xian Mei, Purna, even Logan. You need a place to stay, money, we'll fix you up, you don't have to worry about that.'

'Thanks,' said Jin. 'I appreciate it.' She yawned. 'I suppose I ought to try and get some sleep.'

'You and me both,' said Sam. 'Another long day tomorrow.'

They stood up. Before heading inside, Jin put a hand on Sam's arm. 'Thanks for not lying to me,' she said.

'Lying to you?'

'By telling me that everything will be all right. Because things are a long way from all right, aren't they? If this infection spreads, things may never be all right again.'

Sam looked at her for a long moment, his face grim.

'Ain't *that* the truth,' he muttered finally.

Chapter 19

THE SURVIVOR

'Something's wrong.'

Logan looked at Purna in surprise. 'You got spidey senses or something? Looks quiet enough to me.'

'That's what I mean,' said Purna. 'Where are the guards?'

From the far side of the clearing they all stared across at the high-security fence and the blocky grey buildings beyond it.

'Maybe they're on a break?' suggested Xian Mei unconvincingly.

Purna shot her a withering look. 'All at the same time?'

'OK, people,' Logan said almost wearily, 'lock and load.'

Guns at the ready, the six of them moved across the clearing, scanning the surrounding jungle for anything unusual.

Purna's verdict was not based purely on the lack of guards. She had tried calling West that morning, without success. It had been decided before they had set out for Mowen's village yesterday that if West's overnight attempts to develop a vaccine proved unsuccessful, Mowen would take Purna, Sam and the rest straight over to the prison island without them first making a pointless detour back to the research facility.

However, West's unavailability had meant they had *had* to come here first, after all; if it was even *possible* that a vaccine had been developed then they couldn't afford not to. Purna knew she would be angry if it turned out they had had a wasted journey, but it probably wasn't West's fault. The communications network had not exactly been reliable these past couple of days, and although the phone at the research facility had *seemed* just to ring out over and over again without reply, that didn't necessarily mean nobody could be bothered to pick up.

They were about five metres away from the security fence when Sam said, 'Aw, shit.'

'What is it, big guy?' asked Logan.

'Purna's right. We got trouble.'

Moving up to the fence, he pointed through the vertical metal slats to a patch of grass several metres away. Lying in the grass, among several pools of blood, was an AK 47.

'Must've been a prison breakout,' said Logan.

'Where do you think they are now?'

'Inside, I guess.'

'Maybe they wandered off into the jungle,' said Xian Mei, looking around nervously.

Purna shook her head. 'The infected don't climb, and there's no other way out.'

'So what's our next move?' asked Sam. 'We go in there after them?'

'Don't see that we've got much choice,' Purna replied. 'But we're not going in there after *them*. We're going in there looking for the vaccine.'

'If there is one,' Xian Mei whispered, as if to herself.

Purna pulled a face, as if that was a possibility she didn't want to consider.

'We also need to look for survivors,' said Logan. 'Could be they've locked themselves in somewhere the infected can't get to them.'

Purna nodded.

'So how we gonna do this?' asked Sam. 'Who's going in?'

After some discussion, it was decided that Purna, Sam, Logan and Xian Mei would check out the facility while Mowen and Jin would wait outside the perimeter fence with the backpacks of provisions they had all brought along with them.

'Keep your rifle ready, just in case,' Purna advised Mowen.

He looked at her as if she had insulted him. 'I always ready.'

'And look after Jin,' added Sam, glancing at the girl.

Mowen nodded.

Without guards to warn them off, scaling the security fence was relatively easy. They all climbed over at the same time, while Mowen covered them in case of a sudden unexpected appearance by one or more of the infected. Purna was the first to reach the top of the fence and to land, cat-like, on the ground inside the compound. Seconds later they were all inside, moving forward quickly but warily in a tight formation, checking in every direction as they did so.

The first door they came to was slightly ajar and had a bloody handprint smeared across it, close to the ground, as if someone had tripped and had put out a hand to break their fall. There was more blood on the grass around the door, and a *lot* more just inside the building. From the streaks and spatters on the walls and floor, it looked as though a struggle had taken place, during which the wounded victim had been dragged at least several metres. After the long bloody smear, however, there was nothing but a trail of red spots meandering up the corridor.

Purna stared at the marks for a few seconds, then said, 'Looks as though someone was attacked outside and then the fight spilled over into here.' She pointed at the spots. 'I'm guessing the victim was infected himself and after lying around for a while, eventually stood up and wandered off down the corridor in search of food.'

'If everyone's infected, how many people are we talking about?' asked Xian Mei.

'Couple of dozen,' Purna estimated.

'That's six each,' said Logan. 'No problem.'

'That depends whether they come one at a time or all together,' said Sam.

The words were barely out of his mouth when a trio of dark shapes appeared at the end of the corridor. One of the shapes let out a hideous caterwauling screech and then all three started to run towards them.

Sam barely had time to register that one was a security guard and the other two were Kuruni tribesmen before the shooting began. The corridor reverberated to the deafening rattle of rifle fire, the attacking zombies throwing up their arms in a jerky macabre dance as they were ripped apart.

Within seconds it was over and the infected were lying in a torn heap, blood and lumps of matter trickling down the pock-marked walls.

'Jeez,' said Logan, a slight tremor in his voice, 'that was—'

'Look out!' screamed Xian Mei.

Sam and Logan jerked up their guns in unison. Almost too late Sam realized there had not been three of the infected in the group that had attacked them, but four. The one at the back, a small Kuruni child no older than five or six, had managed to sneak in under the radar. It had evidently escaped unharmed from the hail of bullets, not only because it had been shielded by the three adults but also because most of them had passed over its head.

It came at them now, though, fast as a panther cub but far more deadly. It leaped over the mound of dead zombies and was almost upon them before they could react. Purna raised her rifle and fired just as the child launched itself through the air. The shot ripped the left half of its head and face away in a welter of blood and brains. The impact spun the child round in mid-air, Logan and Xian Mei jumping back as its body hit the wall close to them with a wet smack and slithered to the ground.

'Stay alert,' Purna snapped, barely giving the crumpled body of the child a second glance. 'Don't let your guard down for a moment.'

The rest of them nodded and they moved forward, Sam holding his breath against the rank smell as they cautiously stepped over the slowly spreading pool of blood seeping from under the tangled bodies of the four zombies. He had thought the research facility was cramped before, but now it seemed positively claustrophobic. The ceilings were too low and there were too many intersections; the grey walls seemed to suck in light despite the stark glare of the overheads, and to cast too many shadows.

As they headed for the laboratory, more of the infected suddenly appeared from a door in a corridor to their left. There were six of them this time, and the reflected light made them appear gimlet-eyed, which seemed to bestow them with an eerie, savage intelligence. At their head was a security guard, hunched over like an ape. His blood-streaked upper teeth were bared in a snarl, and the entire left side of his face was an oozing red mask, due to the fact that one of the infected had clearly taken hold of his top lip and wrenched upwards, ripping most of the flesh away. Without eyelids his left eye seemed to bulge and glare as it fixed upon them. Then, snarling and screeching, the six-strong group began to blunder and lope towards them.

Not exactly calmly, but certainly with an efficiency and precision acquired both through practice and necessity, Purna, Sam, Logan and Xian Mei stood their ground and opened fire. The air turned red as the heads of the infected were punctured, shattered, torn apart. The first two zombies – the security guard and a Kuruni tribesman – went down and the others scrambled over them and were themselves cut down in their turn. Again the whole thing was over in less than a minute, the corridor echoing with the din and stink of battle.

Ten down, Sam thought, then something crashed into the back of him, knocking him to the ground.

He fell forward, landing on his gun. Although the thing at his back was a screeching, slashing dervish of activity, his first fearful thought was that the gun might go off with him lying on top of it. If that happened, then the cartridges would rip into his body like a series of minor explosions, causing untold – and almost certainly lethal – damage. Above him he was aware of shouting, running, of people crowding around him. The animal-like snarling was right by his ear, then something slashed across his cheek with a stinging shock.

Though he was pinned to the ground with a weight on his back, Sam did his best to shake his attacker from his body. He bucked and wriggled, pistoned back his elbow and felt it connect with something solid and fleshy.

All at once he was aware of the weight being lifted from him, of the spitting and snarling retreating from close by his ear to somewhere further away. Free to move, he rolled to one side, grabbed his gun and pulled it out from under his body. Then he rolled right over on to his back and sat up, pointing his gun at where he judged his attacker to be.

It was a young infected Kuruni woman, blood smeared around her mouth and clogging the nails of her hooked fingers. Xian Mei and Logan had pulled her off his back and were now wrestling with her, holding on to an arm each, trying to evade her snapping jaws. The tribeswoman was writhing and thrashing like an angry snake, and they were clearly finding it difficult to maintain a grip. Puffing out air to clear his head, Sam took aim and pulled the trigger.

The top of the woman's head disintegrated, spattering all three of them with blood and brains. Instantly the zombie went limp, falling back against the wall and sliding to the floor as Logan and Xian Mei let go of her arms.

Grimacing with distaste, Logan brushed clots of blood and gobbets of brain from his face and clothes. 'Way to go, buddy,' he said.

'Sorry,' said Sam, using his sleeve to wipe blood off his forehead.

'Are you OK?' asked Xian Mei.

Sam fingered the slash on his face. He would have an impressive scar there once it healed. 'I guess so. Bruised my ribs when I landed on my gun.'

Purna stepped forward, offered Sam a hand and hauled him to his feet. 'Making a habit of the old hand-to-hand combat, aren't you?' she said with a grim smile.

Sam snorted a humourless laugh. 'Guess I'm just the tastiest of us all.'

'Yeah, you know what? I'm not even remotely jealous,' said Logan.

Suddenly Xian Mei held up a hand. 'Listen everyone.'

They all froze and raised their heads. Faintly they heard someone shouting for help.

'That's Yerema,' said Sam.

'She must have heard the gunfire,' said Logan.

'Guess we'd better go rescue her,' said Sam, and raised his eyebrows at Purna. 'That's getting to be a habit too.'

'It came from that direction,' said Xian Mei, pointing.

'The laboratory,' Purna confirmed. 'If Yerema's still alive, then that's probably where the rest of the infected will be. Remember everyone, there are potentially still around a dozen of them in here with us, so stay alert and be careful.'

Logan gave her a mock-salute, earning himself a disapproving glance, and they moved towards the laboratory.

As they approached the door they could see it was open. Purna put a finger to her lips and crept forward, the others a step or two behind. Yerema was still calling for help, though now that they were right outside the lab they could tell she was still a couple of rooms away. Sam guessed she must be in the cell area and that she had probably locked herself into one of the cages. He wondered if she was the only survivor, and what had happened to West.

As soon as they entered the laboratory his question was answered. West had been torn apart; there were gnawed pieces of him scattered all over the room. His legs, still clad in designer jeans and Timberland boots, were up against the far wall. There was one of his chewed arms, a still-ticking watch around its wrist, on the counter, and a torso, partly clad in a red and black checked shirt like a huge fleshy cushion, in the middle of the floor, trailing guts like stuffing. His head was resting against one of the now-empty animal cages, his surprisingly unmarked face turned towards them. His mouth was open in a frozen scream, his pale blue eyes glaring at them accusingly.

You caused this, he seemed to be saying. *You brought them here. I'm dead because of you.*

The floor was awash with West's blood and the white walls were covered with it. Some of the equipment had been swept to the floor and smashed, and all the animal cages were open and their occupants gone – eaten by zombies, Sam wondered, or fled back into the jungle?

The door on the far side of the laboratory was also open and, as Sam had expected, it was from beyond here that Yerema's voice was coming. There were other sounds in there with Yerema too – grunts and snarls and dull metallic thumps.

'Yerema!' Sam shouted.

There was a high-pitched gasp. 'Sam? Is that you?'

'Yeah. Listen, you OK in there?'

As he had expected, she shouted, 'I'm locked in one of the cages. The infected are throwing themselves against the bars, trying to get in.'

'How many of them are down there with you?' Purna shouted.

'I don't know. About . . . twelve?'

Purna nodded; it was what she had expected. 'Are there any close to the door?'

'No. They're all trying to get at me.'

Turning to the others, Purna said, 'I'm going in there to draw them out. I want you three to get them in a

274

cross-fire as they emerge – but just do me one favour, OK?'

'What's that?' asked Xian Mei.

Purna smiled faintly. 'Try not to be too trigger-happy. Give me time to get clear before you start firing.'

They took up their positions, Logan to the left of the door, Sam in the middle and Xian Mei to the right. Unhesitatingly Purna passed through the open doorway into the cell area, and they heard her descending the steps and striding determinedly along the corridor towards the second door at the far end, her footsteps fading as she got further away. For a minute or so there was silence, then they heard her shouting defiantly, 'Hey, you lot! Why don't you pick on someone your own size?'

The snarls and grunts of the infected changed pitch, suddenly becoming more urgent, more eager. Then they heard Purna's rapidly approaching footsteps, in the wake of which came the bestial clamour of pursuit. The footsteps grew louder, reaching a crescendo as Purna clattered up the steps. She burst through the doorway, almost slipping in West's blood before regaining her balance.

'They're right . . . behind me . . .' she gasped.

She had barely made it out of the line of fire before the infected were spilling into the room. As soon as they appeared, Logan, Sam and Xian Mei started firing, cutting down men, women and children alike. Blood, flesh and bone flew everywhere. In less than a minute the doorway was clogged with bodies. Yet still the infected came, uncaringly clambering over their fallen comrades, stamping on their faces and slipping in their blood, in their desperate desire for warm, living meat.

As the firing continued and the last of the infected collapsed on top of the tangle of once-human bodies, so the wave of blood leaking and spurting from dozens of wounds and ruptures fanned out across the floor. Grimly Logan, Sam and Xian Mei continued to stand their ground as the blood tide lapped against their boots, oozing around them like something alive.

Finally, however, it was over, and the guns fell silent. Sam, enervated, felt his arms droop to his sides, that sense of numbness, of unreality, of faint self-loathing creeping over him again. He shuddered, shaking it off, and stepped backwards out of the blood, the soles of his boots making a sticky squelching sound as he did so. From what seemed like the bowels of the earth, Yerema's voice called out, 'What's happening up there?'

Sam tried to reply, but for a second his voice wouldn't come. It was Purna who answered, 'We're all OK.'

'What about the infected?' asked Yerema.

Purna hesitated, as if searching for some way of describing what had happened without making it sound as ugly and brutal as it had been. Finally, however, she simply said, 'They're dead. We got them all.'

'So I'm the last then,' said Yerema, a hint of disbelief creeping into her voice. 'The last of the Kuruni.'

For the next few minutes the four of them occupied themselves with the grim task of dragging aside the sprawled and mangled bodies blocking the doorway.

No one spoke, and by the time they were done their hands were gloved in red and their clothes were once again stained and stinking with zombie blood.

Though Yerema was grateful to be rescued and hugged each of them in turn, she was not jubilant, recognizing that theirs was a hollow victory.

'So what happened?' asked Purna.

Yerema shook her head. 'It was one of the guards. A Kuruni child was sick, having seizures, so he opened the cage. Either he hadn't been fully informed about the virus or he simply didn't appreciate how dangerous it was. Anyway, he was attacked and the infected got free. I guess the other guards must have been reluctant to use their guns at first – they probably thought the infected would respond to threats. By the time they realized their mistake, it would have been too late.'

'But you were smart enough to lock yourself in one of the cages,' said Xian Mei.

To their surprise Yerema shook her head. 'I didn't lock *myself* in,' she said. 'Dr West locked me in earlier.'

'West?' exclaimed Logan. 'Why?'

'He wanted to use me as a guinea pig, give me a shot of the vaccine he had developed to see how it affected the dormant virus in my system. But I didn't want him to. I thought it was too dangerous. He'd admitted earlier that if he didn't get it right the vaccine could have the opposite effect and kick-start the virus into fighting back. He tried to inject me by force, but I knocked the hypodermic out of his hand and stamped on it. So he dragged me down to the cells and locked me in, telling me that once he'd prepared another hypodermic he'd be back. But a few minutes later the guard arrived to feed the prisoners and made the mistake of opening the cage, and that's when everything started to go wrong. The infected got out and killed everyone and then they came back for me. I didn't know what had happened to West until now. Despite everything, I was kind of hoping he'd managed to get away.'

'So he *did* develop a working vaccine before he died?' said Purna.

'That's what he told me. But I don't know how safe or effective it was. I know he hadn't properly tested it.'

'Even so, it's the best we've got,' said Purna, looking around the laboratory. There was plenty of equipment still intact on the work surfaces, but nothing that jumped out at her, nothing obvious.

'So where is it?' she asked.

Yerema shook her head. 'I've no idea.'

'We've got to find it,' said Purna firmly. 'We can't leave until we do.'

Chapter 20

ENEMY MINE

'Go to the left.'

Xian Mei relayed the instruction to Mowen as the hand-held mine detector, not much bigger than a TV remote control, began to beep insistently. The detector consisted of a mostly black display screen, which depicted Mowen's boat as a slowly moving white dot. Whenever they got close to one of the hidden under-water mines surrounding the prison island, a flashing red dot would appear, accompanied by a high-pitched beep. The closer they were to the mine, the more frantic both the flashing and the beeping would become. Mowen had told them that he sometimes ran errands for the prison governor and had been given the device to enable him to move safely through the waters between Banoi and the smaller island a couple of miles offshore. He didn't elaborate on the nature of the errands, and no one asked.

Because they had to be almost on top of a mine before the detector picked up its signal, progress through the water was slow. For a while it seemed that the black island jutting from the sea, dominated by its forbidding grey tower like the domain of an evil sorcerer in a fairy story, wasn't getting any closer. Not that Sam, for one, minded at all. Despite their destination, he was just glad to be heading away from Banoi and to be breathing fresh air untainted by the stench of corruption. It was a glorious day, the eggshell-blue of the sky reflected in the deeper blue of the calm and glittering ocean. Odd to think that, like Banoi itself, the sea's beauty concealed such deadly danger lurking beneath its surface.

Inevitably, however, they *did* eventually draw closer to the island, the jagged black rocks that fringed the shoreline like the beckoning claws of some vast leviathan. The island itself, which rose to a plateau on which the prison was built, appeared to swell from the ocean. As Mowen slowly and skilfully steered his boat through the rocks towards a small inlet, Purna dialled Ryder White's number.

'We're here,' she said when her call was answered. 'How do we get in?'

Reception was poor, a mass of white noise through which White's voice could barely be heard. 'Climb over elec . . . fence. I'll cut off . . . tricity supply for an hour once you're up on the plateau . . . give you chance to—'

A prolonged burst of static drowned out his next words. Purna winced and held the phone away from her ear. 'I'm losing you, White,' she shouted. 'What did you say?'

For a moment there was simply more white noise, then it died away a little and Purna heard White's voice, faint and distorted, rising up through it again.

'. . . make for Sector Seven. I repeat, Sector Seven. But be care . . . fected everywhere.'

'Got it,' said Purna. 'See you soon.'

She rang off and told the others what White had said. They drifted into shore and Mowen cut the engine. Before them, clear water lapped gently at a stony, sloping beach. Beyond that rose a gentle cliff face, levelling out to the plateau perhaps thirty metres above. Ringing the plateau was a four-metre-tall security fence topped with metal spikes. Signs at five-metre intervals depicted a skull beneath a zig-zagging lightning bolt, white on red. Though the fence was high above them, they could hear it humming faintly, and through it they could just make out vague dark shapes wandering aimlessly about – the infected with nothing to attack.

Purna sighed. Her life seemed to have boiled down to little more than a succession of obstacles, and here were more of them. She looked at her fellow survivors – a patched-up, motley bunch of strangers, who in the past couple of days had been through hell, both collectively and individually, and who had been forced to mould themselves into a ruthless fighting unit in order to stay alive. She fervently hoped that their ordeal was now, finally, coming to an end, that soon they would be able to return to their old lives and (as much as they were able) put this terrible episode behind them. However, in her heart of hearts she suspected that the outcome would *not* be quite as simple and straightforward as that, and that even if everything *did* eventually work out, there were still battles ahead to be fought and won.

They disembarked, each of them carrying a weapon and a backpack of provisions. She, Sam, Logan and Xian Mei still had the assault rifles they had liberated from the police station and in whose use they had become reasonably proficient over the past couple of days. The younger girls, Jin and Yerema, each carried Smith and Wesson semi-automatic pistols. Since her terrible ordeal in the police station, Jin had abandoned her pacifist principles and seemed to have accepted that the only way she would survive was to arm herself and be prepared to fight. Although Purna was glad the girl's attitude had changed, she wouldn't have wished the cause of it on her worst enemy, and even now she kept going over and over the episode in her mind, wishing she had made better decisions.

Once they were ashore, Mowen raised a hand in farewell. 'I go now.'

Logan stepped forward and shook the trader's hand. 'Take it easy, man,' he said. 'Thanks for everything.'

Mowen nodded, implacable as ever, his eyes still hidden behind his shades. 'Good luck,' he said.

'You too,' said Sam, also shaking Mowen's hand, while Xian Mei, Jin and Yerema smiled and nodded in agreement. Purna, however, simply gave a single curt nod, acknowledging Mowen's help, but knowing that the relationship between themselves and the trader was fragile and temporary at best. It was based – on Mowen's part – not on mutual respect and a genuine willingness to help, but purely on monetary gain.

They watched Mowen's boat chug slowly away, then they turned back to the matter at hand. Purna led the way, as she so often did, as they trudged towards the gently sloping cliff face and began to climb.

It was neither a long nor particularly arduous journey to the summit, but the heat of the sun and the weight of their backpacks were more than enough to sap their strength. By the time they reached the plateau they were each panting and sweating and grateful for a drink. As they sipped water and looked through the buzzing electric fence at the drearily ominous prison building across the two-hundred-metre square expanse of a flat and dusty exercise yard, those infected who had been milling outside began – based on their physical ability – to shamble or run or crawl towards them.

'Here we go again,' Sam said almost wearily and unshouldered his rifle. At the same moment the low humming of the electric fence ceased.

'White's turned it off. That gives us an hour,' said Purna.

'How did he know we were here?' asked Jin.

Purna pointed silently up at one of many CCTV cameras mounted high enough on the prison walls that they couldn't be damaged or disabled. A second later the first of the infected threw himself against the security fence with a metallic crash.

He was a big shaven-headed man with a rearing cobra tattoo on the side of his neck. Like most of the zombies here, he was wearing orange prison overalls. To everyone's surprise it was Yerema who raised her pistol and shot the man in the head. He fell like a sack of cement, face turning slack and almost baby-like as the savagery abruptly went out of him.

'You done that before?' Purna asked, regarding the girl shrewdly.

Yerema shook her head, trying not to look shocked at her own actions. 'No, but I knew that to survive I was going to have to kill. And I also knew that the more I put it off the harder it would be.'

Purna nodded in grim approval and tried not to flash a knowing look at Jin.

'If it helps, try not to think of it as killing,' said Sam. 'Try to think of it as switching off a dangerous machine. Whoever that guy was, he died a while ago. All you've done is stopped the virus from using his body.'

Yerema nodded her thanks as more of the infected hurled themselves against the security fence. They rammed their faces between the bars, growling and snapping like vicious but frustrated guard dogs.

No one needed to be told that the creatures would have to be dealt with before the six of them could even *think* of climbing the fence into the prison. Like kids at a shooting gallery, they silently arranged themselves into a line, raised their guns and began to pick off the infected one by one.

There were around sixty of them, maybe more, but it was over in a matter of minutes. As soon as the last of the infected had fallen, Purna, Sam and the rest lowered their weapons and moved further along the fence, stopping at a spot far enough away from the carnage that they wouldn't be trying to avoid landing in the spreading pool of blood when they climbed over.

Purna went first, scaling the fence with ease, then

Sam and Logan gave the other three girls a leg up before tackling the barrier themselves. Both men gritted their teeth as the effort of climbing stretched and tensed the muscles in their arms and legs, making their various bites – Logan's in his shoulder, Sam's in his calf – throb with pain. However, each spurred on by the other's determination, they eventually made it over.

As soon as they began to hurry across the open ground towards the prison building, a chorus of different sounds erupted into life. For one crazy moment Sam thought they had set off some kind of alarm, then he realized the noise was coming from *them*, and was the combined ringtones of their cell phones.

'What the fuck?' said Logan, looking down at his pocket as if a scorpion had just crawled out of it.

Purna, however, already had her cell phone in her hand. 'Yep?' she snapped without breaking stride.

The others could hear nothing but the crackle of white noise and the hint of a tinny voice.

'OK, thanks,' Purna said before breaking the connection and slipping the phone back into her pocket.

'White?' guessed Sam.

Purna nodded.

'What did he say?' Xian Mei asked.

'He said to move to our left and that the first door we come to should be entrance number 4. Once we're there he'll unlock it for us.'

Sam glanced up and around. 'I don't like the thought of being watched,' he said. 'It gives me the creeps.'

'If it makes our task easier then personally I'm all for it,' said Purna.

They moved quickly across to the building and followed the line of the wall until they came to an alcove that resembled a short, high-sided alleyway. At the end of the alleyway was a grey metal door with a black number 4 stencilled on it, mounted above which was a security camera in a protective cage. As soon as they came within sight of the camera, a series of hefty *chunking* sounds suggested that several heavy-duty locks were being disengaged. With barely a glance at the overhead camera, Purna moved to the door, shoved down the handle and pushed.

It groaned open slowly and heavily like the door of a bank vault. Beyond was a short featureless corridor, the floor made of some black vinyl-like substance, the bare stone walls painted an institutional cream. At the end of this corridor was another metal door with another security camera mounted above it. Again there was a series of heavy *chunking* sounds.

'Open sesame,' murmured Sam.

'Anyone else get the feeling this is almost *too* easy?' asked Logan.

Purna shot him a stern look. 'Don't get complacent. White said the place was swarming with the infected.'

'I'm suspicious, not complacent,' said Logan.

'The man's only helping us because he's desperate for the vaccine,' said Xian Mei.

At the back of the group, Yerema called, 'Shall we close the outside door or leave it open?'

Purna considered a moment, then said, 'Leave it

open. It makes us more vulnerable to attack, but on balance I'd rather have an escape route.'

Cautiously she opened the second door. Beyond was a large dining room, containing ugly, functional rows of tables and chairs that had been bolted to the floor. Along the left-hand wall was a line of stainless-steel serving units, which at meal times no doubt contained tin trays of gristly meat, overcooked vegetables and sloppy mashed potatoes – or whatever the Banoi prison equivalent was.

All was quiet here too, though on the far side of the room were two sets of barred metal doors, beyond which could faintly be heard an uncoordinated chorus of echoing thumps and clangs accompanied by low groans.

'Happy now?' Purna said to Logan as the two of them moved cautiously across the room.

'Delirious,' muttered Logan.

'Let's call White,' said Sam, 'see what we're—'

Before he could finish his sentence, one of the girls behind him screamed. He, Logan and Purna spun round, guns jerking up instinctively. Xian Mei too was turning to face the door through which they had entered, as was Yerema. What they saw was Jin, who had fallen back to the rear of the group, and a black-bearded man in prison overalls. With his left hand the man had twisted Jin's arms behind her back, causing her to drop her gun, and was now holding her in front of him like a human shield. In his right hand he held a large and very sharp-looking carving knife, the blade pressed against Jin's throat.

'Hey!' Sam shouted angrily and started forward, but

halted when the man simply tightened his grip on Jin. At the same time he nicked the skin of her throat just enough to draw both blood and a high-pitched sob of terror from her. Purna raised a hand to indicate that everyone, including the man himself, should stay calm.

The prisoner licked his lips and grinned nastily, clearly relishing the fact that – despite being armed with nothing more than a knife – he was fully in charge of this situation.

'Drop your fucking guns and back off,' he sneered, 'or I'll cut your friend open like a fucking pig.'

288

Chapter 21

HOSTAGE SITUATION

'Look, let's talk about this.'

Purna's voice was calm, her manner relaxed. She allowed the barrel of her gun to droop a little and glanced casually at Sam, Logan and Xian Mei to indicate they should do the same.

By contrast the man looked twitchy, nervous. Beads of sweat stood out on his forehead, and the knife was clenched so tightly in his right hand that the points of his knuckles were white with tension. He gave another clenched-teeth grin and shook his head.

'Don't need to talk,' he said. 'You just need to drop your fucking guns or I swear I'll kill her.'

Purna sighed. 'You know we can't do that.'

The prisoner stared at her bug-eyed. 'You can and you fucking will.'

'See, the thing is,' said Purna reasonably, 'if we let you have our guns, what's to stop you killing us all anyway? What's your name?'

The question seemed to throw the man. 'What do you want to know that for?' he snapped.

'Just trying to be friendly. I think we can help each other out here.'

'Don't need your help,' the man said, his voice high-pitched with tension. Suddenly he screamed at them, *'Now drop your fucking weapons or I'll kill the bitch!'*

'Whoa,' said Sam. 'Take it easy, man.' Moving slowly he placed his gun on the floor. 'There you go.'

Purna glanced at him, tight-lipped. 'Sam, what are you doing?'

Sam looked across at her angrily and gestured towards the shaking and clearly terrified Jin. 'Don't you think she's been through enough?'

'We've *all* been through a lot,' said Purna. 'This isn't the way to do it.'

Ignoring her, Sam said to the man, 'OK, buddy, here's the deal. We lay down our weapons and back off a little, and you let Jin go. Then we talk. What do you say?'

The man stared at him, eyes narrowed, suspicious.

'I'm guessing you're trapped in here because of those things out there?' Sam pointed towards the thuds and groans coming from behind the barred metal doors on the far side of the room.

'Keep talking,' the man said.

'We can help you with that. We can kill those fuckers for you. How you think we got in here in the first place?'

'In fact,' said Xian Mei, 'you can leave right now if you want to. The doors are open and the yard is clear. The infected that were out there are all dead.'

The man shot her a contemptuous look. 'Yeah, and go where? There's an electric fence out there and then

290

two miles of mined ocean, if you hadn't fucking noticed.'

'So what's *your* plan?' asked Logan.

The man hesitated, then to their surprise the question was answered by a voice on the far side of the room.

'I'm thinking maybe we should hear *your* plan first.'

They turned to see a man rising from behind the row of steel serving units off to their left. Another prisoner, this man was tall and skinny, his inquisitive fox-like face and dark-framed spectacles giving him a studious air. In contrast to his colleague with the knife he seemed calm and composed, though Sam got the immediate impression that beneath his cool exterior his mind was working away, that even now he was assessing the situation and how best to turn it to his advantage.

The man with the knife gaped at the skinny guy. 'What the fuck you doing? What you showing yourself for?'

The skinny guy shot the knife-man an almost dismissive look. 'I thought an exchange of information might be mutually beneficial.'

'But we coulda got their guns!' protested the knife-man.

The skinny guy smirked and jerked his head at Purna. 'That one would never have given up her gun. She's too pragmatic for that. And too ruthless.' He gave a thin smile. 'I'm right, aren't I?'

Instead of answering his question, Purna asked, 'Are there just the two of you?'

The man smiled again, as if this was not a tense

stand-off between two groups of desperate people, but simply a game of strategy. Glancing down to either side of him, he murmured, 'Gentlemen?'

Bemusedly, bad-temperedly, more men in orange overalls began to rise up on both sides of the skinny guy – three on his right and four on his left, making nine prisoners in all.

'Do you want us to put up our hands?' the skinny guy asked mildly.

Again Purna ignored him. Glancing to her right she said pointedly, 'Xian Mei, check there's no one else hiding down there. They could be keeping a couple of men in reserve. We wouldn't want to be lulled into a false sense of security, would we?'

The skinny guy chuckled as Xian Mei nodded and moved forward.

'Do I need to say that if anyone tries to grab Xian Mei's gun I'll shoot them?' Purna added.

The skinny guy looked amused. 'No. I don't think you do.'

'All clear,' Xian Mei called a few seconds later.

'Good,' said Purna. 'In that case, gentlemen, I think we'll have you out here. Why not make yourselves comfortable at one of these tables so we can chat?'

The men resentfully shuffled out from behind the counter and sat at the table she had indicated. When they were all seated, the skinny guy nodded at the knife-man and said, 'You asked my friend his name earlier.'

Purna nodded. 'He was reluctant to give it.'

'He's cripplingly shy,' said the skinny guy, 'whereas I am not. My name's Kevin. I won't embarrass either of us by offering you my hand. So what's *your* name?' He gave Purna a piercing look.

'Purna,' she told him.

'Purna.' He rolled the word around in his mouth as though tasting it. 'That's a new one on me.'

'It's Australian,' she said. 'I'm half Aborigine.'

'How exotic,' said Kevin. 'So tell me, Purna, why are you and your friends here?'

Purna looked at him for a long moment, as though deciding what – if anything – she should tell him. Then she said, 'We were contacted by a man called Ryder White. He told us that if we could make our way to this island, he could get access to a helicopter and get us all out of here.'

Kevin regarded her shrewdly. 'Why should White help *you*?'

'His wife's sick,' replied Sam. 'We got something for him.'

'Oh? And what's that?'

'A vaccine. We hope,' said Purna.

'You hope?'

'It hasn't been properly tested,' she admitted.

'We had a whole bunch of stuff going on at the time,' added Logan. 'We just never got round to it.'

Kevin glanced at the other prisoners, who were sitting stoically, allowing him to do the talking. 'Maybe we *can* help each other,' he said.

'No offence, but how can *you* help *us*?' said Sam.

'I'm pretty sure Ryder White will be holed up in Sector Seven,' Kevin said.

Xian Mei nodded. 'Sector Seven, yes. That's where he said we had to make for.'

'In that case, I can show you the way there,' said Kevin, 'though in return I'd need a guarantee from you that as part of the deal for the vaccine you get White to agree to safe passage for myself and my friends off the island. As things stand, we're trapped in here and rapidly running out of food and water, and no one seems to know or care. From the little I've been able to glean, I gather the situation on Banoi isn't much better – in which case I doubt we'll be high on anyone's list of priorities.'

'We don't need you to show us the way,' said Sam. 'We got Ryder White to do that.'

Kevin sighed. 'In that case, let me put it another way. If you don't help us I'll order Rafa there to cut your friend's throat.'

'He does that, we'll shoot the lot of you,' retorted Logan.

Kevin raised his eyebrows. 'Will you really? You'd be prepared to gun down nine men in cold blood? If so, then frankly you'd be doing us a favour. Better to die quickly in a hail of bullets than slowly from starvation.'

Purna sighed. 'No one needs to die. You described me as ruthless earlier, but I wouldn't leave you to starve to death. You have my word on that.'

'Your word,' said Kevin. 'Well, that's wonderful. I'm sure that has set *all* our minds at rest.'

A couple of the prisoners sniggered.

'Why not ring White now?' Xian Mei suggested.

'Yeah, do the deal so *everyone* can hear,' added Logan.

Purna shrugged, took out her phone and punched in

White's number. All that came through, however, was static. She tried again with the same result.

'Shit, I can't get through,' she said.

'How *convenient*,' mocked Kevin.

'So how's he gonna help you get through to Sector Seven now?' one of the other prisoners said snidely.

Purna glanced at him. 'He's monitoring our progress on CCTV, unlocking doors for us as we reach them.'

Kevin looked thoughtful. Finally he said, 'All righty, here's what's going to happen. We'll keep your friend there as insurance just in case you decide to run out on us. Don't worry, she won't come to any harm. You have my personal guarantee on that.'

Hearing his words, Jin whimpered. Sam said, 'No way. She's coming with us.'

Kevin raised his hands and said mildly, 'Now come on, be reasonable. Do you honestly think—'

'Fuck reasonable!' barked Sam.

Raising a hand to take the heat out of the exchange, Purna explained, 'We tried that once before. It didn't work out for any of the parties concerned.'

Kevin sighed. 'If *this* particular girl is the issue, then we'll happily take that one.' He nodded at Yerema.

'No way.' Sam shook his head. 'We all stay together. No one gets left behind.'

Kevin pursed his lips, his brow furrowing slightly as if he were puzzling out a tricky conundrum. 'In that case, that leaves only one alternative.'

'Oh yeah? And what's that?' said Logan.

'I'll tag along personally. Make sure you do the deed.'

There was a rumble of discontent among the prisoners sitting around the table. One, a heavy-set black man with elaborate swirls shaved into the stubble at the side of his head, said, 'What good that do? Soon as you leave this room, they shoot you dead.'

Kevin shook his head, his eyes never leaving Purna's. 'No,' he said quietly, 'I really don't think they will. This one is the most dangerous, but she's not dishonest. In fact, she's a woman of *honour*.'

'How you know that?' said the black man.

Kevin flashed a smile that was almost charming. 'I'm an excellent judge of character.'

'What about the crazies?' said another of the prisoners, a raddled, balding man in his fifties with a prominent Adam's apple.

'What do you think these are?' Logan said, brandishing his gun. 'Designer accessories?'

'There're too many of those things out there,' said a rat-like man with spiky yellow hair. 'They bite you, they even *drool* on you, you're fucked, dude.'

'Not us,' said Sam. 'We're immune.' He rolled up the leg of his jeans, peeled back the bandage on his calf and showed them his bite. 'Check it out.'

There were murmurs both of wonder and disquietude. 'You *all* immune?' said the big black guy.

'All except for Jin,' said Purna. 'Speaking of which . . .'

'Oh, of course. Sorry,' said Kevin. He raised a hand and flicked a finger. 'Unhand the young lady please, Rafa.'

Rafa did so, albeit reluctantly, and Jin gasped and

dashed forward, all but collapsing into Xian Mei's arms.

'I don't think this is a good idea,' Rafa muttered.

'Yes, well, thinking's never been your strong suit, has it, Rafa?' Kevin said, eliciting a few titters from the other men.

He stood up slowly, then clapped his hands together and smiled, like a vicar contemplating a church outing.

'Right then,' he said. 'Shall we go?'

Chapter 22

BATTLEFIELD

'So what's directly behind this door?'

'Let me draw you a diagram,' Kevin said in answer to Purna's question. 'Rafa, if I could borrow your knife for a moment?'

Eyeing Purna, Sam and the rest of the group with the sullen resentment of a small boy who fears he is about to have his favourite toy taken away from him, Rafa pulled the knife from his belt and passed it across the table to Kevin.

'Thank you,' Kevin said, and turned briefly to beam at Purna. Waving the knife casually he said, 'I promise I won't try anything silly with this. Just in case you were wondering.'

'I wasn't,' Purna replied.

Smirking as if at some private joke, Kevin turned back to the table and began to scratch a pattern into its surface with the knife's tip. Working patiently and laboriously he said, 'It's ironic, isn't it, that because pens and pencils are regarded as dangerous weapons in our sweaty little hands, I have to resort to using a knife as a writing implement. What a crazy world we live in.'

When he was finished he passed the knife back to Rafa and stood back, revealing his handiwork with a flourish. Purna glanced suspiciously at the seated men before stepping forward. What Kevin had drawn was a series of five circles – two at the top and two at the bottom, with a smaller one in the middle – linked by a series of spokes she assumed were corridors. A longer spoke leading away from the central circle led to a sixth circle on the right.

'If I may explain?' said Kevin, holding up his hands to show he had nothing in them.

'Go ahead,' said Purna.

'Although it doesn't look it from the outside,' Kevin said, 'the interior of the prison is built "in the round", by which I mean the cell areas and the dayroom areas are circular. Apparently this design functions more efficiently as an incarcerating facility. There are no shadowy corners, which means that sight lines are clear and there's a better view of all that goes on. Now, we're currently in this area,' he pointed at the top left-hand circle, 'though as you can see *this* particular room isn't round, because it's simply one element of the space – a square within a circle, so to speak.' He looked up and smiled. 'Still with me so far?'

'Go on,' muttered Purna.

'We need to get to Sector Seven, which is here.' His finger moved across to the larger circle on the right. 'This is the tower you can see from Banoi, and it's connected to the rest of the facility primarily by this long corridor here. However, although this is the most direct route, it will also be the most populated. What I propose, therefore, is that we move diagonally across the central Panopticon here, and down to the door leading into the high-security section through here.' He pointed at the lower right-hand circle. 'There is access through a corridor here into the lower left quadrant of the tower. Where we're aiming for is here.' He indicated a cross at the end of the long corridor, which extended almost halfway into the right-hand circle depicting the tower.

'What's that?' asked Purna.

'A lift,' said Kevin. 'It will take us up into the operating heart of the facility. And that's where we need to be. That's Sector Seven.'

Purna studied the diagram carefully. 'Explain the layout of these circular areas to me,' she said.

'They're very simple,' said Kevin. 'Cells on four levels around the outside and a large central area in the middle where inmates congregate during the day. Right in the middle of each central area, like the hub of a wheel, is a security tower, maybe ten metres high. The tower has a door at the bottom, opening on to steps which lead up to a panoramic viewing area.'

'Are there individual windows?' Purna asked.

Kevin nodded and narrowed his eyes, visualizing it. 'Eight in all, I think.'

'And can they be opened?'

'I don't know. I guess.' He smirked again. 'I've never been up there. I'm an observ*ee* not an observ*er*.'

'I'm guessing these areas will be crawling with the infected?' said Logan.

Kevin nodded almost gleefully. 'Oh, absolutely *swarming* with them.'

'What do you think our chances are of getting through?' asked Xian Mei.

'Honestly? I'd say the chances of us *all* making it through are slim. We'd have to run very fast and shoot very accurately. And even then some of us would probably be overwhelmed by sheer numbers.'

'Yet you're still prepared to come with us,' said Purna suspiciously.

Kevin looked at her without blinking. 'Yes.'

'Why?'

''Cos he crazy,' muttered the black man.

Kevin looked pained. 'Thank you, Clarence, for that pithy character assassination.' He turned the full force of his gaze on Purna. 'Because I honestly think you're our only chance of survival, minimal though that may be. And because I'd rather go down fighting than sit here and rot.'

Purna stared at him and Kevin stared back. It was as if they were trying to see into each other's souls. Finally she said, 'I'm not sure I believe you.'

'But you'll still allow me to tag along?'

She shrugged. 'If you really want to. But you're not getting a gun.'

He seemed to accept her pronouncement with equanimity. 'In that case, may I ask one small favour?'

'Depends what it is.'

'If any of you see me getting into . . . difficulties with my fellow inmates out there, please put me out of my misery. Being eaten alive by those *things*, or even worse, turning *into* one of them –' He shuddered. 'Well, it would be so undignified.'

'If those things get you,' said Sam heavily, 'it will be my personal pleasure to shoot you in the head.'

Kevin placed a hand on his chest. 'Your kindness overwhelms me.'

Purna, meanwhile, had crossed to another table and was swinging her backpack from her shoulders. Placing it in front of her, she said, 'I've got something in here which may even up the odds a little . . .'

Three minutes later they were good to go. After discussing and agreeing on their strategy, Purna had tried calling White again without success. Frustrated by her inability to get through, she had crossed to the nearest wall-mounted CCTV camera, stared up into it and carefully outlined the route they were planning to take.

'I hope you can see and hear me,' she said, 'because if you can't, we're probably dead, which means your wife is too.'

It was as she was walking back across the room that they all heard the doors on the far side unlock with a series of *chunks*. Sam, Logan, Yerema and Jin were already kneeling by the door in readiness, and Xian Mei was standing behind them, her rifle trained on the door, pointing over their heads. Kevin was waiting with his hand on the handle and looked round almost casually as Purna approached.

'I presume you heard that?'

Purna nodded. 'Everyone ready?'

They all muttered in affirmation.

'OK,' she said, and jerked her head at Kevin.

He pushed down the handle and rammed his shoulder against the heavy metal door, leaning against

302

it with all his wiry strength. Even so, it opened agonizingly slowly, the widening gap giving them a gradually expanding glimpse into a hellish world.

The circular cathedral-like room was packed with zombies. They milled like sheep, snarling and groaning, blundering into one another as they each moved in their own pointlessly meandering fashion. Occasionally one would stumble and fall, sometimes knocking down others, but there were no recriminations, no hostility. Indeed, the infected seemed barely aware of each other, barely even operational. It was only ever food, or the prospect of food, that coaxed any sort of reaction from them.

It wasn't, therefore, the opening door that drew the creatures' attention, but the glimpse or smell of living meat beyond it. As Sam crouched in front of the door, he became aware of bodies turning clumsily around, heads snapping in his direction. He could almost see the creatures' primitive thought processes sparking into life, their blotchy discoloured faces twisting into the only expressions they were capable of – rage and hunger. As the infected moved en masse towards them, like water flowing towards a crack in a dam wall, Xian Mei started firing, carefully and precisely eradicating the closest and most immediate threats.

'Now!' shouted Purna, whereupon she, Sam, Logan, Jin and Yerema pulled the pins from the grenades they were clutching in their hands and hurled them, in five different directions, into the room beyond. Instantly Sam snatched up the second grenade from the floor by his feet and, peripherally aware that the others were doing the same, pulled the pin from it and hurled that one too.

As soon as all ten grenades had been thrown, he jumped up and helped Kevin wrestle the door closed, Xian Mei still firing through the gradually narrowing gap. By this time mottled grey-blue hands, the fingernails black and splintered, were curling round the edge of the door, trying to haul it open again or simply swipe at the tasty morsels on the other side. As Sam and Kevin struggled with the door, Yerema, Jin and Logan battered at the grasping fingers as best they could with the butts of their guns. Purna joined Xian Mei in firing through the gap, her face as calm and concentrated as ever, despite the proximity of the ravening dead.

Then the first of the grenades went off, and was followed in quick succession by several others. Kevin, Sam and the girls were thrown back as the blast slammed the door shut in a super-heated gust of air. They were picking themselves up, a little dazed, when Jin cried out in disgust. As the door had banged shut, a zombie hand had been severed at the wrist and was now lying on the floor, convulsively opening and closing like a beetle on its back. For a few seconds they all remained motionless, watching the thing's death-throes. Despite everything they had been through, everything they had seen, the frantically wriggling fingers held a particular revulsion. At last the hand stopped moving, whereupon Purna stepped decisively forward and kicked it across the room, where it came to rest under a table like a dead crab.

All the time they had been watching the hand, the

grenades in the other room had been going off. Accompanying the first wave of blasts had been the tinkle of breaking glass and numerous wet thuds against the closed doors. The echoes were still thrumming in their ears when the second wave kicked in, five enormous explosions, one after the other. The room shook, and a large crack appeared in the thick stone wall from floor to ceiling. Then there was silence.

It was the prisoners, still sitting around the table fifteen metres away, who reacted first. They began to whoop and laugh; a couple of them high-fived each other.

Irritably Purna raised a hand for silence, pressing her ear against the door. After a few seconds, she said, 'Still some movement, but I think we should go now, while those that haven't been blown to bits are still recovering.'

Though Sam's ears were still throbbing, he nodded and looked around. 'Everyone ready?'

There were further nods and mutters of confirmation.

'Come on,' said Purna.

She opened the door with a shove, took one look around and started running. Sam, a step behind her, did the same, feeling not unlike a soldier crossing a battlefield. The circular room – Panopticon, Kevin had called it – was a wreck, the floor scattered with twisted metal and shattered glass. Even more of a wreck were its occupants, the majority blown to pieces. There were body parts everywhere, and the floor was so awash with blood that it resembled a red lake choked with flesh and debris.

Despite this, some of the infected were still active. A

good proportion of these, however, were so badly injured they could do little more than drag themselves around on shattered limbs. One man, his arms nothing but stumps from which spikes of splintered bone stuck out like vestigial wings, ran at Sam, gnashing his teeth. Sam swivelled and shot him in the head, barely breaking his stride. He jumped over the grasping hand of a man whose innards were oozing from a gaping hole in his midriff. Nearby a head, attached to little more than a spinal column and half a torso, was growling and grinding its teeth.

It had earlier been agreed that if a good proportion of the infected survived the blast, the seven of them would make for the observation tower in the centre of the room and re-enact 'Operation Fish in a Barrel', picking off the zombies from above. However the grenades – two dozen of which had been liberated, along with their guns, from the police armoury on Banoi – had done considerably more damage than Sam suspected even Purna had hoped. As a result of this the Australian girl turned briefly and shouted, 'Keep going!' She gestured towards the door diagonally across from the one through which they had entered.

As soon as she reached the door, just a little ahead of the others, she tried the handle. Satisfied the door would open, she yelled, 'Xian Mei, cover us! The rest of you – grenades!'

None of them needed any further explanation. As Xian Mei turned and began firing at the few zombies still able-bodied enough to lurch towards them (a quick glance confirmed to Sam that none of the remaining creatures were actually running), he,

Logan, Jin and Yerema were fumbling in their pockets. Sam helped Purna shove the door open, and then as the infected on the other side began to register their presence, the five of them pulled the pins on their second batch of grenades and hurled them into what Kevin had earlier told them was the high-security wing. Purna began firing at the creatures closest to the door while Sam and the others grabbed their remaining grenades and repeated the process. Then Purna and Sam swapped places, Sam keeping the infected back while Purna threw *her* last grenade.

Once again it was the first, almost simultaneous round of blasts that slammed the door closed. This time Sam and the others were already moving back in readiness, but that didn't prevent them from being liberally spattered with zombie blood when one of the infected, who had been squeezing himself through the narrow gap between door and frame, was all but sliced in half lengthways when the first grenade went off. Choking and spluttering, Sam was at least secretly gratified to see that Kevin too had had a liberal dousing. The skinny guy was looking down at his gore-streaked overalls with the appalled expression of a kid at a party whose best friend had just vomited all over his favourite T-shirt. Still wiping the stinking, dripping fluid from his face, Sam said, 'Welcome to the club, buddy.'

For a split-second, which coincided with the second batch of grenades going off in the next room, Kevin looked at him with an expression of pure venom. And then his face abruptly and creepily slipped back into its familiar, slightly secretive smile, and he said, 'I'll look forward to receiving my membership badge.'

With Xian Mei and Logan still picking off zombies behind them, Purna and Sam reopened the door to check what damage the second batch of grenades had wrought. As before the results were both impressive and appalling. Though some of the infected had survived, most had been torn to pieces, and the room now looked like the aftermath of a train wreck. To add to this impression the central observation tower had collapsed, which meant that as well as severed limbs and mangled bodies, the floor was strewn with an obstacle course of tangled metal and broken glass.

Purna began to cross the room, picking her way through and over the wreckage, heading for the door Kevin had indicated on his diagram, which stood between two rows of cells on the far wall. As she advanced she gunned down approaching zombies with ruthless efficiency, and Sam, a few steps behind her, did the same. Just behind Sam came Jin and Yerema, firing their pistols when they needed to, and just behind *them*, keeping his head low, was Kevin.

At the back of the group Logan and Xian Mei wrestled the door closed to shut out the straggle of approaching zombies left in the previous room. Turning, they found themselves cut off from the rest of the group, as at least two dozen of the infected closed in from all sides. Some of the creatures had been injured in the blast, but most were still able-bodied enough to remain dangerous.

'Er ... guys,' Logan shouted as he and Xian Mei,

standing back to back, began firing at the fastest of the approaching zombies. Suddenly something dropped from above, and although it only caught them a glancing blow, it was enough to knock Xian Mei off her feet and send her gun flying out of her hand. Logan barely had time to register that what had hit them was one of the infected, which had apparently been so desperate to attack that it had taken the most direct route from an upper balcony, before the rest of the zombies converged on them.

'*Guys!*' he yelled again, firing desperately into the mass of clawing hands and viciously snarling faces. Somewhere close to him he heard Xian Mei screaming in terror and pain, and then, wrenched and buffeted from all sides, he went down. He began to struggle frantically, punching and kicking, as faces lunged in at him. He felt a sharp pain in his leg, and then another in his upper arm.

No! he thought. *I won't fucking die like this!*

Then there were gunshots, running feet, a confusion of noise, and suddenly he was showered with blood and brains as the hideous, rage-filled faces above him were blasted apart one by one. A couple of seconds later those faces were replaced by one he recognized. It was Sam, his wide eyes alive with anxiety and concern.

'Hey, man, you OK?' he asked.

'Apart from nearly becoming a Happy Meal, I'm great,' replied Logan. He tried to rise and felt pain shoot through his left arm and right leg. 'Ow! Fuck! That hurts!'

'You're bitten, man,' said Sam. 'Can you stand?'

Logan gritted his teeth. 'Yes, I can stand. If I can't I'm fucking dead, right?'

With Sam's and – surprisingly – Kevin's help, Logan rose to his feet. Vaguely, through the swimming pain in his head, he was still aware of gunshots being fired, of zombies dropping like cattle in an abattoir.

'How's Xian Mei?' he gasped.

'She'll be fine. Come on.'

'Where we going?'

'No questions. Just *come on*.'

Staggering, limping, supported on one side by Kevin and on the other by Sam, who was firing from the hip, blowing advancing zombies aside as they went, they made it to the door at the far side of the room.

When they were through, Sam quickly but gently lowered Logan to the ground. Logan sat with his back against the wall, wondering where his gun had gone, willing his head to stop spinning. Everything was still a blur, however, a mush of noise and activity. He was aware of people running towards him, of more shots being fired, and then what sounded like whimpers of pain. He tried to focus, to concentrate, but the sounds ran together, became distorted, and he felt as if he was sinking into a deep well. He tried to claw his way back towards the light, but thick velvety blackness swamped him, rolling over him in waves. Finally, unable to find the strength to fight it any longer, he passed out . . .

. . . and woke what seemed like seconds later, gasping in shock. 'How you doing?' asked a voice.

Sam. It was Sam. Logan blinked at him.

'Where am I?'

'In prison,' Sam said, and with that it all came flooding back.

Logan rubbed a hand over his face and groaned. 'Figures. My mom always said I'd end up in jail. How's Xian Mei?'

'Worse than you,' said Sam, 'but she'll be OK.'

'What'd they do to her?'

'They tore a lot of the skin off her arm. Purna bandaged her up pretty good. Here.'

Sam offered Logan a bottle of water. He took it gratefully, chugging it down. The water helped revive him and he looked around. They were in a corridor. It was featureless, kind of depressing, but quiet. Blessedly quiet.

Everyone was sitting around, taking a breather, getting over what had happened. They looked like the remains of an army after a very tough battle – exhausted, blood-stained, shell-shocked. Xian Mei, her left arm heavily bandaged from fingertips to shoulder like the Bride of Frankenstein, had dark rings around her eyes and an expression so pasty her lips looked bloodless.

'Hey,' Logan said to her, and she rewarded him with a weary smile.

The only person not sitting down was Purna. She glanced at Logan and then at Xian Mei.

'Are you two OK to carry on?'

In any other situation Logan would have laughed and told her to take a hike, but now he simply nodded and with Sam's help rose to his feet.

'It's OK,' Sam mumbled. 'There ain't no more zombies.'

311

'Good,' said Logan, 'because I think I lost my gun. I hope Purna doesn't make me pay for it.'

Led by Kevin, the seven of them made their way slowly along the long corridor to a door at the far end. This one was open like the others (*Thank you, Ryder White*, Logan thought) and led through a number of empty administrative offices and linking corridors to a central lobby area where several corridors converged. There was no sign of the infected in this part of the building, and indeed no sign they had ever been here. The left-hand wall was dominated by a lift with metal doors.

'This is it,' said Kevin. 'Sector Seven awaits.'

He pressed the button and the downward-facing arrow lit up. For a few seconds they waited, not speaking, like strangers in a hotel lobby. There was a ping and the lift doors slowly opened. They shuffled inside and Kevin pressed a button marked 7. As soon as the lift doors closed, Logan heard a hissing sound, which at first he thought was something to do with the lift mechanism. Then Purna said, 'What's that?'

'That's the gas,' said Kevin, his voice oddly muffled.

Logan turned, bemused, and saw that Kevin had released a small catch next to the lift buttons, which had caused a flap to drop down. Behind the flap was a compartment, like a tiny locker, from which Kevin, shielded by the people standing next to him, had produced a gas mask. He was now wearing the mask and the hissing was getting louder.

'What—' Purna said, then her legs folded under her and she slid unconscious to the floor.

Gas? Logan thought, trying to make sense of what

was happening, but all at once his mind felt slow and syrupy, his head heavy as a boulder. The last thing he saw, before his body shut down and he blacked out for the second time in an hour, was Kevin's masked face goggling down at him.

Chapter 23

SECRETS AND LIES

'So this is what it's all about. It really doesn't look like much, does it?'

The words tugged Sam up from a black pool of unconsciousness. He opened first one eye and then the other, his head pounding as if he was suffering from the worst ever hangover. He was vaguely aware he was sitting in a chair, but had no idea how he had got there. The last thing he remembered was . . .

The lift! The memory snapped him fully awake and he tried to jump to his feet.

But he couldn't move. He was paralysed. Kevin's gas had paralysed him! Then he realized his back was aching, and there was a glassy cramped feeling in his shoulders, and something was cutting into his wrists.

Not paralysed then. Thank God. Not paralysed, but immobile all the same. Tied to a chair.

He blinked to clear his blurred vision, turned his head towards the source of the words he had heard echoing in his mind. He saw a smear of orange (*Hallowe'en pumpkin orange*, he thought, and felt a sudden pang of nostalgia for his childhood). Then the smear tightened, coalesced, and he realized he was looking at Kevin in his orange prison overalls.

The skinny man was leaning against a control desk, backlit by the icy glare from a wall of TV screens. The screens depicted different static views of the prison – corridors and cell areas, kitchens, shower blocks, the library, the exercise yard. Sam could see that most of the places were deserted, but in a few the infected milled about like sleepwalkers. He turned his attention back to Kevin. The man was holding up a vial of yellowish liquid that resembled weak tea or piss.

'What's going on?' Sam mumbled and Kevin glanced across at him.

'Oh, welcome back,' he said. 'Enjoy your little nap?'

Sam ignored him, looking around to take in his surroundings. He was relieved to see his friends were all here, and apparently OK – aside from the fact that, like him, they had been manacled to chairs and had had their backpacks and weapons taken away.

Of the others, Purna and Xian Mei were the only ones who were conscious. Logan, Jin and Yerema were still slumped forward, eyes closed, breathing heavily.

Xian Mei looked ill, her skin clammy, her face and body tense as if the slightest movement caused her pain. The thick bandage around her arm was stained red where blood had seeped through from the wound beneath.

'You OK?' Sam asked her.

She licked her lips and gave a tiny unconvincing nod.

In contrast to Xian Mei, Purna looked fighting fit, her dark eyes blazing with anger.

'What do you hope to gain from this, *Kevin*?' she said, making his name sound like an insult.

'Oh, I've already gained it,' he said.

She scowled. 'What are you talking about?'

Smiling and slipping the vial into his pocket, he said, 'Let me tell you a little story.'

'Oh, is this the bit where the bad guy gloats about how clever he's been and the good guys get bored?' Sam said.

Kevin looked for a moment as if he was contemplating whether to punch Sam in the face, and then he snorted a laugh and settled himself more comfortably against the desk, folding his arms.

'Not exactly,' he said. 'It's more the bit where the little unimportant people discover how the world really works, and how they can do absolutely nothing about it.'

'That sounds even more boring,' Sam muttered.

'So tell us,' said Purna with weary contempt, 'how *does* the world work? In *your* estimation?'

Kevin smirked. 'Why do you think you're really here on Banoi?'

'Because we're immune,' said Purna. 'Because we were brought here to be manipulated, to be used as guinea pigs.'

Kevin nodded. 'And why are you here now? In the prison, I mean?'

''Cos this guy, Ryder White, said he'd get us off the island if we brought him the vaccine,' said Sam.

Clearly amused, Kevin raised a hand and waggled it from side to side. 'Well . . . that's *partly* right,' he said. 'But I'm afraid that's not the *full* story.'

'All right,' Purna conceded, 'so why don't you *tell* us the full story? I can see you're dying for the opportunity to let us know how clever you've been. Why don't you start by telling us who you really are, because you sure as hell aren't a regular prisoner?'

Kevin pursed his lips, as though inwardly debating how much to reveal. Eventually he said, 'My name is Charon. I'm a sleeper agent for the Organization—'

'The *Organization*?' Purna interrupted mockingly. 'Ooh, how mysterious.'

The man now called Charon shrugged, unmoved by the taunt. 'It doesn't have a name because it doesn't officially exist. It's a secret association of the world's wealthiest individuals, who make their money by exploiting certain financial opportunities that arise in areas of global conflict.'

'So they're like vultures?' asked Sam. 'Feeding on the misery and destruction of innocent people?'

Charon sneered. 'I wouldn't expect you to understand.'

'Oh, we understand more than you think,' Purna's voice dripped contempt. 'I know how people like that operate, and they're not opportunists. They might have been once, but when your financial profile achieves a certain level, you no longer passively sit around, waiting for something to happen. You *make* things happen. You stoke the fires. And if misery and chaos is big business, then you make damn sure you're the one creating it.'

'So they start wars?' asked Sam. 'And they created this virus to use as a weapon they can sell to the highest bidder?'

317

'Of course they did.' Purna shot Charon a contemptuous look. 'Isn't that right?'

Charon inclined his head. 'Partly. But the Organization didn't *create* the virus. The virus was already here, on Banoi. The Organization invests a huge amount of money in research and development. They probe every branch of science looking for potential new weapons, and they have eyes and ears everywhere.'

'And they heard about the virus?' said Sam.

Kevin nodded. 'The first of the infected to come back from the dead were taken off the island and tested.'

'Yerema's rapists,' said Purna, glancing at the girl.

'Precisely,' replied Kevin. 'And tests showed that in all three of them the virus – Pathogen K – could not be isolated because it was constantly mutating. And so in order to create a usable biological weapon, a stable form of Pathogen K had to be found so that a vaccine could be developed.'

'Because without a vaccine the virus would be useless as a biological weapon,' said Purna.

'Which is where you guys came in,' said Charon, spreading his hands expansively. 'It was discovered that, despite the aggressive nature and constantly mutating state of the virus, a tiny percentage of people were completely immune. The Organization therefore used its resources to scan blood records the world over. They even created a multi-national blood drive event under a variety of banners and initiatives to cast their net still further. Ultimately you four were selected from millions of potential subjects. It was discovered that you possessed the most vigorously resistant immune systems, strong enough to withstand close proximity engagement with the infection. Plus you fitted the required demographic survival profile.'

'You mean we were young and fit and we wouldn't get sick,' said Sam.

'Precisely.'

'So you dropped us into the middle of all this shit just so we'd get the original stable form of the virus for you?'

'Dropping a trail of crumbs for you to follow along the way, yes,' replied Charon smugly.

'I assume West was in on this?' asked Purna.

Charon smirked. 'Mowen too. Such a shame about poor Dr West, though he served his purpose. I'm sure the vaccine he developed, combined with his notes – which you were thoughtful enough to bring along with you – will prove invaluable.'

'So all that shit about Ryder White's wife—' said Sam.

'Oh, that's all true,' said Charon, still smirking. 'It's always more convincing if you conceal a few droplets of truth in an ocean of subterfuge.'

Sam frowned. 'So this Ryder White guy works for the Organization too?'

'No.'

Sam stared at Charon for a long moment and then shook his head. 'I don't get it.'

'I think I do,' said Purna. Narrowing her eyes, she said, 'It wasn't Ryder White who contacted us, was it? It was you.'

'Guilty as charged,' said Charon, holding up his hands.

'So Ryder White don't know squat about us?' asked Sam.

'Oh, he knows there are operatives on Banoi, trying to locate a stable form of the virus in order to develop a vaccine that he hopes will save his wife. If he hadn't been furnished with *that* information, the island would have been destroyed and all our hard work would have been for nothing.'

'All your hard work?' yelled Sam. 'You make it sound like this fucking virus is some kind of achievement.'

'And so it is,' said Charon. 'The ultimate biological weapon, for which potential buyers will be willing to pay untold sums of money?' He laughed. 'What's not to like?'

Sam looked as if he was about to explode, but before he could say anything, Purna glanced at him quickly. 'Hang on, Sam.' Turning back to Charon, she said, 'What do you mean, if White hadn't known we were looking for a vaccine, the island would have been destroyed? Destroyed by who?'

Charon sighed, as if her lack of understanding was becoming tiresome. 'After analysing the virus, scientists working for the Organization were able to predict that once the plague was introduced into the general population, it would spread quickly. Exactly *how* quickly they weren't sure – and in the event it achieved pandemic proportions far more rapidly than anyone had anticipated – but they at least knew that the *potential* was there, and so were able to instigate various precautionary measures.'

'Such as?'

'It's not a widely known fact, for obvious reasons,

but for some time now western governments have been running scared of the possibility of terrorist groups developing biological and chemical weapons so devastating that, if unleashed, they would decimate the populations of entire countries. In order to counteract this, certain measures have been agreed upon, measures that would be met with widespread horror and condemnation if their existence were made public. Suffice to say that a pandemic with no foreseeable cure – such as the one currently rampant on Banoi – would ordinarily trigger the execution of security protocols, resulting in the nuclear cleansing of the infected area.'

'Nuclear cleansing?' sneered Sam. 'You mean they'd blow the fucking place sky high? Murder thousands of innocent people?'

'In order to protect the majority, yes,' said Charon. 'But I'm only the messenger boy, not the instigator here – so let's not get bogged down quibbling about the moral issues.'

'You said "ordinarily",' said Purna, 'which I'm guessing means that because of these "precautionary measures" you mentioned, what was supposed to happen hasn't happened in this case?'

Charon nodded.

Purna looked as though she was about to ask him another question, then her eyes widened. 'Oh my God.'

'What?' asked Sam.

Looking intently at Charon, Purna said, 'Let me take a wild guess: Ryder White would be the man in charge of ordering the nuclear strike on Banoi, right?'

Charon's smile was confirmation enough.

'Don't you see?' said Purna to a stillbemused Sam. 'The reason Banoi hasn't been wiped off the face of the earth is because Ryder White's wife is sick, and he's delayed the order because he thinks the cure might be on the island. But the question is, why did she get sick in the first place?'

Sam felt like the kid in class who doesn't get what everyone else seems able to grasp – and then all at once he *did* get it. 'Because *they* made her sick,' he said, nodding at Charon.

'Exactly.'

Sam shook his head in disbelief. 'Bastards.'

'Oh, please,' said Charon wearily, 'less of the bleeding heart bullshit. It was purely a practical decision. The Organization simply needed a way to buy some time. It was discovered that Ryder White's wife was the physician here, so the infection was planted in the prison. As the doctor treating the sick prisoners it was inevitable she would contract the virus sooner rather than later – and hence the nuclear threat, luckily for you, was allayed.'

'So where are White and his wife now?' asked Purna.

'In the sick bay, waiting for news that you've arrived with the vaccine. As soon as your friends wake up, I'll give him a call, whereupon he will radio for a helicopter to take us all far, far away from here.'

'And what happens then?' said Purna. 'What happens to *us*?'

Charon patted his pocket. 'You're my insurance,' he said, 'in case the vaccine doesn't work.'

Insurance. Purna was growing to hate that word. The

men in the police station had kept Jin as 'insurance'.
'And if it does work?' she said.

'You'll still be assets,' Charon replied. 'Once news of
the virus gets out, I'm sure there will be plenty of
factions desperate for immunity.'

'So what you saying?' said Sam. 'That you'll sell us
like cattle to the highest bidder?'

'Maybe. But don't worry, I'll see that you go to a
good home.'

'I thought you worked for the *Organization*?'

'That doesn't mean there isn't room for a little free
enterprise.'

Purna gave him a disgusted look. 'You're nothing
but a chancer, are you, *Kevin* or *Charon* or whatever
your name is?'

'I prefer to think of myself as an entrepreneur,'
Charon said.

'Dealing in human lives?' asked Purna.

'Why not?' Charon replied. 'Is there a product more
precious?'

Before anyone could answer, there was a groan and
Yerema leaned back in her seat, screwing up her eyes
in an attempt to open them.

'Ah, and here's Patient Zero,' he said, 'the most
precious asset of all.'

Suddenly, briskly, he strode across to the line of
chairs on which they sat and shook first Logan and
then Jin roughly by the shoulder.

'Wake up,' he barked. 'It's time to go.'

Chapter 24

ÜBER ZOMBIE

'You must be the people who brought the vaccine.'

Strong-jawed and broad-shouldered, Colonel Ryder White looked every inch the capable and efficient army man. Even standing beneath the blazing sun, and despite his straitened circumstances, his green army fatigues were immaculate – every button fastened, trousers tucked neatly into the tops of his gleaming, tightly-laced army boots, red beret folded precisely beneath the epaulette on his left shoulder.

His wife's demeanour, however, could not have provided more of a contrast. Strapped to a gurney with thick leather constraints, the clearly once slim and pretty blonde woman in the beautifully-tailored white suit was a snarling spitting harridan. Her eyes had already taken on the familiar milky glaze of the terminally infected and her skin was grey and discoloured. Even her suit looked grubby and dishevelled, as if she had been scrabbling around in the dirt, or as if the corruption of her body was seeping through her clothes.

One look was enough for Sam to tell there was no

way back for her. If White believed that some miracle vaccine was going to restore his wife to life and health, then he was sorely deluded.

'That's us,' said Logan in response to White's question.

'Why are you handcuffed?'

'You better ask him,' said Sam, jerking his head towards Charon, who was at the rear of the group, herding them across the wide expanse of the tower roof with the aid of what had previously been Yerema's handgun.

'Despite the successful conclusion to what you no doubt perceive as a heroic mission, Colonel, these people are ruthless mercenaries and should be treated with the utmost caution,' Charon said.

Purna barked a laugh. 'That's a prime example of the pot calling the kettle black if I ever heard one.'

Despite asking the question, White seemed uninterested in either Charon's explanation or Purna's response. Looking at Charon with barely concealed desperation, he demanded, 'Where is the vaccine now?'

Charon patted the pocket of his overalls. 'Don't worry, Colonel. I have it here, safe and sound.'

'Show it to me.'

'I don't think that's really nece—'

'Show it to me,' the Colonel insisted, employing what Sam guessed was his parade-ground bark, a tone that invited no argument. 'I need to *know* it exists, that there's still a chance . . .'

His voice choked off, and Sam realized how raw the Colonel's emotions were, how hard he was fighting to hold himself together. Walking forward a few paces,

Charon sighed and reached into his pocket, producing the stoppered vial of yellowish liquid.

'There you are,' he said, as if speaking to a spoiled child. 'Happy now?'

White produced a Beretta M9 from his holster and pointed it at Charon. 'Hand it over.'

Sam glanced at Charon, who was now standing to his right. The Organization agent rolled his eyes. 'Oh, come on, Colonel, put that away. You're embarrassing yourself.'

'Give it to me.'

'Why?' asked Charon. 'So you can feed it to your wife like medicine? Don't be ridiculous. It has to be fully tested and an antidote manufactured. That's going to take time.'

'We don't *have* time,' White insisted, and he seemed twitchy now, agitated. Beads of sweat stood out on his broad forehead. 'My wife's sick, can't you see that?'

'Your wife's *dead*, Colonel,' Purna piped up. She jerked her head towards Charon. 'And *he* killed her.'

'Dead?' White shook his head angrily. 'No . . . no, she's very ill. But she's going to be fine.'

Charon laughed. 'Of course she is, Colonel. Don't listen to this woman. She's just trying to drive a wedge between us.'

'It's true, Colonel,' Purna called across the gap between them. 'This man – Charon or Kevin or whatever he calls himself – introduced the virus into the hospital, knowing that your wife would contract it. He did it to delay your order to destroy the island if the infection achieved pandemic proportions – which, of course, it quickly did.'

Charon laughed even harder. 'I've never heard such nonsense.'

'It's all true,' Logan called. 'He told us so himself. We all heard it, right everyone?'

They all nodded.

'He's been stringing you along, Colonel,' Sam shouted. 'Every step of the way. He and the people he works for want to use the virus as a weapon. They only wanted a vaccine so they could control it.'

White gaped at them, clearly not sure what to believe. Apparently unruffled, Charon said, 'Of *course* they're going to say that, Colonel. But we both know it's not true, don't we? It's just a pathetic attempt to divide and conquer. But it's not going to work, is it? We're both stronger, more intelligent than that.'

'Look at your wife, Colonel,' Purna shouted. 'Look at what Charon did to her.'

White looked down at his wife, bemused and indecisive, his capable and efficient demeanour of a few minutes before having crumbled completely. 'You did this?' he asked.

'Of course not,' snapped Charon, exasperated. 'They're just—'

And that was when Sam hit him.

Taking advantage of Charon's momentary distraction, Sam threw himself sideways, his hands still cuffed in front of him. His 190 pounds of almost solid muscle smashed into the skinnier man's midriff and knocked him off his feet. Both men landed in a heap, Charon on his back, Sam crashing down on the ground next to him and taking the full impact on his shoulder. Although Charon kept a grip on his gun, the vial of vaccine flew from his hand and hit the ground about five metres away. Despite being made of glass, it didn't break, but instead rolled along the tower's flat concrete roof. Furiously Charon kicked out at Sam, then brought his gun hand round and smashed him in the side of the head. Sam, who had been struggling to rise, groaned and slumped back down, dazed. Charon jumped to his feet, teeth bared in a feral snarl.

While Sam and Charon had been scrabbling on the ground, Jin, acting largely on impulse, had broken away from the captive group and sprinted towards the rolling vial. Dropping to her knees, she leaned forward and awkwardly snatched it up in one of her cuffed hands, scrambled back to her feet and ran towards the Colonel and his wife. She had a vague notion that the vaccine would be better off in White's hands than in Charon's, that under the army's jurisdiction it would be put to good use, rather than simply being sold, along with the virus itself, to the highest bidder. She had covered around two-thirds of the distance, and was no more than ten metres away from the still uncertain-looking Colonel, when Charon shot her.

There was no warning. The skinny man merely raised his gun and fired. There were cries of horror from the captive group as blood erupted from the ragged wound that appeared in Jin's back. Arms outstretched, she was thrown forward, as if hit with a sledgehammer, and crashed down on to her face. Her body convulsed for a moment and then relaxed as the life went out of her.

There was a moment of stunned silence. Xian Mei's

face was etched with shock, her mouth open in disbelief. Purna's eyes burned with anger. Logan spun
round to face Charon, his face blazing red.

'What the fuck did you do that for?' he yelled. 'You
killed her! You fucking killed her, you murdering
fuck!'

With vicious intent, Charon swung the gun round,
aiming it at Logan's face. 'I'll shoot you too if you
don't shut your mouth.'

Still somewhat dazed, Sam struggled up into a
sitting position and spat out a mouthful of blood.
Looking numbly at Jin's motionless body, he said in a
low voice, 'First chance I get, I swear I'm gonna
fucking kill *you*.'

'Is that so?' sneered Charon. 'In that case, I'd better
make sure you don't *get* that chance, hadn't I?' Then he
swung away from Sam and pointed his gun at a fresh
target. 'Get back, Colonel,' he warned.

While everyone had been reacting to Jin's death,
White had moved forward and plucked the vial from
the girl's lifeless hand. He held it up in front of him
now, looking at it with something like wonder.
Ignoring Charon's warning, he turned and walked
back to his wife.

'Colonel, I mean it!' Charon snapped.

Almost casually White glanced round, raised his
gun and fired. The bullet went high, but they all threw
themselves to the ground, Charon included. By the
time they lifted their heads, White had re-holstered his
gun and was pulling the stopper from the vial.

'Colonel, don't!' Charon cried, an edge of panic in
his voice. With his weapon held high he began to run

across the thirty metres of open space between them.

White was tipping the contents of the vial towards his wife's mouth when Charon fired. Fearful that shooting White would cause him to drop the vial and spill its contents, Charon aimed his bullet deliberately over the Colonel's head. He hoped the threat alone would be enough to make him freeze, perhaps even to bring him to his senses.

'The next bullet *won't* miss!' Charon promised, his voice raw. 'Give me back the vial *now* or I'll kill you *and* your wife.'

But White wasn't listening. Driven by an obsessive desire to save the woman he loved, the Colonel was now lost in his own world, deaf both to threats and reason. Charon could only watch, appalled, as White poured the entire contents of the vial into his wife's snarling snapping mouth.

'*No!*' Charon roared. 'What have you done?'

Enraged, he raised his gun and squeezed the trigger, again and again and again.

White twitched and bucked, blood spurting from him as bullets ripped into his body. He crashed against his wife's gurney and slid to the floor. Coldly Charon swung the gun round, aimed it at the Colonel's wife and pulled the trigger. It clicked empty. Swearing, Charon rooted for extra ammunition in the pocket of his overalls.

Reduced for the moment to mere spectators, Purna, Sam and the others watched from thirty metres away. Sam felt a savage satisfaction in seeing Charon's carefully laid plans going up in smoke, but he couldn't help wondering how the loss of the vaccine would affect not only his and his friends' long-term prospects, but also those of the rest of the world, should the virus spread beyond the island.

All at once Logan called, 'Hey, check out Mrs White.'

'What's happening to her?' muttered Yerema.

'Must be the vaccine,' said Sam.

Still strapped to the gurney, the Colonel's wife was shaking violently, as if she was having some kind of seizure. The gurney itself was rattling, in danger of tipping over. And then Mrs White began to change. Her body seemed to swell, to bulk out with strange mis-shapen growths. They erupted all over her, her clothes ripping as her limbs and torso expanded. It was almost like watching a violent chemical reaction, thought Sam, or maybe an accelerated film of chronic steroid abuse. The infected woman screeched in either rage or agony as her face also began to dilate and distort. Within seconds she had enlarged to twice, maybe three times her normal size, and had become so grossly malformed that she was barely recognizable as human.

'Shit,' said Logan in awe as the hideous creature thrashed from side to side, snapping the gurney's thick leather constraints like cotton thread. 'She's become a fucking *über* zombie.'

What once had been the Colonel's wife bellowed again and clambered to its feet, pulverizing the gurney into twisted metal and sweeping it aside with a single blow from its massive arm.

Charon, meanwhile, had succeeded in reloading his gun and was backing away in disbelief, looking up at

331

the creature as it rose to its full height. It stood, swaying for a moment, like a gnarled, ancient tree made not
of bark and sap, but of compacted, hideously swollen
lumps of dead flesh.

Then it charged.

It thundered towards Charon like a bull elephant, its
terrible ratcheting cry a jagged blade of sound that
ripped the air apart. Sam had to hand it to the skinny
guy – if nothing else, the man had balls. Most people
would have turned and run, but Charon stood his
ground, levelled his gun and began to fire. Arm
ramrod-straight, he pumped bullet after bullet into the
creature's head – or at least, into the grotesquely
swollen protuberance on its shoulders that now *passed*
for a head. Each shot ripped away dough-like chunks
of flesh, thick blackish fluid gushing from the gaping
wounds. The first few bullets barely slowed the
creature down, but then the barrage began to take its
toll. Punctured in a dozen or more places, the creature
started to stagger and sway, leaving a black trail like
engine oil behind it. Still Charon backed away before
its advance; still he fired his gun, reloading quickly
when he needed to. Eventually he could back away no
more. He came to a halt a metre from the edge of the
tower roof. The creature was stumbling now, wheez-
ing as it came. Charon stopped firing his gun and
slowly raised his arms, like a high diver preparing for
a plunge into the water below.

'Come on,' he shouted. And then he screamed at it:
'*Come on!*'

As if reacting to the taunt, the creature broke into a
renewed run, putting the last of its energy into a final

attack. Charon waited until it was no more than a couple of metres away from him, then he hurled himself to one side. With a final screech the creature, unable to halt its forward momentum, plunged over the edge of the tower and plummeted to the ground far below. There was a moment of silence followed by a sizzling bang, like a massive electrical circuit shorting out.

Before anyone could react, there came the faint drone of an engine from somewhere overhead. Sam looked up and saw a black speck in the sky, growing steadily larger. Even though Charon had been occupied by the creature for the past couple of minutes, the rest of them had simply stood and watched. If they had been anywhere else they might have used the distraction to try to escape, but up here on the roof there had been nowhere to escape *to*. Now Charon was walking back towards them almost casually, his gun trained on them.

'Stand well back,' he shouted. 'Give him room to land.'

Sam didn't know much about helicopters, but he could see this was a pretty big one. It was black and fat-bodied like a gigantic well-fed fly. As it descended towards them the downdraught from its whickering rotors caused their clothes to flap and the girls' hair to whip and thrash around their faces. It landed gracefully, its wheels barely kissing the concrete before it came to rest. Charon gestured again with the gun.

'Get in,' he yelled.

'Where are we going?' Purna's voice was almost lost in the noise.

He smiled a crooked smile. 'Magical mystery tour.'

Still handcuffed, the five of them, with Charon bringing up the rear, trooped towards the chopper. The helmeted, black-goggled pilot barely glanced at them as they climbed aboard. Inside they sat on two rows of three seats, Logan and Xian Mei at the back, Sam, Purna and Yerema at the front. Charon sat up front, next to the pilot, though he swivelled in his seat so he could keep his gun trained on them. Nodding to the pilot, he said mockingly, 'Ladies and gentlemen, we are now leaving paradise.'

With a deafening roar of engines, the helicopter lifted away from the roof of the tower. Sam's stomach lurched as it banked slightly, swooping to one side. Looking out of a window, he saw the creature that had once been Dana White impaled on the electric fence. She was burning, the bulbous mass of her head hanging down, her vast arms spread as if crucified. As they headed up towards the clouds, Sam saw the island of Banoi receding below him. Turning away, he looked into the cold staring eyes of Charon, and wondered what the future would bring.

DEAD ISLAND